PENGUIN CLASSICS

THE MINISTRY OF FEAR

GRAHAM GREENE, whose long life (1904–1991) nearly spanned the twentieth century, was one of its greatest novelists. Educated at Berkhamsted School and Balliol College, Oxford, he started his career as a subeditor of *The Times* in London. He began to attract notice as a novelist with his fourth book, *Orient Express,* in 1932. In 1935, he trekked across northern Liberia, his first experience in Africa, told in *A Journey Without Maps.* He converted to Catholicism in 1926 and reported on religious persecution in Mexico in 1938 in *The Lawless Roads,* which served as a background for his famous *The Power and the Glory,* one of several "Catholic" novels (*Brighton Rock, The Heart of the Matter, The End of the Affair*). During the war he worked for the British secret service in Sierra Leone; afterward, he began wide-ranging travels as a journalist, reflected in novels such as *The Quiet American, Our Man in Havana, The Comedians, Travels with My Aunt, The Honorary Consul, The Human Factor, Monsignor Quixote* and *The Captain and the Enemy.* As well as his many novels, Graham Greene wrote several collections of short stories, four travel books, six plays, two books of autobiography, *A Sort of Life* and *Ways of Escape,* two of biography, and four books for children. He also contributed hundreds of essays and film and book reviews to *The Spectator* and other journals, many of which appear in the late collection *Reflections.* Most of his novels have been filmed, including *The Third Man,* which was first written as a film treatment. Graham Greene was named Companion of Honour and received the Order of Merit and many other awards.

ALAN FURST is widely known as the author of historical spy novels, which take place in Europe during the period 1933–1945. These include *Night Soldiers, Dark Star, The Polish Officer, The World at Night, Red Gold, Kingdom of Shadows, Blood of Victory,* and, most recently, *Dark Voyage.* He has written as a journalist for *Esquire* magazine and *The International Herald Tribune.* Born in New York, he has lived for long periods in France, especially Paris. He now lives on Long Island, New York.

GRAHAM GREENE

The Ministry of Fear

AN ENTERTAINMENT

Introduction by ALAN FURST

PENGUIN BOOKS

PENGUIN BOOKS
Published by the Penguin Group
Penguin Group (USA) Inc., 375 Hudson Street, New York, New York 10014, U.S.A.
Penguin Group (Canada), 90 Eglinton Avenue East, Suite 700, Toronto, Ontario,
Canada M4P 2Y3 (a division of Pearson Penguin Canada Inc.)
Penguin Books Ltd, 80 Strand, London WC2R 0RL, England
Penguin Ireland, 25 St Stephen's Green, Dublin 2, Ireland
(a division of Penguin Books Ltd)
Penguin Group (Australia), 250 Camberwell Road, Camberwell, Victoria 3124,
Australia (a division of Pearson Australia Group Pty Ltd)
Penguin Books India Pvt Ltd, 11 Community Centre, Panchsheel Park,
New Delhi – 110 017, India
Penguin Group (NZ), 67 Apollo Drive, Rosedale, North Shore 0632, New Zealand
(a division of Pearson New Zealand Ltd)
Penguin Books (South Africa) (Pty) Ltd, 24 Sturdee Avenue,
Rosebank, Johannesburg 2196, South Africa

Penguin Books Ltd, Registered Offices: 80 Strand, London WC2R 0RL, England

First published in Great Britain by William Heinemann Ltd 1943
First published in the United States of America by The Viking Press 1943
Published in Penguin Books (U.K.) 1963
Published in Penguin Books (U.S.A.) 1978
This edition with an introduction by Alan Furst published in Penguin Books (U.S.A.) 2005

CIP data available
ISBN 978-0-14-303911-2

Printed in the United States of America
Set in Sabon

Contents

Contents

Introduction

On a Sunday afternoon in the late summer of 1941, in London, Arthur Rowe, an ordinary man with an ordinary name, comes upon a church bazaar in progress. Caught by memories of childhood, he cannot resist—the fortune teller, the small military band the tepid games of chance; he simply must, in the words of the local vicar, have "a little flutter in a good cause."

This is not, however, an ordinary summer afternoon. Britain is at war with Germany, and the bazaar will end early because of the blackout, and then, heralded by air-raid sirens, the bombers will arrive—flying up the Thames estuary from the southeast, the drumming of their engines calling "where are you, where are you," to the people of the city. And Arthur Rowe is not quite an ordinary man: memories of the crucial, life-changing event in his history, the mercy-killing of his wife some years earlier, visit him hourly. At one of the booths in the bazaar, Arthur Rowe guesses the weight of a prize cake, "made with real eggs," and wins it. And so, once again, his life is changed forever.

Graham Greene was born in what turned out to be a lucky year: 1904. This made him too young for the First World War, which slaughtered the generation ahead of him, and thirty-five years old in 1939, when Britain declared war on Germany. Just the right age for a successful intellectual—Balliol College at Oxford, seventeen books already in print—to get a good job in the war. This he did, according to his colleague Malcolm Muggeridge, with help from his sister Liza, who "worked for someone important in the Secret Service." Thus Greene became, in 1941, chief of the British Secret Intelligence Service station at Freetown, Sierra Leone.

It was there that he discovered the eccentricities of the SIS cipher book, which listed standard groups of numbers for commonly used expressions, and still retained a group for the word *eunuch,* a survival of Empire diplomacy, when eunuchs were often powerful advisors in the courts of eastern potentates. An amused Greene determined to use it and, in 1942, receiving a coded telegram from a colleague in England which included an invitation to visit over the Christmas holidays, wired back, in code, his regrets: "Like the Eunuch, I cannot come." Much of his other work in Freetown was likely far less amusing.

It was in Freetown that Greene wrote *The Ministry of Fear,* the only book he produced during the war, and the reader's awareness of his employment at that time may lend a particular resonance to certain passages in the novel. On the run for a murder he did not commit, Arthur Rowe has a dream, a dream of childhood innocence, a dream about his mother. "This isn't real life any more," he tells her. Then goes on:

> Tea on the lawn, evensong, croquet, the old ladies calling, the gentle unmalicious gossip, the gardner trundling the wheelbarrow full of leaves and grass. People write about it as if it still went on; lady novelists describe it over and over again in books of the month, but it's not there any more. . . . People want to kill me because I know too much, I'm hiding underground, and up above the Germans are methodically smashing London to bits . . . It sounds like a thriller, doesn't it, but the thrillers are like life—more like life than you are, this lawn, your sandwiches, that pine. You used to laugh at the books Miss Savage read—about spies, and murders, and violence, and wild motor-car chases, but dear, that's real life: it's what we've made of the world since you died. . . . The world has been remade by William Le Queux.

William Le Queux was an early practicioner of the British spy novel, publishing *England's Peril: A Story of the Secret Service* in 1900 and *Spies of the Kaiser: Plotting the Downfall of England* in 1909. The villain of the latter was the chief of the French Secret Service. "Today he would be heard of in savage Africa, a week later he would be seen sipping his *mazagran* before the Grand Café in Paris, and a few days afterwards one would read that he had sailed from Havre, Brest or Marseilles to some other quarter of the globe." In other words, a supervillain: powerful, omnipresent, and determined. But more a literary ancestor of the evil plotters created by Ian Fleming—another civilian who joined the fray, as a naval intelligence officer, in 1939—with little relation to the shabby little men of Eric Ambler or Graham Greene.

The real horror of the political brutality of the twentieth century, to Greene and Ambler, and their precursors, Somerset Maugham and Joseph Conrad, was that its practicioners were perfect exemplars of what Hannah Arendt was to call "the banality of evil," not monsters of superhuman cunning. Early on, Le Queux established one of the two narrative strategies that spy novels follow—mythic evil, as opposed to quotidian evil. But for Greene, there was never any question of where the truth of it lay. Speaking through Arthur Rowe, in *Ministry of Fear*, Greene says, "the Devil—and God too—had always used comic people, futile people, little suburban natures and the maimed and warped to serve his purposes. When God used them you talked emptily of Nobility and when the devil used them of Wickedness, but the material was only dull shabby human mediocrity in either case."

Thus *Ministry of Fear* follows the classic path of the literary spy novel: a hero must confront, and overcome, his own private darkness to confront, and defeat, the dark side of the world. Old as storytelling, this idea; back up far enough and extend the focus to infinity and you have Arthur Rowe and Homer's Achilles—with his *hubris*, and vulnerable heel—in the same class photograph. The strength and durability of this idea means that it summons a human experience so common and ancient that it never changes. Like the chase, which almost always concludes a spy novel—and *Ministry of Fear* is no different—it is a base element of genre fiction, and plays on very deep instincts and we like, as humans, to hear about such things.

A situation that perhaps did not entirely please Graham Greene, *The Ministry of Fear* is subtitled "An Entertainment." What on earth did he mean by this? That the novel was a throwaway, feeding the low appetites of the reading mob? That, if he chose, he could be far more complex and insightful on the subject of the human condition? Perhaps, but *Ministry of Fear*, along with all the other novels of intrigue, does not suffer in comparison to Greene's novels of faith; it isn't less sophisticated, serious, or forceful, the subtitle simply acknowledges that the novel is a certain kind of genre fiction which had not, by 1941, had its reputation elevated by the work of Graham Greene, though Maugham and Ambler had already published sophisticated, high-quality spy novels.

Greene achieved his part in the elevation in two ways: with good writing—Swiss-watch narrative, which you aren't supposed to notice, and great lines, which you are—and by the fictional deployment of politics. What he learned in Freetown, and what enriches his novels for the rest of his career, is that the spy novel at its best is not a thriller, but a political novel.

So, in *The Third Man, Our Man in Havana, The Honorary Consul, The Quiet American,* and, finally, *The Human Factor,* it is *politics* that is the antidote, the ingredient that adds the serious and seductive dimension to a genre that people read on trains. But this he could not do in 1941. There is even, midway through the novel, a rather tartly managed tribute to Winston Churchill. "And of course in one great case a man who was considered too brilliant and too reckless ever to be trusted with major office was the leader of his country. One of [Rowe's] last memories was of hearing him hissed from the public gallery of a law court because he had told an abrupt unpalatable truth about an old campaign. Now he had taught the country to love his unpalatable truths."

Spy novels are, at some level, always political novels—patriotic or agnostic—but for Greene, politics meant opposition, opposition to governments and bureaucracies as the natural enemies of individual freedom. In an interview with John R. MacArthur, late in life, Greene says, "ever since the age of nineteen I've been on the Left, but I don't know if it means anything or whether it's just my way of thinking. I think it means being against dictatorship. And it's against the extremes of capitalism, which I think is represented by the United States."

The hero who must fight the amoral schemes of his own government, or its intelligence service, has become a convention of the Greene/Ambler line in espionage novels. It is everywhere, by the 1960s, in John le Carré and Len Deighton, and Greene works his way there over the four-decade course of his spy fiction—from *Stamboul Train* in 1932 to *The Human Factor* in 1978. By the time he gets to *The Quiet American,* in 1955, it is the American intelligence service that is the villain. In *Our Man in Havana*, it's his own national service—bumbling and destructive almost by accident. Eventually, with *The Human Factor* in 1978, he produces the double-agent, betrayal novel, with a hero who winds up defecting to the other side.

Greene was likely concerned with that idea—the tension between moral choice and national obligation—as he sketched the outlines of *Ministry of Fear*. Could Greene have considered his very own employers, the SIS, to be such a ministry? Was there, in the planning stages, a different novel lurking behind this title—a title so good it had to be used? One can't know, but the evil opposition in this novel does not turn out to be a real ministry—instead it's a cabal, a fifth-column conspiracy, its name a metaphor conceived by the hero.

And if the title of *The Ministry of Fear* subverts the reader's expectations, there's more where that came from, as Greene fights the constraints, the conventions of the genre, throughout the novel. He removes the hero's memory and gives him, for a time, another name. He comes to the edge of a conclusive action, then ends the chapter and suspends time—advancing beyond the climactic moment and letting the reader know what happened only in retrospect, and at leisure. Such tricks can be dislocating, even, momentarily, confusing. It's almost as if he's mad at the reader for buying a suspense novel, and mad at himself for writing it.

And at the end of *The Ministry of Fear*, the hero, whom Greene has forced to choose between love and national duty, makes a decision that may be described as unexpected. This denouement can be taken as a statement of the author's moral position, but it is also the tactic of a novelist trying to write a better spy story, and steering violently away from cliché, away from what other writers would be expected to do.

In time, he learned not to care. *The Ministry of Fear*, like all of Graham Greene's novels, is the work of a man with a God-given talent to write the English language. The pleasure of this novel, of all novels, is never the ethical position of the author, it's not in *what* they are about, it's in *how* they are about it. If you don't believe that love conquers all when you sit down to read the novel, you won't believe it when you're done. What will happen to you is that you will watch, with the author, as "the sun came

into the room like pale green underwater light." When a policeman is to take notes of Arthur Rowe's interrogation, he has "an
odd air of muted shame like a bull who has begun to realize that
he is out of place in a china shop. When he held the pencil to the
pad you expected one or the other to suffer in his awkward grasp,
and you felt too that he knew and feared the event." And when a
German bomber with a slightly mistimed engine flies over London, Greene gives it a voice, "where are you, where are you," so
that the reader will know how it sounds, and, simultaneously,
what it means. These images, and hundreds of others as good or
better, are the real heart of the genre novel, and the reason these
books are still read.

And if, along the way, love conquers all, it can generally be
counted on to do so in all genre novels. What else? You will
search in vain for a novel that tells you to do what the government wants, or tells you to take care of number one and let the
world go to hell. The best you can hope for is an amoral hero
who survives in an amoral world, and these novels are either
grounded in an implicit sigh that it's all come to this, or they're
comedies.

For a novelist writing anywhere in the intrigue genre—from
the village police station to the president's office—the pleasure is
in the strange characters, the gloomy weather, the dark streets
and sinister neighborhoods, the shabby offices and shabbier hotel
rooms, and the sharp bite of muted dialogue. That's where *The
Ministry of Fear* lives, and triumphs, becomes a novel that readers have always loved to read. Which may not be the love that
conquers all, but it can conquer a few hours on a plane or a train,
and that is, in 1941 or now, some way down the road toward
conquering the rest of it.

Suggestions for Further Reading

Norman Sherry's *Life of Graham Greene* is now complete in three volumes; the first, which appeared in 1989, covers Greene's life from 1904 to 1939, the second (1995) covers the period from 1939 to 1955, and the third (2003) takes the story from 1955 until the writer's death in 1991. There is a competing, and prosecutorial, one-volume life by Michael Shelden, *Graham Greene: The Enemy Within* (London: Heinemann, 1994). Two of Greene's own books provide a useful context for his fiction. His comments on other novelists invariably supply a commentary on his practice, and he was also an acute critic of his own work. See the *Collected Essays* (New York: Viking, 1969) and *Ways of Escape* (New York: Simon and Schuster, 1980). The essential critical volume remains the collection edited by Samuel Hynes, *Graham Greene: A Collection of Critical Essays* (Englewood Cliffs, NJ: Prentice-Hall, 1973). It reprints seminal essays by Morton Dauwen Zabel, R.W.B. Lewis, and Richard Hoggart; reviews by Evelyn Waugh and George Orwell; a fine essay on the theology of *The End of the Affair* by Ian Gregor; and an overview of Greene's career by Frank Kermode. Interested readers may also find the following of use:

Adamson, Judith. *Graham Greene and Cinema.* Norman, OK: Pilgrim Books, 1984.

———. *Graham Greene: The Dangerous Edge.* New York: St. Martin's, 1990.

Baldridge, Cates. *Graham Greene's Fictions: The Virtues of Extremity.* Columbia and London: University of Missouri Press, 2000.

Lodge, David. *Graham Greene.* New York and London: Columbia Univ. Press, 1966.

Mudford, Peter. *Graham Greene*. Plymouth, England: Northcote House in assoc. with the British Council, 1996.

Sharrock, Roger. *Saints, Sinners and Comedians: The Novels of Graham Greene*. Notre Dame, IN: University of Notre Dame Press, 1984.

Smith, Grahame. *The Achievement of Graham Greene*. Sussex: The Harvester Press, 1986.

Spurling, John. *Graham Greene*. London and New York: Methuen, 1983.

'Have they brought home the haunch?'
CHARLOTTE M. YONGE
The Little Duke

The Ministry of Fear

BOOK ONE
THE UNHAPPY MAN

CHAPTER I
THE FREE MOTHERS

'None passes without warrant.'
The Little Duke

I

There was something about a fête which drew Arthur Rowe irre-
sistibly, bound him a helpless victim to the distant blare of a
band and the knock-knock of wooden balls against coconuts. Of
course this year there were no coconuts because there was a war
on: you could tell that too from the untidy gaps between the
Bloomsbury houses—a flat fireplace half-way up a wall, like the
painted fireplace in a cheap dolls' house, and lots of mirrors and
green wall-papers, and from round a corner of the sunny afternoon the sound of glass being swept up, like the lazy noise of the
sea on a shingled beach. Otherwise the square was doing its very
best with the flags of the free nations and a mass of bunting
which had obviously been preserved by somebody ever since the
Jubilee.

Arthur Rowe looked wistfully over the railings—there were
still railings. The fête called him like innocence: it was entangled
in childhood, with vicarage gardens and girls in white summer
frocks and the smell of herbaceous borders and security. He had
no inclination to mock at these elaborately naïve ways of making
money for a cause. There was the inevitable clergyman presiding
over a rather timid game of chance; an old lady in a print dress
that came down to her ankles and a floppy garden hat hovered
officially, but with excitement, over a treasure-hunt (a little plot
of ground like a child's garden was staked out with claims), and
as the evening darkened—they would have to close early because
of the blackout—there would be some energetic work with trow-
els. And there in a corner, under a plane tree, was the fortune-
teller's booth—unless it was an impromptu outside lavatory. It all
seemed perfect in the late summer Sunday afternoon. 'My peace

I give unto you. Not as the world knoweth peace . . .' Arthur
Rowe's eyes filled with tears, as the small military band they had
somehow managed to borrow struck up again a faded song of the
last war: *Whate'er befall I'll oft recall that sunlit mountainside.*

Pacing round the railings he came towards his doom: pennies
were rattling down a curved slope on to a chequer-board—not
very many pennies. The fête was ill-attended; there were only three
stalls and people avoided those. If they had to spend money they
would rather try for a dividend—of pennies from the chequer-
board or savings-stamps from the treasure-hunt. Arthur Rowe
came along the railings, hesitantly, like an intruder, or an exile
who has returned home after many years and is uncertain of his
welcome.

He was a tall stooping lean man with black hair going grey
and a sharp narrow face, nose a little twisted out of the straight
and a too sensitive mouth. His clothes were good but gave the
impression of being uncared for; you would have said a bachelor
if it had not been for an indefinable married look . . .

'The charge,' said the middle-aged lady at the gate, 'is a
shilling, but that doesn't seem quite fair. If you wait another five
minutes you can come in at the reduced rate. I always feel it's
only right to warn people when it gets as late as this.'

'It's very thoughtful of you.'

'We don't want people to feel cheated—even in a good cause,
do we?'

'I don't think I'll wait, all the same. I'll come straight in. What
exactly is the cause?'

'Comforts for free mothers—I mean mothers of the free nations.'

Arthur Rowe stepped joyfully back into adolescence, into
childhood. There had always been a fête about this time of the
year in the vicarage garden, a little way off the Trumpington
Road, with the flat Cambridgeshire field beyond the extempo-
rized bandstand, and at the end of the fields the pollarded willows by the stickleback stream and the chalk-pit on the slopes of
what in Cambridgeshire they call a hill. He came to these fêtes
every year with an odd feeling of excitement—as if anything
might happen, as if the familiar pattern of life that afternoon
might be altered for ever. The band beat in the warm late sunlight, the brass quivered like haze, and the faces of strange young

women would get mixed up with Mrs Troup, who kept the general store and post office, Miss Savage the Sunday School teacher, the publicans' and the clergy's wives. When he was a child he would follow his mother round the stalls—the baby clothes, the pink woollies, the art pottery, and always last and best the white elephants. It was always as though there might be discovered on the white elephant stall some magic ring which would give three wishes or the heart's desire, but the odd thing was that when he went home that night with only a second-hand copy of *The Little Duke*, by Charlotte M. Yonge, or an out-of-date atlas advertising Mazawattee tea, he felt no disappointment: he carried with him the sound of brass, the sense of glory, of a future that would be braver than today. In adolescence the excitement had a different source; he imagined he might find at the vicarage some girl whom he had never seen before, and courage would touch his tongue, and in the late evening there would be dancing on the lawn and the smell of stocks. But because these dreams had never come true there remained the sense of innocence . . .

And the sense of excitement. He couldn't believe that when he had passed the gate and reached the grass under the plane trees nothing would happen, though now it wasn't a girl he wanted or a magic ring, but something far less likely—to mislay the events of twenty years. His heart beat and the band played, and inside the lean experienced skull lay childhood.

'Come and try your luck, sir?' said the clergyman in a voice which was obviously baritone at socials.

'If I could have some coppers.'

'Thirteen for a shilling, sir.'

Arthur Rowe slid the pennies one after the other down the little inclined groove and watched them stagger on the board.

'Not your lucky day, sir, I'm afraid. What about another shilling's-worth? Another little flutter in a good cause?'

'I think perhaps I'll flutter further on.' His mother, he remembered, had always fluttered further on, carefully dividing her patronage in equal parts, though she left the coconuts and the gambling to the children. At some stalls it had been very difficult to find anything at all, even to give away to the servants . . .

Under a little awning there was a cake on a stand surrounded by a small group of enthusiastic sightseers. A lady was explaining, 'We clubbed our butter rations—and Mr Tatham was able to get hold of the currants.'

She turned to Arthur Rowe and said, 'Won't you take a ticket and guess its weight?'

He lifted it and said at random, 'Three pounds five ounces.'

'A very good guess, I should say. Your wife must have been teaching you.'

He winced away from the group. 'Oh no, I'm not married.'

War had made the stall-holders' task extraordinarily difficult: second-hand Penguins for the Forces filled most of one stall, while another was sprinkled rather than filled with the strangest second-hand clothes—the cast-offs of old age—long petticoats with pockets, high lacy collars with bone supports, routed out of Edwardian drawers and discarded at last for the sake of the free mothers, and corsets that clanked. Baby clothes played only a very small part now that wool was rationed and the second-hand was so much in demand among friends. The third stall was the traditional one—the white elephant—though black might have described it better since many Anglo-Indian families had surrendered their collections of ebony elephants. There were also brass ash-trays, embroidered match-cases which had not held matches now for a very long time, books too shabby for the bookstall, two post-card albums, a complete set of Dickens cigarette-cards, an electro-plated egg-boiler, a long pink cigarette-holder, several embossed boxes for pins from Benares, a signed post-card of Mrs Winston Churchill, and a plateful of mixed foreign copper coins . . . Arthur Rowe turned over the books and found with an ache of the heart a dingy copy of *The Little Duke*. He paid sixpence for it and walked on. There was something threatening, it seemed to him, in the very perfection of the day. Between the plane trees which shaded the treasure-ground he could see the ruined section of the square; it was as if Providence had led him to exactly this point to indicate the difference between then and now. These people might have been playing a part in an expensive morality for his sole benefit . . .

He couldn't, of course, not take part in the treasure-hunt, though it was a sad declension to know the nature of the prize, and afterwards there remained nothing of consequence but the fortune-teller—it was a fortune-teller's booth and not a lavatory. A curtain made of a cloth brought home by somebody from Algiers dangled at the entrance. A lady caught his arm and said, 'You must. You really must. Mrs Bellairs is quite wonderful. She told my son . . .' and clutching another middle-aged lady as she went by, she went breathlessly on, 'I was just telling this gentleman about wonderful Mrs Bellairs and my son.'

'Your younger son?'

'Yes. Jack.'

The interruption enabled Rowe to escape. The sun was going down: the square garden was emptying: it was nearly time to dig up the treasure and make tracks, before darkness and blackout and siren-time. So many fortunes one had listened to, behind a country hedge, over the cards in a liner's saloon, but the fascination remained even when the fortune was cast by an amateur at a garden fête. Always, for a little while, one could half-believe in the journey overseas, in the strange dark woman, and the letter with good news. Once somebody had refused to tell his fortune at all—it was just an act, of course, put on to impress him—and yet that silence had really come closer to the truth than anything else.

He lifted the curtain and felt his way in.

It was very dark inside the tent and he could hardly distinguish Mrs Bellairs, a bulky figure shrouded in what looked like cast-off widow's weeds—or perhaps it was some kind of peasant's costume. He was unprepared for Mrs Bellairs' deep powerful voice: a convincing voice. He had expected the wavering tones of a lady whose other hobby was water-colours.

'Sit down, please, and cross my hand with silver.'

'It's so dark.'

But now he could just manage to make her out: it was a peasant's costume with a big head-dress and a veil of some kind tucked back over her shoulder. He found a half-crown and sketched a cross upon her palm.

'Your hand.'

He held it out and felt it gripped firmly as though she intended to convey: expect no mercy. A tiny electric night-light was reflected down on the girdle of Venus, the little crosses which should have meant children, the long, long line of life . . .

He said, 'You're up-to-date. The electric nightlight, I mean.'

She paid no attention to his flippancy. She said, 'First the character, then the past: by law I am not allowed to tell the future. You're a man of determination and imagination and you are very sensitive—to pain, but you sometimes feel you have not been allowed a proper scope for your gifts. You want to do great deeds, not dream them all day long. Never mind. After all, you have made one woman happy.'

He tried to take his hand away, but she held it too firmly: it would have been a tug of war. She said, 'You have found the true contentment in a happy marriage. Try to be more patient, though. Now I will tell you your past.'

He said quickly, 'Don't tell me the past. Tell me the future.'

It was as if he had pressed a button and stopped a machine. The silence was odd and unexpected. He hadn't hoped to silence her, though he dreaded what she might say, for even inaccuracies about things which are dead can be as painful as the truth. He pulled his hand again and it came away. He felt awkward sitting there with his hand his own again.

Mrs Bellairs said, 'My instructions are these. What you want is the cake. You must give the weight as four pounds eight and a half ounces.'

'Is that the right weight?'

'That's immaterial.'

He was thinking hard and staring at Mrs Bellairs' left hand which the light caught: a square ugly palm with short blunt fingers prickly with big art-and-crafty rings of silver and lumps of stone. Who had given her instructions? Did she refer to her familiar spirits? And if so, why had she chosen him to win the cake? or was it really just a guess of her own? Perhaps she was backing a great number of weights, he thought, smiling in the dark, and expected at least a slice from the winner. Cake, good cake, was scarce nowadays.

'You can go now,' Mrs Bellairs said.

'Thank you very much.'

At any rate, Arthur Rowe thought, there was no harm in trying the tip—she might have stable information, and he returned to the cake-stall. Although the garden was nearly empty now except for the helpers, a little knot of people always surrounded the cake, and indeed it was a magnificent cake. He had always liked cakes, especially rich Dundees and dark brown home-made fruit-cakes tasting elusively of Guinness. He said to the lady at the stall, 'You won't think me greedy if I have another six-pennyworth?'

'No. Please.'

'I should say, then, four pounds eight and a half ounces.'

He was conscious of an odd silence, as if all the afternoon they had been waiting for just this, but hadn't somehow expected it from him. Then a stout woman who hovered on the outskirts gave a warm and hearty laugh. 'Lawks,' she said. 'Anybody can tell you're a bachelor.'

'As a matter of fact,' the lady behind the stall rebuked her sharply, 'this gentleman has won. He is not more than a fraction of an ounce out. That counts,' she said, with nervous whimsical-ity, 'as a direct hit.'

'Four pounds eight ounces,' the stout woman said. 'Well, you be careful, that's all. It'll be as heavy as lead.'

'On the contrary, it's made with real eggs.'

The stout woman went away laughing ironically in the direc-tion of the clothing stall.

Again he was aware of the odd silence as the cake was handed over: they all came round and watched—three middle-aged ladies, the clergyman who had deserted the chequer-board, and looking up Rowe saw the gypsy's curtain lifted and Mrs Bellairs peering out at him. He would have welcomed the laughter of the stout outsider as something normal and relaxed: there was such an in-tensity about these people as though they were attending the main ceremony of the afternoon. It was as if the experience of childhood renewed had taken a strange turn, away from inno-cence. There had never been anything quite like this in Cam-bridgeshire. It was dusk and the stall-holders were ready to pack up. The stout woman sailed towards the gates carrying a corset (no paper wrappings allowed). Arthur Rowe said, 'Thank you. Thank you very much.' He felt so conscious of being sur-rounded that he wondered whether anyone would step aside and let him out. Of course the clergyman did, laying a hand upon his upper arm and squeezing gently. 'Good fellow,' he said, 'good fellow.'

The treasure-hunt was being hastily concluded, but this time there was nothing for Arthur Rowe. He stood with his cake and *The Little Duke* and watched. 'We've left it very late, very late,' the lady wailed beneath her floppy hat.

But late as it was, somebody had thought it worth while to pay for entrance at the gate. A taxi had driven up, and a man made hastily for the gypsy tent rather as a mortal sinner in fear of immediate death might dive towards a confessional-box. Was this another who had great faith in wonderful Mrs Bellairs, or was it perhaps Mrs Bellairs' husband come prosaically to fetch her home from her unholy rites?

The speculation interested Arthur Rowe, and he scarcely took in the fact that the last of the treasure-hunters was making for the garden gate and he was alone under the great planes with the stall-keepers. When he realized it he felt the embarrassment of the last guest in a restaurant who notices suddenly the focused look of the waiters lining the wall.

But before he could reach the gate the clergyman had intercepted him jocosely. 'Not carrying that prize of yours away so soon?'

'It seems quite time to go.'

'Wouldn't you feel inclined—it's usually the custom at a fête like this—to put the cake up again—for the Good Cause?'

Something in his manner—an elusive patronage as though he were a kindly prefect teaching to a new boy the sacred customs of the school—offended Rowe. 'Well, you haven't any visitors left surely?'

'I meant to auction—among the rest of us.' He squeezed Rowe's arm again gently. 'Let me introduce myself. My name's Sinclair. I'm supposed, you know, to have a touch—for touching.' He gave a small giggle. 'You see that lady over there—that's Mrs Fraser—*the* Mrs Fraser. A little friendly auction like this gives her the opportunity of presenting a note to the cause—unobtrusively.'

'It sounds quite obtrusive to me.'

'They're an awfully nice set of people. I'd like you to know them, Mr . . .'

Rowe said obstinately, 'It's not the way to run a fête—to prevent people taking their prizes.'

'Well, you don't exactly come to these affairs to make a profit, do you?' There were possibilities of nastiness in Mr Sinclair that had not shown on the surface.

'I don't want to make a profit. Here's a pound note, but I fancy the cake.'

Mr Sinclair made a gesture of despair towards the others openly and rudely.

Rowe said, 'Would you like *The Little Duke* back? Mrs Fraser might give a note for that just as unobtrusively.'

'There's really no need to take that tone.'

The afternoon had certainly been spoiled: brass bands lost their associations in the ugly little fracas. 'Good afternoon,' Rowe said.

But he wasn't to be allowed to go yet; a kind of deputation advanced to Mr Sinclair's support—the treasure-hunt lady flapped along in the van. She said, smiling coyly, 'I'm afraid I am the bearer of ill tidings.'

'You want the cake too,' Rowe said.

She smiled with a sort of elderly impetuosity. 'I must *have* the cake. You see—there's been a mistake. About the weight. It wasn't—what you said.' She consulted a slip of paper. 'That rude woman was right. The real weight was three pounds seven ounces. And that gentleman,' she pointed towards the stall, 'won it.'

It was the man who had arrived late in the taxi and made for Mrs Bellairs' booth. He kept in the dusky background by the cake-stall and let the ladies fight for him. Had Mrs Bellairs given him a better tip?

Rowe said, 'That's very odd. He got the exact weight?'

There was a little hesitation in her reply—as if she had been cornered in a witness-box undrilled for that question. 'Well, not exact. But he was within three ounces.' She seemed to gain confidence. 'He guessed three pounds ten ounces.'

'In that case,' Rowe said, 'I keep the cake because you see I guessed three pounds five the first time. Here is a pound for the cause. Good evening.'

He'd really taken them by surprise this time; they were wordless, they didn't even thank him for the note. He looked back from the pavement and saw the group from the cake-stall surge forward to join the rest, and he waved his hand. A poster on the railings said: 'The Comforts for Mothers of the Free Nations Fund. A fête will be held . . . under the patronage of royalty . . .'

2

Arthur Rowe lived in Guilford Street. A bomb early in the blitz had fallen in the middle of the street and blasted both sides, but Rowe stayed on. Houses went overnight, but he stayed. There were boards instead of glass in every room, and the doors no longer quite fitted and had to be propped at night. He had a sitting-room and a bedroom on the first floor, and he was done for by Mrs Purvis, who also stayed—because it was her house. He had taken the rooms furnished and simply hadn't bothered to make any alterations. He was like a man camping in a desert. Any books there were came from the two-penny or the public library except for *The Old Curiosity Shop* and *David Copperfield*, which he read, as people used to read the Bible, over and over again till he could have quoted chapter and verse, not so much because he liked them as because he had read them as a child, and they carried no adult memories. The pictures were Mrs Purvis's— a wild water-colour of the Bay of Naples at sunset and several steel engravings and a photograph of the former Mr Purvis in the odd dated uniform of 1914. The ugly arm-chair, the table covered with a thick woollen cloth, the fern in the window—all were Mrs Purvis's, and the radio was hired. Only the packet of cigarettes on the mantelpiece belonged to Rowe, and the tooth-brush and shaving tackle in the bedroom (the soap was Mrs Purvis's), and inside a cardboard box his sleeping pills. In the sitting-room there was not even a bottle of ink or a packet of stationery: Rowe didn't write letters, and he paid his income tax at the post office.

You might say that a cake and a book added appreciably to his possessions.

When he reached home he rang for Mrs Purvis. 'Mrs Purvis,' he said, 'I won this magnificent cake at the fête in the square. Have you by any chance a tin large enough?'

'It's a good-sized cake for these days,' Mrs Purvis said hungrily.

It wasn't the war that had made her hungry; she had always, she would sometimes confide to him, been like it from a girl. Small and thin and bedraggled she had let herself go after her husband died. She would be seen eating sweets at all hours of the day: the stairs smelt like a confectioner's shop: little sticky pape~ ¹ would be found mislaid in corners, and if she ~~ ᵢ ered in the house, you might be suᵢ
for fruit gums. 'It weighs two and
ounce,' Mrs Purvis said.

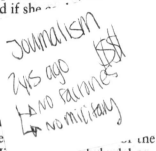

'It weighs nearly three and a half.
'Oh, it couldn't do that.'
'You weigh it.'
When she was gone he sat down in
his eyes. The fête was over: the imme   ᵤₗ ᵢne
week ahead stretched before him. Hi   ᵤₗ work had been
journalism, but that had ceased two years ago. He had four hundred a year of his own, and as the saying goes, he didn't have to
worry. The army wouldn't have him, and his short experience of
civil defence had left him more alone than ever—they wouldn't
have him either. There were munition factories, but he was tied
to London. Perhaps if every street with which he had associations were destroyed, he would be free to go—he would find a
factory near Trumpington. After a raid he used to sally out and
note with a kind of hope that this restaurant or that shop existed
no longer—it was like loosening the bars of a prison cell one
by one.

Mrs Purvis brought the cake in a large biscuit-tin. 'Three and
a half!' she said scornfully. 'Never trust these charities. It's just
under three.'

He opened his eyes. 'That's strange,' he said, 'that's very
strange.' He thought for awhile. 'Let me have a slice,' he said.
Mrs Purvis hungrily obeyed. It tasted good. He said, 'Put it away
in the tin now. It's the kind of cake that improves with keeping.'

'It'll get stale,' Mrs Purvis said.

'Oh no, it's made with real eggs.' But he couldn't bear the yearn-
ing way in which she handled it. 'You can give yourself a slice, Mrs
Purvis,' he said. People could always get things out of him by
wanting them enough; it broke his precarious calm to feel that
people suffered. Then he would do anything for them. Anything.

3

It was the very next day that the stranger moved in to Mrs Purvis's back room on the third floor. Rowe met him in the evening of the second day on the dusk of the stairs; the man was talking to Mrs Purvis in a vibrant undertone, and Mrs Purvis stood back against the wall with an out-of-depth scared expression. 'One day,' the man was saying, 'you'll see.' He was dark and dwarfish and twisted in his enormous shoulders with infantile paralysis.

'Oh, sir,' Mrs Purvis said to Rowe with relief, 'this gentleman wants to hear the news. I said I thought perhaps you'd let him listen . . .'

'Come in,' Rowe said, and opened his door and ushered the stranger in—his first caller. The room at this time of the evening was very dim; beaverboard in the windows kept out the last remains of daylight and the single globe was shaded for fear of cracks. The Bay of Naples faded into the wallpaper. The little light that went on behind the radio dial had a homely effect like a nightlight in a child's nursery—a child who is afraid of the dark. A voice said with hollow cheeriness, 'Good night, children, good night.'

The stranger hunched down in one of the two easy-chairs and began to comb his scalp with his fingers for scurf. You felt that sitting was his natural position; he became powerful then with his big out-of-drawing shoulders in evidence and his height disguised. He said, 'Just in time,' and without offering his case he lit a cigarette; a black bitter tang of Caporal spread over the room.

'Will you have a biscuit?' Rowe asked, opening his cupboard door. Like most men who live alone, he believed his own habits to be the world's; it never occurred to him that other men might not eat biscuits at six.

'Wouldn't you like the cake?' Mrs Purvis asked, lingering in the doorway.

'I think we had better finish the biscuits first.'

'Cakes,' said the stranger, 'are hardly worth eating these days.'

'But this one,' Mrs Purvis said with vicarious pride, 'was made with real eggs. Mr Rowe won it in a raffle.' And just at that moment the news began—'and this is Joseph Macleod reading it.' The

stranger crouched back in his chair and listened; there was something supercilious in his manner, as though he were listening to
stories of which only he was in a position to know the real truth.

'It's a little more cheerful tonight,' Rowe said.

'They feed us,' the stranger said.

'You won't want the cake?' Mrs Purvis asked.

'Well, perhaps this gentleman would rather have a biscuit . . .?'

'I'm very fond of cake,' the stranger said sharply, 'when it's
good cake,' as though his taste were the only thing that mattered,
and he stamped out his Caporal on the floor.

'Then fetch it, Mrs Purvis, and a pot of tea.'

The stranger hoisted his deformed figure round in the chair to
watch the cake brought in. Certainly he was fond of cake: it was
as though he couldn't keep his eyes off it. He seemed to hold his
breath until it reached the table safely; then he sat impatiently
forward in his chair.

'A knife, Mrs Purvis?'

'Oh dear, oh dear. This time of night,' Mrs Purvis explained, 'I
always get forgetful. It's the sirens.'

'Never mind,' Rowe said, 'I'll use my own.' He brought tenderly
out of his pocket his last remaining treasure—a big schoolboy's
knife. He couldn't resist displaying its beauties to a stranger—the
corkscrew, the tweezers, the blade that shot open and locked
when you pressed a catch. 'There's only one shop you can get
these in now,' he said, 'a little place off the Haymarket.' But the
stranger paid him no attention, waiting impatiently to see the
knife slide in. Far away on the outskirts of London the sirens began their nightly wail.

The stranger's voice said, 'Now you and I are intelligent men.
We can talk freely . . . about things.' Rowe had no idea what he
meant. Somewhere two miles above their heads an enemy bomber
came up from the estuary. 'Where are you? Where are you?' its
uneven engine-beat pronounced over and over again. Mrs Purvis
had left them; there was a scrambling on the stairs as she
brought her bedding down, a slam of the front door: she was
making for her favourite shelter down the street. 'There's no
need for people like you and me to get angry,' the stranger said,
'about things.'

He pushed his great deformed shoulder into the light, getting nearer to Rowe, sidling his body to the chair's edge. 'The stupidity of this war,' he said. 'Why should you and I . . . intelligent men . . .?' He said, 'They talk about democracy, don't they. But you and I don't swallow stuff like that. If you want democracy— I don't say you do, but if you want it—you must go to Germany for it. What do you want?' he suddenly inquired.

'Peace,' Rowe said.

'Exactly. So do we.'

'I don't suppose I mean your kind of peace.'

But the stranger listened to nobody but himself. He said, 'We can give you peace. We are working for peace.'

'Who are we?'

'My friends and I.'

'Conscientious objectors?'

The deformed shoulder moved impatiently. He said, 'One can worry too much about one's conscience.'

'What else could we have done? Let them take Poland too without a protest?'

'You and I are men who know the world.' When the stranger leant forward, his chair slid an inch with him, so that he bore steadily down on Rowe like something mechanized. 'We know that Poland was one of the most corrupt countries in Europe.'

'Who are we to judge?'

The chair groaned nearer. 'Exactly. A Government like the one we had . . . and have . . .'

Rowe said slowly, 'It's like any other crime. It involves the innocent. It isn't any excuse that your chief victim was . . . dishonest, or that the judge drinks . . .'

The stranger took him up. Whatever he said had an intolerable confidence. 'How wrong you are. Why, even murder can sometimes be excused. We've all known cases, haven't we . . .?'

'Murder . . .' Rowe considered slowly and painfully. He had never felt this man's confidence about anything. He said, 'They say, don't they, that you shouldn't do evil that good may come.'

'Oh, poppycock,' sneered the little man. 'The Christian ethic. You're intelligent. Now I challenge you. Have you ever really followed that rule?'

'No,' Rowe said. 'No.'

'Of course not,' the stranger said. 'Haven't we checked up on you? But even without that, I could have told . . . you're intelligent . . .' It was as if intelligence was the password to some small exclusive society. 'The moment I saw you, I knew you weren't— one of the sheep.' He started violently as a gun in a square nearby went suddenly off, shaking the house, and again faintly up from the coast came the noise of another plane. Nearer and nearer the guns opened up, but the plane pursued its steady deadly tenor until again one heard, 'Where are you? Where are you?' overhead and the house shook to the explosion of the neighbouring gun. Then a whine began, came down towards them like something aimed deliberately at this one insignificant building. But the bomb burst half a mile away: you could feel the ground dent. 'I was saying,' the stranger said, but he'd lost touch, he had mislaid his confidence: now he was just a cripple trying not to be frightened of death. He said, 'We're going to have it properly tonight. I hoped they were just passing . . .'

Again the drone began.

'Have another piece of cake?' Rowe asked. He couldn't help feeling sorry for the man: it wasn't courage in his own case that freed him from fear so much as loneliness. 'It may not be . . .' he waited till the scream stopped and the bomb exploded—very near this time—probably the end of the next street: *The Little Duke* had fallen on its side . . . 'much.' They waited for a stick of bombs to drop, pounding a path towards them, but there were no more.

'No, thank you—that's to say, please, yes.' The man had a curious way of crumbling the cake when he took a slice: it might have been nerves. To be a cripple in wartime, Rowe thought, is a terrible thing; he felt dangerous pity stirring in the bowels. 'You say you checked me up, but who are you?' He cut himself a piece of cake and felt the stranger's eyes on him all the time like a starving man watching through the heavy plate-glass window the gourmet in the restaurant. Outside an ambulance screamed by, and again a plane came up. The night's noise and fires and deaths were now in train; they would go on like a routine till three or four in the morning: a bombing pilot's eight-hour day. He said, 'I was telling you about this knife . . .' During the intense preoccupation of a raid it was hard to stick to any one line of thought.

The stranger interrupted, laying a hand on his wrist—a nervous bony hand attached to an enormous arm. 'You know there's been a mistake. That cake was never meant for you.'

'I won it. What do you mean?'

'You weren't meant to win it. There was a mistake in the figures.'

'It's a bit late now to worry, isn't it?' Rowe said. 'We've eaten nearly half.'

But the cripple took no notice of that. He said, 'They've sent me here to get it back. We'll pay in reason.'

'Who are they?'

But he knew who *they* were. It was comic; he could see the whole ineffective rabble coming across the grass at him: the elderly woman in the floppy hat who almost certainly painted water-colours, the intense whimsical lady who had managed the raffle, and wonderful Mrs Bellairs. He smiled and drew his hand away. 'What are you all playing at?' he asked. Never had a raffle, surely, been treated quite so seriously before. 'What good is the cake to you now?'

The other watched him with gloom. Rowe tried to raise the cloud. 'I suppose,' he said, 'it's the principle of the thing. Forget it and have another cup of tea. I'll fetch the kettle.'

'You needn't bother. I want to discuss . . .'

'There's hardly anything left to discuss, and it isn't any bother.'

The stranger picked at the scurf which had lodged below his finger-nail. He said, 'There's no more to say then?'

'Nothing at all.'

'In that case . . .' the stranger said: he began to listen as the next plane beat towards them. He shifted uneasily as the first guns fired, far away in East London. 'Perhaps I will have another cup.'

When Rowe returned the stranger was pouring out the milk—and he had cut himself another piece of cake. He was conspicuously at home with his chair drawn nearer to the gas fire. He waved his hand towards Rowe's chair as if *he* were the host, and he seemed quite to have forgotten the squabble of a moment ago. 'I was thinking,' he said, 'while you were out of the room that it's intellectuals like ourselves who are the only free men. Not bound

by conventions, patriotic emotions, sentimentality . . . we haven't
what they call a stake in the country. We aren't shareholders and
it doesn't matter to us if the company goes on the rocks. That's
quite a good image, don't you think?'

'Why do you say "we"?'

'Well,' the cripple said, 'I see no sign that you are taking any
active part. And of course we know why, don't we?' and suddenly, grossly, he winked.

Rowe took a sip of tea: it was too hot to swallow . . . an odd
flavour haunted him like something remembered, something unhappy. He took a piece of cake to drown the taste, and looking
up caught the anxious speculative eyes of the cripple, fixed on
him, waiting. He took another slow sip and then he remembered.
Life struck back at him like a scorpion, over the shoulder. His
chief feeling was astonishment and anger, that anybody should
do this to *him*. He dropped the cup on the floor and stood up.
The cripple trundled away from him like something on wheels:
the huge back and the long strong arms prepared themselves . . .
and then the bomb went off.

They hadn't heard the plane this time; destruction had come
drifting quietly down on green silk cords: the walls suddenly
caved in. They were not even aware of noise.

Blast is an odd thing; it is just as likely to have the effect of an
embarrassing dream as of man's serious vengeance on man, landing you naked in the street or exposing you in your bed or on
your lavatory seat to the neighbours' gaze. Rowe's head was
singing; he felt as though he had been walking in his sleep; he
was lying in a strange position, in a strange place. He got up and
saw an enormous quantity of saucepans all over the floor: something like the twisted engine of an old car turned out to be a re-
frigerator. He looked up and saw Charles's Wain heeling over an
arm-chair which was poised thirty feet above his head: he looked
down and saw the Bay of Naples intact at his feet. He felt as
though he were in a strange country without any maps to help
him, trying to get his position by the stars.

Three flares came sailing slowly, beautifully, down, clusters of
spangles off a Christmas tree: his shadow shot out in front of
him and he felt exposed, like a gaolbreaker caught in a search-
light beam. The awful thing about a raid is that it goes on: your

own private disaster may happen early, but the raid doesn't stop. They were machine-gunning the flares: two broke with a sound like cracking plates and the third came to earth in Russell Square; the darkness returned coldly and comfortingly.

But in the light of the flares Rowe had seen several things; he had discovered where he was—in the basement kitchen: the chair above his head was in his own room on the first floor, the front wall had gone and all the roof, and the cripple lay beside the chair, one arm swinging loosely down at him. He had dropped neatly and precisely at Rowe's feet a piece of uncrumbled cake. A warden called from the street, 'Is anyone hurt in there?' and Rowe said aloud in a sudden return of his rage, 'It's beyond a joke: it's beyond a joke.'

'You're telling me,' the warden called down to him from the shattered street as yet another raider came up from the south-east muttering to them both like a witch in a child's dream, 'Where are you? Where are you? Where are you?'

CHAPTER 2
PRIVATE INQUIRIES

'There was a deep scar long after the pain had ceased.'
The Little Duke

I

Orthotex—the Longest Established Private Inquiry Bureau in the Metropolis—still managed to survive at the unravaged end of Chancery Lane, close to a book auctioneer's, between a public house which in peace-time had been famous for its buffet and a legal bookshop. It was on the fourth floor, but there was no lift. On the first floor was a notary public, on the second floor the office of a monthly called *Fitness and Freedom,* and the third was a flat which nobody occupied now.

Arthur Rowe pushed open a door marked Inquiries, but there was no one there. A half-eaten sausage-roll lay in a saucer beside an open telephone directory: it might, for all one knew, have lain there for weeks. It gave the office an air of sudden abandonment, like the palaces of kings in exile where the tourist is shown the magazines yet open at the page which royalty turned before fleeing years ago. Arthur Rowe waited a minute and then explored further, trying another door.

A bald-headed man hurriedly began to put a bottle away in a filing cabinet.

Rowe said, 'Excuse me. There seemed to be nobody about. I was looking for Mr Rennit.'

'I'm Mr Rennit.'

'Somebody recommended me to come here.'

The bald-headed man watched Rowe suspiciously with one hand on the filing cabinet. 'Who, if I may ask?'

'It was years ago. A man called Keyser.'

'I don't remember him.'

'I hardly do myself. He wasn't a friend of mine. I met him in a train. He told me he had been in trouble about some letters . . .'

'You should have made an appointment.'

'I'm sorry,' Rowe said. 'Apparently you don't want clients. I'll say good morning.'

'Now, now,' Mr Rennit said. 'You don't want to lose your temper. I'm a busy man, and there's ways of doing things. If you'll be brief . . .' Like a man who deals in something disreputable—pornographic books or illegal operations—he treated his customer with a kind of superior contempt, as if it was not he who wanted to sell his goods, but the other who was over-anxious to buy. He sat down at his desk and said as an afterthought, 'Take a chair.' He fumbled in a drawer and hastily tucked back again what he found there; at last he discovered a pad and pencil. 'Now,' he said, 'when did you first notice anything wrong?' He leant back and picked at a tooth with his pencil point, his breath whistling slightly between the uneven dentures. He looked abandoned like the other room: his collar was a little frayed and his shirt was not quite clean. But beggars, Rowe told himself, could not be choosers.

'Name?' Mr Rennit went on. 'Present address?' He stubbed the paper fiercely, writing down the answers. At the name of a hotel he raised his head and said sombrely, 'In your position you can't be too careful.'

'I think perhaps,' Rowe said, 'I'd better begin at the beginning.'

'My good sir,' Mr Rennit said, 'you can take it from me that I know all the beginnings. I've been in this line of business for thirty years. Thirty years. Every client thinks he's a unique case. He's nothing of the kind. He's just a repetition. All I need from you is the answer to certain questions. The rest we can manage without you. Now then—when did you notice anything wrong, wife's coldness?'

'I'm not married,' Rowe said.

Mr Rennit shot him a look of disgust; he felt guilty of a quibble. 'Breach of promise, eh?' Mr Rennit asked. 'Have you written any letters?'

'It's not breach of promise either.'

'Blackmail?'

'No.'

'Then why,' Mr Rennit asked angrily, 'do you come to me?' He added his tag, 'I'm a busy man,' but never had anyone been so palpably unemployed. There were two trays on his desk marked

In and Out, but the Out tray was empty and all the In tray held was a copy of *Men Only*. Rowe might perhaps have left if he had known any other address, and if it had not been for that sense of pity which is more promiscuous than lust. Mr Rennit was angry because he had not been given time to set his scene, and he could so obviously not afford his anger. There was a kind of starved nobility in the self-sacrifice of his rage.

'Doesn't a detective deal with anything but divorces and breaches of promise?'

Mr Rennit said, 'This is a respectable business with a tradition. I'm not Sherlock Holmes. You don't expect to find a man in my position, do you, crawling about floors with a microscope looking for blood-stains?' He said stiffly, 'If you are in any trouble of that kind, I advise you to go to the police.'

'Listen,' Rowe said, 'be reasonable. You know you can do with a client just as much as I can do with you. I can pay, pay well. Be sensible and unlock that cupboard and let's have a drink on it together. These raids are bad for the nerves. One has to have a little something . . .'

The stiffness drained slowly out of Mr Rennit's attitude as he looked cautiously back at Rowe. He stroked his bald head and said, 'Perhaps you're right. One gets rattled. I've never objected to stimulants *as* stimulants.'

'Everybody needs them nowadays.'

'It was bad last night at Purley. Not many bombs, but the waiting. Not that we haven't had our share, and land-mines . . .'

'The place where I live went last night.'

'You don't say,' Mr Rennit said without interest, opening the filing cabinet and reaching for the bottle. 'Now last week . . . at Purley . . .' He was just like a man discussing his operations. 'Not a hundred yards away . . .'

'We both deserve a drink,' Rowe said.

Mr Rennit—the ice broken—suddenly became confiding. 'I suppose I was a bit sharp. One does get rattled. War plays hell with a business like this.' He explained. 'The reconciliations—you wouldn't believe human nature could be so contrary. And then, of course, the registrations have made it very difficult. People daren't go to hotels as they used to. And you can't *prove* anything from motor-cars.'

'It must be difficult for you.'

'It's a case of holding out,' Mr Rennit said, 'keeping our backs to the wall until peace comes. Then there'll be such a crop of divorces, breaches of promise . . .' He contemplated the situation with uncertain optimism over the bottle. 'You'll excuse a teacup?' He said, 'When peace comes an old-established business like this—with connections—will be a gold-mine.' He added gloomily, 'Or so I tell myself.'

Listening Rowe thought, as he often did, that you couldn't take such an odd world seriously, and yet all the time, in fact, he took it with a mortal seriousness. The grand names stood permanently like statues in his mind: names like Justice and Retribution, though what they both boiled down to was simply Mr Rennit, hundreds and hundreds of Mr Rennits. But of course if you believed in God—and the Devil—the thing wasn't quite so comic. Because the Devil—and God too—had always used comic people, futile people, little suburban natures and the maimed and warped to serve his purposes. When God used them you talked emptily of Nobility and when the devil used them of Wickedness, but the material was only dull shabby human mediocrity in either case.

'. . . new orders. But it will always be the same world, I hope,' Mr Rennit was saying.

'Queer things do happen in it, all the same,' Rowe said. 'That's why I'm here.'

'Ah yes,' Mr Rennit said. 'We'll just fill our cups and then to business. I'm sorry I have no soda-water. Now just tell me what's troubling you—as if I was your best friend.'

'Somebody tried to kill me. It doesn't sound important when so many of us are being killed every night—but it made me angry at the time.'

Mr Rennit looked at him imperturbably over the rim of his cup. 'Did you say you were *not* married?'

'There's no woman in it. It all began,' Rowe said, 'with a cake.' He described the fête to Mr Rennit, the anxiety of all the helpers to get the cake back, the stranger's visit . . . and then the bomb. 'I wouldn't have thought twice about it,' Rowe said, 'if it hadn't been for the taste the tea had.'

'Just imagination, probably.'

'But I knew the taste. It was—hyoscine,' he admitted reluctantly.

'Was the man killed?'

'They took him to hospital, but when I called today he'd been fetched away. It was only concussion and his friends wanted him back.'

'The hospital would have the name and address.'

'They had a name and address, but the address—I tried the London Directory—simply didn't exist.' He looked up across the desk at Mr Rennit expecting some sign of surprise—even in an odd world it was an odd story, but Mr Rennit said calmly, 'Of course there are a dozen explanations.' He stuck his fingers into his waistcoat and considered. 'For instance,' he said, 'it might have been a kind of confidence trick. They are always up to new dodges, those people. He might have offered to take the cake off you—for a large sum. He'd have told you something valuable was hidden in it.'

'Something hidden in it?'

'Plans of a Spanish treasure off the coast of Ireland. Something romantic. He'd have wanted you to give him a mark of confidence in return. Something substantial like twenty pounds while he went to the bank. Leaving you the cake, of course.'

'It makes one wonder . . .'

'Oh, it would have worked out,' Mr Rennit said. It was extraordinary, his ability to reduce everything to a commonplace level. Even air-raids were only things that occurred at Purley.

'Or take another possibility,' Mr Rennit said. 'If you are right about the tea. I don't believe it, mind. He might have introduced himself to you with robbery in mind. Perhaps he followed you from the fête. Did you flourish your money about?'

'I did give them a pound when they wanted the cake.'

'A man,' Mr Rennit said, with a note of relief, 'who gives a pound for a cake is a man with money. Thieves don't carry drugs as a rule, but he sounds a neurotic type.'

'But the cake?'

'Pure patter. He hadn't really come for the cake.'

'And your next explanation? You said there were a dozen.'

'I always prefer the Straightforward,' Mr Rennit said, running his fingers up and down the whisky bottle. 'Perhaps there was a genuine mistake about the cake and he had come for it. Perhaps it contained some kind of a prize . . .'

'And the drug was imagination again?'

'It's the straightforward explanation.'

Mr Rennit's calm incredulity shook Rowe. He said with resentment, 'In all your long career as a detective, have you never come across such a thing as murder—or a murderer?'

Mr Rennit's nose twitched over the cup. 'Frankly,' he said, 'no. I haven't. Life, you know, isn't like a detective story. Murderers are rare people to meet. They belong to a class of their own.'

'That's interesting to me.'

'They are very, very seldom,' Mr Rennit said, 'what we call gentlemen. Outside of story-books. You might say that they belong to the lower orders.'

'Perhaps,' Rowe said, 'I ought to tell you that I am a murderer myself.'

2

'Ha-ha,' said Mr Rennit miserably.

'That's what makes me so furious,' Rowe said. 'That they should pick on me, me. They are such amateurs.'

'You are—a professional?' Mr Rennit asked with a watery and unhappy smile.

Rowe said, 'Yes, I am, if thinking of the thing for two years before you do it, dreaming about it nearly every night until at last you take the drug out from the unlocked drawer, makes you one . . . and then sitting in the dock trying to make out what the judge is really thinking, watching each one of the jury, wondering what *he* thinks . . . there was a woman in pince-nez who wouldn't be separated from her umbrella, and then you go below and wait hour after hour till the jury come back and the warder tries to be encouraging, but you know if there's any justice left on earth there can be only one verdict . . .'

'Would you excuse me one moment?' Mr Rennit said. 'I think I heard my man come back . . .' He emerged from behind his desk and then whisked through the door behind Rowe's chair with surprising agility. Rowe sat with his hands held between his

knees, trying to get a grip again on his brain and his tongue . . .
'Set a watch, O Lord, before my mouth and a door round about
my lips . . .' He heard a bell tinkle in the other room and followed
the sound. Mr Rennit was at the phone. He looked piteously at
Rowe and then at the sausage-roll as if that were the only
weapon within reach.

'Are you ringing up the police?' Rowe asked, 'or a doctor?'

'A theatre,' Mr Rennit said despairingly, 'I just remembered
my wife . . .'

'You are married, are you, in spite of all your experience?'

'Yes.' An awful disinclination to talk convulsed Mr Rennit's
features as a thin faint voice came up the wires. He said, 'Two
seats—in the front row,' and clapped the receiver down again.

'The theatre?'

'The theatre.'

'And they didn't even want your name? Why not be reasonable?' Rowe said. 'After all, I had to tell you. You have to have all
the facts. It wouldn't be fair otherwise. It might have to be taken
into consideration, mightn't it, if you work for me.'

'Into consideration?'

'I mean—it might have a bearing. That's something I discovered when they tried me—that everything may have a bearing.
The fact that I had lunch on a certain day alone at the Holborn
Restaurant. Why was I alone, they asked me. I said I liked being
alone sometimes, and you should have seen the way they nodded
at the jury. It had a bearing.' His hands began to shake again. 'As
if I really wanted to be alone for life . . .'

Mr Rennit cleared a dry throat.

'Even the fact that my wife kept love-birds . . .'

'You *are* married?'

'It was my wife I murdered.' He found it hard to put things in
the right order; people oughtn't to ask unnecessary questions: he
really hadn't meant to startle Mr Rennit again. He said, 'You
needn't worry. The police know all about it.'

'You were acquitted?'

'I was detained during His Majesty's pleasure. It was quite a
short pleasure: I wasn't mad, you see. They just had to find an excuse.' He said with loathing, 'They pitied me, so that's why I'm
alive. The papers all called it a mercy killing.' He moved his hand

in front of his face as though he were troubled by a thread of cobweb. 'Mercy to her or mercy to me. They didn't say. And I don't know myself.'

'I really don't think,' Mr Rennit said, swallowing for breath in the middle of a sentence and keeping a chair between them, 'I can undertake . . . It's out of my line.'

'I'll pay more,' Rowe said. 'It always comes down to that, doesn't it?' and as soon as he felt cupidity stirring in the little dusty room, over the half-eaten sausage-roll and the saucer and the tattered telephone-directory, he knew he had gained his point. Mr Rennit after all could not afford to be nice. Rowe said, 'A murderer is rather like a peer: he pays more because of his title. One tries to travel incognito, but it usually comes out . . .'

CHAPTER 3
FRONTAL ASSAULT

'It were hard he should not have one faithful
comrade and friend with him.'
The Little Duke

I

Rowe went straight from Orthotex to the Free Mothers. He had
signed a contract with Mr Rennit to pay him fifty pounds a week
for a period of four weeks to carry out investigations; Mr Rennit
had explained that the expenses would be heavy—Orthotex employed only the most experienced agents—and the one agent he
had been permitted to see before he left the office was certainly
experienced. (Mr Rennit introduced him as A.2, but before long
he was absent-mindedly addressing him as Jones.) Jones was
small and at first sight insignificant, with his thin pointed nose,
his soft brown hat with a stained ribbon, his grey suit which
might have been quite a different colour years ago, and the pencil and pen on fasteners in the breast pocket. But when you
looked a second time you saw experience; you saw it in the small
cunning rather frightened eyes, the weak defensive mouth, the
wrinkles of anxiety on the forehead—experience of innumerable
hotel corridors, of bribed chamber-maids and angry managers,
experience of the insult which could not be resented, the threat
which had to be ignored, the promise which was never kept.
Murder had a kind of dignity compared with this muted second-
hand experience of scared secretive passions.

An argument developed almost at once in which Jones played
no part, standing close to the wall holding his old brown hat,
looking and listening as though he were outside a hotel door. Mr
Rennit, who obviously considered the whole investigation the
fantastic fad of an unbalanced man, argued that Rowe himself
should not take part. 'Just leave it to me and A.2,' he said. 'If it's
a confidence trick . . .'

He would not believe that Rowe's life had been threatened. 'Of course,' he said, 'we'll look into the chemists' books—not that there'll be anything to find.'

'It made me angry,' Rowe repeated. 'He said he'd checked up—and yet he had the nerve.' An idea came to him and he went excitedly on, 'It was the same drug. People would have said it was suicide, that I'd managed to keep some of it hidden . . .'

'If there's anything in your idea,' Mr Rennit said, 'the cake was given to the wrong man. We've only got to find the right one. It's a simple matter of tracing. Jones and I know all about tracing. We start from Mrs Bellairs. She told you the weight, but why did she tell you the weight? Because she mistook you in the dark for the other man. There must be some resemblance . . .' Mr Rennit exchanged a look with Jones. 'It all boils down to finding Mrs Bellairs. That's not very difficult. Jones will do that.'

'It would be easiest of all for me to ask for her—at the Free Mothers.'

'I'd advise you to let Jones see to it.'

'They'd think he was a tout.'

'It wouldn't do at all for a client to make his own investigations, not at all.'

'If there's nothing in my story,' Rowe said, 'they'll give me Mrs Bellairs' address. If I'm right they'll try to kill me, because, though the cake's gone, I know there was a cake, and that there are people who want the cake. *There's* the work for Jones, to keep his eye on me.'

Jones shifted his hat uneasily and tried to catch his employer's eye. He cleared his throat and Mr Rennit asked, 'What is it, A.2?'

'Won't do, sir,' Jones said.

'No?'

'Unprofessional, sir.'

'I agree with Jones,' Mr Rennit said.

All the same, in spite of Jones, Rowe had his way. He came out into the shattered street and made his sombre way between the ruins of Holborn. In his lonely state to have confessed his identity to someone was almost like making a friend. Always before it had been discovered, even at the warden's post; it came out sooner or later, like cowardice. They were extraordinary the tricks and turns of fate, the way conversations came round, the long

memories some people had for names. Now in the strange torn
landscape where London shops were reduced to a stone ground-
plan like those of Pompeii he moved with familiarity; he was part
of this destruction as he was no longer part of the past—the long
weekends in the country, the laughter up lanes in the evening, the
swallows gathering on telegraph wires, peace.

Peace had come to an end quite suddenly on an August the
thirty-first—the world waited another year. He moved like a bit
of stone among the other stones—he was protectively coloured,
and he felt at times, breaking the surface of his remorse, a kind
of evil pride like that a leopard might feel moving in harmony
with all the other spots on the world's surface, only with greater
power. He had not been a criminal when he murdered; it was afterwards that he began to grow into criminality like a habit of
thought. That these men should have tried to kill him who had
succeeded at one blow in destroying beauty, goodness, peace—it
was a form of impertinence. There were times when he felt the
whole world's criminality was his; and then suddenly at some
trivial sight—a woman's bag, a face on an elevator going up as
he went down, a picture in a paper—all the pride seeped out of
him. He was aware only of the stupidity of his act; he wanted to
creep out of sight and weep; he wanted to forget that he had ever
been happy. A voice would whisper, 'You say you killed for pity;
why don't you have pity on yourself?' Why not indeed? except
that it is easier to kill someone you love than to kill yourself.

2

The Free Mothers had taken over an empty office in a huge white
modern block off the Strand. It was like going into a mechanised
mortuary with a separate lift for every slab. Rowe moved steadily
upwards in silence for five floors: a long passage, frosted glass,
somebody in pince-nez stepped into the lift carrying a file marked
'Most Immediate' and they moved on smoothly upwards. A door
on the seventh floor was marked 'Comforts for Mothers of the
Free Nations. Inquiries.'

He began to believe that after all Mr Rennit was right. The
stark efficient middle-class woman who sat at a typewriter was

so obviously incorruptible and unpaid. She wore a little button
to show she was honorary. 'Yes?' she asked sharply and all his
anger and pride drained away. He tried to remember what the
stranger had said—about the cake not being intended for him.
There was really nothing sinister in the phrase so far as he could
now remember it, and as for the taste, hadn't he often woken at
night with that upon his tongue?

'Yes?' the woman repeated briskly.

'I came,' Rowe said, 'to try and find out the address of a Mrs
Bellairs.'

'No lady of that name works here.'

'It was in connection with the fête.'

'Oh, they were all voluntary helpers. We can't possibly dis-
close addresses of voluntary helpers.'

'Apparently,' Rowe said, 'a mistake was made. I was given a
cake which didn't belong to me . . .'

'I'll inquire,' the stark lady said and went into an inner room.
He had just long enough to wonder whether after all he had been
wise. He should have brought A.2 up with him. But then the normality of everything came back; he was the only abnormal thing
there. The honorary helper stood in the doorway and said, 'Will
you come through, please?' He took a quick glance at her typewriter as he went by; he could read 'The Dowager Lady Crad-
brooke thanks Mrs J. A. Smythe-Philipps for her kind gift of tea
and flour . . .' Then he went in.

He had never become accustomed to chance stabs: only when
the loved person is out of reach does love become complete. The
colour of the hair and the size of the body—something very small
and neat and incapable, you would say, of inflicting pain—this
was enough to make him hesitate just inside the room. There were
no other resemblances, but when the girl spoke—in the slightest
of foreign accents—he felt the kind of astonishment one feels at a
party hearing the woman one loves talking in a stranger's tone to
a stranger. It was not an uncommon occurrence; he would follow
people into shops, he would wait at street corners because of a
small resemblance, just as though the woman he loved was only
lost and might be discovered any day in a crowd.

She said, 'You came about a cake?'

He watched her closely: they had so little in common compared with the great difference, that one was alive and the other dead. He said, 'A man came to see me last night—I suppose from this office.'

He fumbled for words because it was just as absurd to think that this girl might be mixed up in a crime as to think of Alice—except as a victim. 'I had won a cake in a raffle at your fête—but there seemed to be some mistake.'

'I don't understand.'

'A bomb fell before I could make out what it was he wanted to tell me.'

'But no one could have come from here,' she said. 'What did he look like?'

'Very small and dark with twisted shoulders—practically a cripple.'

'There is no one like that here.'

'I thought perhaps that if I found Mrs Bellairs . . .' The name seemed to convey nothing. 'One of the helpers at the fête.'

'They were all volunteers,' the girl explained. 'I dare say we could find the address for you through the organizers, but is it so—important?'

A screen divided the room in two; he had imagined they were alone, but as the girl spoke a young man came round the screen. He had the same fine features as the girl; she introduced him, 'This is my brother, Mr . . .'

'Rowe.'

'Somebody called on Mr Rowe to ask about a cake. I don't quite understand. It seems he won it at our fête.'

'Now let me see, who could that possibly be?' The young man spoke excellent English; only a certain caution and precision marked him as a foreigner. It was as if he had come from an old-fashioned family among whom it was important to speak clearly and use the correct words; his care had an effect of charm, not of pedantry. He stood with his hand laid lightly and affectionately on his sister's shoulder as though they formed together a Victorian family group. 'Was he one of your countrymen, Mr Rowe? In this office we are most of us foreigners, you know.' Smiling he took Rowe into his confidence. 'If health or nationality prevent us fighting for you, we have to do something. My sister and I are—technically—Austrian.'

'This man was English.'

'He must have been one of the voluntary helpers. We have so many—I don't know half of them by name. You want to return a prize, is that it? A cake?'

Rowe said cautiously, 'I wanted to inquire about it.'

'Well, Mr Rowe, if I were you, I should be unscrupulous. I should just "hang on" to the cake.' When he used a colloquialism you could hear the inverted commas drop gently and apologetically around it.

'The trouble is,' Rowe said, 'the cake's no longer there. My house was bombed last night.'

'I'm sorry. About your house, I mean. The cake can't seem very important now, surely?'

They were charming, they were obviously honest, but they had caught him neatly and effectively in an inconsistency.

'I shouldn't bother,' the girl said, 'if I were you.'

Rowe watched them hesitatingly. But it is impossible to go through life without trust: that is to be imprisoned in the worst cell of all, oneself. For more than a year now Rowe had been so imprisoned—there had been no change of cell, no exercise-yard, no unfamiliar warder to break the monotony of solitary confinement. A moment comes to a man when a prison-break must be made whatever the risk. Now cautiously he tried for freedom. These two had lived through terror themselves, but they had emerged without any ugly psychological scar. He said, 'As a matter of fact it wasn't simply the cake which was worrying me.'

They watched him with a frank and friendly interest; you felt that in spite of the last years there was still the bloom of youth on them—they still expected life to offer them other things than pain and boredom and distrust and hate. The young man said, 'Won't you sit down and tell us . . .?' They reminded him of children who liked stories. They couldn't have accumulated more than fifty years' experience between them. He felt immeasurably older.

Rowe said, 'I got the impression that whoever wanted that cake was ready to be—well, violent.' He told them of the visit and the stranger's vehemence and the odd taste in his tea. The young man's very pale blue eyes sparkled with his interest and excitement. He said, 'It's a fascinating story. Have you any idea who's behind it—or what? How does Mrs Bellairs come into it?'

He wished now that he hadn't been to Mr Rennit—these were the allies he needed, not the dingy Jones and his sceptical employer.

'Mrs Bellairs told my fortune at the fête, and told me the weight of the cake—which wasn't the right weight.'

'It's extraordinary,' the young man said enthusiastically.

The girl said, 'It doesn't make sense.' She added almost in Mr Rennit's words, 'It was probably all a misunderstanding.'

'Misunderstanding,' her brother said and then dropped his inverted commas round the antiquated slang, ' "my eye".' He turned to Rowe with an expression of glee. 'Count this Society, Mr Rowe, as far as the secretary's concerned at your service. This is really interesting.' He held out his hand. 'My name—*our* name is Hilfe. Where do we begin?'

The girl sat silent. Rowe said, 'Your sister doesn't agree.'

'Oh,' the young man said, 'she'll come round. She always does in the end. She thinks I'm a romantic. She's had to get me out of too many scrapes.' He became momentarily serious. 'She got me out of Austria.' But nothing could damp his enthusiasm for long. 'That's another story. Do we begin with Mrs Bellairs? Have you any idea what it's all about? I'll get our grim volunteer in the next room on the hunt,' and opening the door he called through. 'Dear Mrs Dermody, do you think you could find the address of one of our voluntary helpers called Mrs Bellairs?' He explained to Rowe, 'The difficulty is she's probably just the friend of a friend—not a regular helper. Try Canon Topling,' he suggested to Mrs Dermody.

The greater the young man's enthusiasm, the more fantastic the whole incident became. Rowe began to see it through Mr Rennit's eyes—Mrs Dermody, Canon Topling . . .

He said, 'Perhaps after all your sister's right.'

But young Hilfe swept on. 'She may be, of course she may be. But how dull if she is. I'd much rather think, until we *know*, that there's some enormous conspiracy . . .'

Mrs Dermody put her head in at the door and said, 'Canon Topling gave me the address. It's 5 Park Crescent.'

'If she's a friend of Canon Topling,' Rowe began and caught Miss Hilfe's eye. She gave him a secret nod as much as to say—now you're on the right track.

'Oh, but let's "hang on" to the stranger,' Hilfe said.

'There may be a thousand reasons,' Miss Hilfe said.

'Surely not a thousand, Anna,' her brother mocked. He asked Rowe, 'Isn't there anything else you can remember which will convince her?' His keenness was more damping than her scepticism. The whole affair became a game one couldn't take seriously.

'Nothing,' Rowe said.

Hilfe was at the window looking out. He said, 'Come here a moment, Mr Rowe. Do you see that little man down there—in the shabby brown hat? He arrived just after you, and he seems to be staying . . . There he goes now, up and down. Pretends to light a cigarette. He does that too often. And that's the second evening paper he's bought. He never comes quite opposite, you see. It almost looks as if you are being trailed.'

'I know him,' Rowe said. 'He's a private detective. He's being paid to keep an eye on me.'

'By Jove,' young Hilfe said—even his exclamations were a little Victorian—'you do take this seriously. We're allies now you know—you aren't "holding out" on us, are you?'

'There is something I haven't mentioned.' Rowe hesitated.

'Yes?' Hilfe came quickly back and with his hand again on his sister's shoulder waited with an appearance of anxiety. 'Something which will wipe out Canon Topling?'

'I think there was something in the cake.'

'What?'

'I don't know. But he crumbled every slice he took.'

'It may have been habit,' Miss Hilfe said.

'Habit!' her brother teased her.

She said with sudden anger, 'One of these old English characteristics you study so carefully.'

Rowe tried to explain to Miss Hilfe, 'It's nothing to do with me. I don't want their cake, but they tried, I'm sure they tried, to kill me. I know it sounds unlikely, now, in daylight, but if you had seen that wretched little cripple pouring in the milk, and then waiting, watching, crumbling the cake . . .'

'And you really believe' Miss Hilfe said, 'that Canon Topling's friend . . .'

'Don't listen to her,' Hilfe said. 'Why not Canon Topling's friend? There's no longer a thing called a criminal class. We can tell you that. There were lots of people in Austria you'd have said couldn't . . . well, do the things we saw them do. Cultured people, pleasant people, people you had sat next to at dinner.'

'Mr Rennit,' Rowe said, 'the head of the Orthotex Detective Agency, told me today that he'd never met a murderer. He said they were rare and not the best people.'

'Why, they are dirt cheap,' Hilfe said, 'nowadays. I know myself at least six murderers. One was a cabinet minister, another was a heart specialist, the third a bank manager, an insurance agent . . .'

'Stop,' Miss Hilfe said, 'please stop.'

'The difference,' Hilfe said, 'is that in these days it really pays to murder, and when a thing pays it becomes respectable. The rich abortionist becomes a gynaecologist and the rich thief a bank director. Your friend is out of date.' He went on explaining gently, his very pale blue eyes unshocked and unshockable. 'Your old-fashioned murderer killed from fear, from hate—or even from love, Mr Rowe, very seldom for substantial profit. None of these reasons is quite—respectable. But to murder for position— that's different, because when you've gained the position nobody has a right to criticize the means. Nobody will refuse to meet you if the position's high enough. Think of how many of your statesmen have shaken hands with Hitler. But, of course, to murder for fear or from love, Canon Topling wouldn't do that. If he killed his wife he'd lose his preferment,' and he smiled at Rowe with a blithe innocence of what he was saying.

When he came out of what wasn't called a prison, when His Majesty's pleasure had formally and quickly run its course, it had seemed to Rowe that he had emerged into quite a different world— a secret world of assumed names, of knowing nobody, of avoiding faces, of men who leave a bar unobtrusively when other people enter. One lived where least questions were asked, in furnished rooms. It was the kind of world that people who attended garden fêtes, who went to Matins, who spent week-ends in the country and played bridge for low stakes and had an account at a good grocer's, knew nothing about. It wasn't exactly a criminal world, though eddying along its dim and muted corridors you might possibly rub shoulders with genteel forgers who had never actually been charged or the corrupter of a child. One attended cinemas at

ten in the morning with other men in macintoshes who had somehow to pass the time away. One sat at home and read *The Old
Curiosity Shop* all the evening. When he had first believed that
someone intended to murder him, he had felt a sort of shocked indignation; the act of murder belonged to him like a personal char-
acteristic, and not the inhabitants of the old peaceful places from
which he was an exile, and of which Mrs Bellairs, the lady in the
floppy hat and the clergyman called Sinclair were so obviously inhabitants. The one thing a murderer should be able to count himself safe from was murder—by one of these.

But he was more shocked now at being told by a young man of
great experience that there was no division between the worlds.
The insect underneath the stone has a right to feel safe from the
trampling superior boot.

Miss Hilfe told him, 'You mustn't listen.' She was watching
him with what looked like sympathy. But that was impossible.

'Of course,' Hilfe said easily, 'I exaggerate. But all the same
you have to be prepared in these days for criminals—everywhere.
They call it having ideals. They'll even talk about murder being
the most merciful thing.'

Rowe looked quickly up, but there was no personal meaning
in the pale blue theoretical eyes. 'You mean the Prussians?' Rowe
asked.

'Yes, if you like, the Prussians. Or the Nazis. The Fascists. The
Reds, the Whites . . .'

A telephone rang on Miss Hilfe's desk. She said, 'It's Lady
Dunwoody.'

Hilfe, leaning quickly sideways, said, 'We are so grateful for
your offer, Lady Dunwoody. We can never have too many woollies. Yes, if you wouldn't mind sending them to this office, or shall
we collect? You'll send your chauffeur. Thank you. Good-bye.'
He said to Rowe, with a rather wry smile, 'It's an odd way for
someone of my age to fight a war, isn't it? collecting woollies
from charitable old dowagers. But it's useful, I'm allowed to do it,
and it's something not to be interned. Only—you do understand,
don't you—a story like yours excites me. It seems to give one an
opportunity, well, to take a more violent line.' He smiled at his
sister and said with affection, 'Of course she calls me a romantic.'

But the odd thing was she called him nothing at all. It was

almost as if she not only disapproved of him, but had disowned him, wouldn't co-operate in anything—outside the woollies. She seemed to Rowe to lack her brother's charm and ease; the experience which had given him an amusing nihilistic abandon had left her brooding on some deeper, more unhappy level. He felt no longer sure that they were both without scars. Her brother had the ideas, but she felt them. When Rowe looked at her it was as if his own unhappiness recognized a friend and signalled, signalled, but got no reply.

'And now,' Hilfe said, 'what next?'

'Leave it alone.' Miss Hilfe addressed herself directly to Rowe—the reply when it did at last come was simply to say that communication was at an end.

'No, no,' Hilfe said, 'we can't do that. This is war.'

'How do you know,' Miss Hilfe said, still speaking only to Rowe, 'that even if there is something behind it, it isn't just—theft, drugs, things like that?'

'I don't know,' Rowe said, 'and I don't care. I'm angry, that's all.'

'What is your theory, though?' Hilfe asked. 'About the cake?'

'It might have contained a message, mightn't it?'

Both the Hilfes were silent for a moment as though that were an idea which had to be absorbed. Then Hilfe said, 'I'll go with you to Mrs Bellairs.'

'You can't leave the office, Willi,' Miss Hilfe said. 'I'll go with Mr Rowe. You have an appointment.'

'Oh, only with Trench. You can handle Trench for me, Anna.' He said with glee, 'This is important. There may be trouble.'

'We could take Mr Rowe's detective.'

'And warn the lady? He sticks out a yard. No,' Hilfe said, 'we must very gently drop him. I'm used to dropping spies. It's a thing one has learned since 1933.'

'But I don't know what you want to say to Mr Trench.'

'Just stave him off. Say we'll settle at the beginning of the month. You'll forgive us talking business, Mr Rowe.'

'Why not let Mr Rowe go alone?'

Perhaps, Rowe thought, she does after all believe there's something in it; perhaps she fears for her brother. She was saying, 'You don't both of you want to make fools of yourselves, Willi.'

Hilfe ignored his sister completely. He said to Rowe, 'Just a moment while I write a note for Trench,' and disappeared behind the screen.

When they left the office together it was by another door; dropping Jones was as simple as that, for he had no reason to suppose that his employer would try to evade him. Hilfe called a taxi, and as they drove down the street, Rowe was able to see how the shabby figure kept his vigil, lighting yet another cigarette with his eyes obliquely on the great ornate entrance, like a faithful hound who will stay interminably outside his master's door. Rowe said, 'I wish we had let him know.'

'Better not,' Hilfe said. 'We can pick him up afterwards. We shan't be long,' and the figure slanted out of sight as the taxi wheeled away; he was lost amongst the buses and bicycles, absorbed among all the other loitering seedy London figures, never to be seen again by anyone who knew him.

CHAPTER 4
AN EVENING WITH
MRS BELLAIRS

'There be dragons of wrong here and everywhere,
quite as venomous as any in my Sagas.'
The Little Duke

Mrs Bellairs' house was a house of character; that is to say it was old and unrenovated, standing behind its little patch of dry and weedy garden among the To Let boards on the slope of Campden Hill. A piece of statuary lay back in a thin thorny hedge like a large block of pumice stone, chipped and grey with neglect, and when you rang the bell under the early Victorian portico, you seemed to hear the sound pursuing the human inhabitants into back rooms as though what was left of life had ebbed up the passages.

The snowy-white cuffs and the snowy-white apron of the maid who opened the door came as a surprise. She was keeping up appearances as the house wasn't, though she looked nearly as old. Her face was talcumed and wrinkled and austere like a nun's. Hilfe said, 'Is Mrs Bellairs at home?'

The old maid watched them with the kind of shrewdness people learn in convents. She said, 'Have you an appointment?'

'Why no,' Hilfe said, 'we were just calling. I'm a friend of Canon Topling's.'

'You see,' the maid explained, 'this is one of her evenings.'

'Yes?'

'If you are not one of the group . . .'

An elderly man with a face of extraordinary nobility and thick white hair came up the path. 'Good evening, sir,' the maid said. 'Will you come right in?' He was obviously one of the group, for she showed him into a room on the right and they heard her announce, 'Dr Forester.' Then she came back to guard the door.

Hilfe said, 'Perhaps if you would take my name to Mrs Bellairs, we might join the group. Hilfe—a friend of Canon Topling's.'

'I'll *ask* her,' the maid said dubiously.

But the result was after all favourable. Mrs Bellairs herself swam into the little jumbled hall. She wore a Liberty dress of shot silk and a toque and she held out both hands as though to welcome them simultaneously. 'Any friend of Canon Topling . . .' she said.

'My name is Hilfe. Of the Free Mothers Fund. And this is Mr Rowe.'

Rowe watched for a sign of recognition, but there was none. Her broad white face seemed to live in worlds beyond them.

'If you'd join our group,' she said, 'we welcome newcomers. So long as there's no settled hostility.'

'Oh, none, none,' Hilfe said.

She swayed in front of them like a figure-head into a drawing-room all orange curtain and blue cushion, as though it had been furnished once and for all in the twenties. Blue blackout globes made the room dim like an Oriental café. There were indications among the trays and occasional tables that it was Mrs Bellairs who had supplied the fête with some of its Benares work.

Half a dozen people were in the room, and one of them immediately attracted Rowe's attention—a tall, broad, black-haired man; he couldn't think why, until he realized that it was his normality which stood out. 'Mr Cost,' Mrs Bellairs was saying, 'this is . . .'

'Mr Rowe.' Hilfe supplied the name, and the introductions went round with a prim formality. One wondered why Cost was here, in the company of Dr Forester with his weak mouth and his nobility; Miss Pantil, a dark young-middle-aged woman with blackheads and a hungry eye; Mr Newey—'Mr Frederick Newey'—Mrs Bellairs made a point of the first name—who wore sandals and no socks and had a grey shock of hair; Mr Maude, a short-sighted young man who kept as close as he could to Mr Newey and fed him devotedly with thin bread and butter, and Collier, who obviously belonged to a different class and had worked himself in with some skill. He was patronized, but at the same time he was admired. He was a breath of the larger life and they were interested. He had been a hotel waiter and a tramp and a stoker, and he had published a book—so Mrs Bellairs whispered to Rowe—of the most fascinating poetry, rough but spiritual. 'He uses words,' Mrs Bellairs said, 'that have never been used in poetry before.' There seemed to be some antagonism between him and Mr Newey.

All this scene became clear to Rowe over the cups of very weak China tea which were brought round by the austere parlourmaid.

'And what,' Mrs Bellairs asked, 'do you do, Mr Rowe?' She had been explaining Collier in an undertone—calling him plain Collier because he was a Player and not a Gentleman.

'Oh,' Rowe said, watching her over his tea-cup, trying to make out the meaning of her group, trying in vain to see her in a dangerous rôle, 'I sit and think.'

It seemed to be the right as well as the truthful answer. He was encircled by Mrs Bellairs' enthusiasm as though by a warm arm. 'I shall call you our philosopher,' she said. 'We have our poet, our critic . . .'

'What is Mr Cost?'

'He is Big Business,' Mrs Bellairs said. 'He works in the City. I call him our mystery man. I sometimes feel he is a hostile influence.'

'And Miss Pantil?'

'She has quite extraordinary powers of painting the inner world. She sees it as colours and circles, rhythmical arrangements, and sometimes oblongs.'

It was fantastic to believe that Mrs Bellairs could have anything to do with crime—or any of her group. He would have made some excuse and gone if it had not been for Hilfe. These people—whatever Hilfe might say—did not belong under the stone with him.

He asked vaguely, 'You meet here every week?'

'Always on Wednesdays. Of course we have very little time because of the raids. Mr Newey's wife likes him to be back at Welwyn before the raids start. And perhaps that's why the results are bad. They can't be driven, you know.' She smiled. 'We can't promise a stranger anything.'

He couldn't make out what it was all about. Hilfe seemed to have left the room with Cost. Mrs Bellairs said, 'Ah, the conspirators. Mr Cost is always thinking up a test.'

Rowe tried out a question tentatively. 'And the results are sometimes bad?'

'So bad I could cry . . . if I knew at the time. But there are other times—oh, you'd be surprised how good they are.'

A telephone was ringing in another room. Mrs Bellairs said, 'Who can that naughty person be? All my friends know they mustn't ring me on Wednesdays.'

The old parlourmaid had entered. She said with distaste, 'Somebody is calling Mr Rowe.'

Rowe said, 'But I can't understand it. Nobody knows . . .'

'Would you mind,' Mrs Bellairs said, 'being very quick?'

Hilfe was in the hall talking earnestly to Cost. He asked, 'For you?' He too was discomposed. Rowe left a track of censorious silence behind him: they watched him following the maid. He felt as though he had made a scene in church and was now being conducted away. He could hear behind him nothing but the tinkle of tea-cups being laid away.

He thought: perhaps it's Mr Rennit, but how can he have found me? or Jones? He leant across Mrs Bellairs' desk in a small packed dining-room. He said, 'Hullo,' and wondered again how he could have been traced. 'Hullo.'

But it wasn't Mr Rennit. At first he didn't recognize the voice—a woman's. 'Mr Rowe?'

'Yes.'

'Are you alone?'

'Yes.'

The voice was blurred; it was as if a handkerchief had been stretched across the mouthpiece. She couldn't know, he thought, that there were no other women's voices to confuse with hers.

'Please will you leave the house as soon as you can?'

'It's Miss Hilfe, isn't it?'

The voice said impatiently, 'Yes. Yes. All right. It is.'

'Do you want to speak to your brother?'

'Please do not tell him. And leave. Leave quickly.'

He was for a moment amused. The idea of any danger in Mrs Bellairs' company was absurd. He realized how nearly he had been converted to Mr Rennit's way of thinking. Then he remembered that Miss Hilfe had shared those views. Something had converted her—the opposite way. He said, 'What about your brother?'

'If you go away, he'll go too.'

The dimmed urgent voice fretted at his nerves. He found himself edging round the desk so that he could face the door, and then he moved again, because his back was to a window. 'Why don't you tell this to your brother?'

'He would want to stay all the more.' That was true. He wondered how thin the walls were. The room was uncomfortably crowded with trashy furniture: one wanted space to move about— the voice was disturbingly convincing—to manoeuvre in. He said, 'Is Jones still outside—the detective?'

There was a long pause: presumably she had gone to the window. Then the voice sprang at him unexpectedly loud—she had taken away the handkerchief. 'There's nobody there.'

'Are you sure?'

'Nobody.'

He felt deserted and indignant. What business had Jones to leave his watch? Somebody was approaching down the passage. He said, 'I must ring off.'

'They'll try to get you in the dark,' the voice said, and then the door opened. It was Hilfe.

He said, 'Come along. They are all waiting. Who was it?'

Rowe said, 'When you were writing your note I left a message with Mrs Dermody, in case anyone wanted me urgently.'

'And somebody did?'

'It was Jones—the detective.'

'Jones?' Hilfe said.

'Yes.'

'And Jones had important news?'

'Not exactly. He was worried at losing me. But Mr Rennit wants me at his office.'

'The faithful Rennit. We'll go straight there—afterwards.'

'After what?'

Hilfe's eyes expressed excitement and malice. 'Something we can't miss—"at any price".' He added in a lower voice, 'I begin to believe we were wrong. It's lots of fun, but it's not—dangerous.'

He laid a confiding hand in Rowe's arm and gently urged him 'Keep a straight face, Mr Rowe, if you can. You mustn't laugh. She *is* a friend of Canon Topling.'

The room when they came back was obviously arranged for something. A rough circle had been formed with the chairs, and everyone had an air of impatience politely subdued. 'Just sit down, Mr Rowe, next Mr Cost,' said Mrs Bellairs, 'and then we'll turn out the lights.'

In nightmares one knows the cupboard door will open: one knows that what will emerge is horrible: one doesn't know what it is . . .

Mrs Bellairs said again, 'If you'll just sit down, so that we can turn out the lights.'

He said, 'I'm sorry. I've got to go.'

'Oh, you can't go now,' Mrs Bellairs cried. 'Can he, Mr Hilfe?'

Rowe looked at Hilfe, but the pale blue eyes sparkled back at him without understanding. 'Of course, he mustn't go,' Hilfe said. 'We'll both wait. What did we come for?' An eyelid momentarily flickered as Mrs Bellairs with a gesture of appalling coyness locked the door and dropped the key down her blouse and shook her fingers at them. 'We always lock the door,' she said, 'to satisfy Mr Cost.'

In a dream you cannot escape: the feet are leaden-weighted: you cannot stir from before the ominous door which almost imperceptibly moves. It is the same in life; sometimes it is more difficult to make a scene than to die. A memory came back to him of someone else who wasn't certain, wouldn't make a scene, gave herself sadly up and took the milk . . . He moved through the circle and sat down on Cost's left like a criminal taking his place in an identity parade. On his own left side was Miss Pantil. Dr Forester was on one side of Mrs Bellairs and Hilfe on the other. He hadn't time to see how the others were distributed before the light went out. 'Now,' Mrs Bellairs said, 'we'll all hold hands.'

The blackout curtains had been drawn and the darkness was almost complete. Cost's hand felt hot and clammy, and Miss Pantil's hot and dry. This was the first séance he had ever attended, but it wasn't the spirits he feared. He wished Hilfe was beside him, and he was aware all the time of the dark empty space of the room behind his back, in which anything might happen. He tried to loosen his hands, but they were firmly gripped. There was complete silence in the room. A drop of sweat formed above his right eye and trickled down. He couldn't brush it away: it hung on his eyelid and tickled him. Somewhere in another room a gramophone began to play.

It played and played—something sweet and onomatopoeic by Mendelssohn, full of waves breaking in echoing caverns. There was a pause and the needle was switched back and the melody began again. The same waves broke interminably into the same hollow. Over and over again. Underneath the music he became aware of breathing on all sides of him—all kinds of anxieties, suspenses, excitements controlling the various lungs. Miss Pantil's had an odd dry whistle in it, Cost's was heavy and regular, but not so heavy as another breath which laboured in the dark, he couldn't tell whose. All the time he listened and waited. Would he hear a step behind him and have time to snatch away his hands? He no longer doubted at all the urgency of that warning—'They'll try to get you in the dark.' This was danger: this suspense was what somebody else had experienced, watching from day to day his pity grow to the monstrous proportions necessary to action.

'Yes,' a voice called suddenly, 'yes, I can't hear?' and Miss Pantil's breath whistled and Mendelssohn's waves moaned and withdrew. Very far away a taxi-horn cried through an empty world.

'Speak louder,' the voice said. It was Mrs Bellairs, with a difference: a Mrs Bellairs drugged with an idea, with an imagined contact beyond the little dark constricted world in which they sat. He wasn't interested in any of that: it was a human movement he waited for. Mrs Bellairs said in a husky voice, 'One of you is an enemy. He won't let it come through.' Something—a chair, a table?—cracked, and Rowe's fingers instinctively strained against Miss Pantil's. That wasn't a spirit. That was the human agency which shook tambourines or scattered flowers or imitated a child's touch upon the cheek—it was the dangerous element, but his hands were held.

'There is an enemy here,' the voice said. 'Somebody who doesn't believe, whose motives are evil . . .' Rowe could feel Cost's fingers tighten round his. He wondered whether Hilfe was still completely oblivious to what was happening: he wanted to shout to him for help, but convention held him as firmly as Cost's hand. Again a board creaked. Why all this mummery, he thought, if they are all in it? But perhaps they were not all in it. For anything he knew he was surrounded by friends—but he didn't know which they were.

'Arthur.'

He pulled at the hands holding him: that wasn't Mrs Bellairs' voice.

'Arthur.'

The flat hopeless voice might really have come from beneath the heavy graveyard slab.

'Arthur, why did you kill . . .' The voice moaned away into silence, and he struggled against the hands. It wasn't that he recognized the voice: it was no more his wife's than any woman's dying out in infinite hopelessness, pain and reproach: it was that the voice had recognized him. A light moved near the ceiling, feeling its way along the walls, and he cried, 'Don't. Don't.'

'Arthur,' the voice whispered.

He forgot everything, he no longer listened for secretive movements, the creak of boards. He simply implored, 'Stop it, please stop it,' and felt Cost rise from the seat beside him and pull at his hand and then release it, throw the hand violently away, as though it were something he didn't like to hold. Even Miss Pantil let him go, and he heard Hilfe say, 'This isn't funny. Put on the light.'

It dazzled him, going suddenly on. They all sat there with joined hands watching him; he had broken the circle—only Mrs Bellairs seemed to see nothing, with her head down and her eyes closed and her breathing heavy. 'Well,' Hilfe said, trying to raise a laugh, 'that was certainly quite an act,' but Mr Newey said, 'Cost. Look at Cost,' and Rowe looked with all the others at his neighbour. He was taking no more interest in anything, leaning forward across the table with his face sunk on the French polish.

'Get a doctor,' Hilfe said.

'I'm a doctor,' Dr Forester said. He released the hands on either side of him, and everyone became conscious of sitting there like children playing a game and surreptitiously let each other go. He said gently, 'A doctor's no good, I'm afraid. The only thing to do is to call the police.'

Mrs Bellairs had half-woken up and sat with leery eyes and her tongue a little protruding.

'It must be his heart,' Mr Newey said. 'Couldn't stand the excitement.'

'I'm afraid not,' Dr Forester said. 'He has been murdered.' His old noble face was bent above the body; one long sensitive delicate hand dabbled and came up stained like a beautiful insect that feeds incongruously on carrion.

'Impossible,' Mr Newey said, 'the door was locked.'

'It's a pity,' Dr Forester said, 'but there's a very simple explanation of that. One of us did it.'

'But we were all,' Hilfe said, 'holding . . .' Then they all looked at Rowe.

'He snatched away his hand,' Miss Pantil said.

Dr Forester said softly, 'I'm not going to touch the body again before the police come. Cost was stabbed with a kind of schoolboy's knife . . .'

Rowe put his hand quickly to an empty pocket and saw a room full of eyes noting the movement.

'We must get Mrs Bellairs out of this,' Dr Forester said. 'Any séance is a strain, but this one . . .' He and Hilfe between them raised the turbaned bulk; the hand which had so delicately dabbled in Cost's blood retrieved the key of the room with equal delicacy. 'The rest of you,' Dr Forester said, 'had better stay here, I think. I'll telephone to Notting Hill police station, and then we'll both be back.'

For a long while there was silence after they had gone; nobody looked at Rowe, but Miss Pantil had slid her chair well away from him, so that he now sat alone beside the corpse, as though they were two friends who had got together at a party. Presently Mr Newey said, 'I'll never catch my train unless they hurry.' Anxiety fought with horror—any moment the sirens might go—he caressed his sandalled foot across his knee, and young Maude said hotly, 'I don't know why *you* should stay,' glaring at Rowe.

It occurred to Rowe that he had not said one word to defend himself: the sense of guilt for a different crime stopped his mouth. Besides, what could he, a stranger, say to Miss Pantil, Mr Newey and young Maude to convince them that in fact it was one of their friends who had murdered? He took a quick look at Cost, half expecting him to come alive again and laugh at them—'one of my tests', but nobody could have been deader than Cost was now. He thought: somebody here *has* killed him—it was fantastic, more fantastic really than that he should have done it himself. After all, he belonged to the region of murder—he was a native of that country. As the police will know, he thought, as the police will know.

The door opened and Hilfe returned. He said, 'Dr Forester is looking after Mrs Bellairs. I have telephoned to the police.' His eyes were saying something to Rowe which Rowe couldn't understand. Rowe thought: I must see him alone, surely he can't believe . . .

He said, 'Would anybody object if I went to the lavatory and was sick?'

Miss Pantil said, 'I don't think anybody ought to leave this room till the police come.'

'I think,' Hilfe said, 'somebody should go with you. As a formality, of course.'

'Why beat about the bush?' Miss Pantil said. 'Whose knife is it?'

'Perhaps Mr Newey,' Hilfe said, 'wouldn't mind going with Mr Rowe . . .'

'I won't be drawn in,' Newey said. 'This has nothing to do with me. I only want to catch my train.'

'Perhaps I had better go then,' Hilfe said, 'if you will trust me.' No one objected.

The lavatory was on the first floor. They could hear from the landing the steady soothing rhythm of Dr Forester's voice in Mrs Bellairs' bedroom. 'I'm all right,' Rowe whispered. 'But Hilfe, I didn't do it.'

There was something shocking in the sense of exhilaration Hilfe conveyed at a time like this. 'Of course you didn't,' he said. 'This is the Real Thing.'

'But why? Who did it?'

'I don't know, but I'm going to find out.' He put his hand on Rowe's arm with a friendliness that was very comforting, urging him into the lavatory and locking the door behind them. 'Only, old fellow, you must be off out of this. They'll hang you if they can. Anyway, they'll shut you up for weeks. It's so convenient for Them.'

'What can I do? It's my knife.'

'They are devils, aren't they,' Hilfe said with the same light-hearted relish he might have used for a children's clever prank. 'We've just got to keep you out of the way till Mr Rennit and I . . . By the way, better tell me who rang you up.'

'It was your sister.'

'My sister . . .' Hilfe grinned at him. 'Good for her, she must have got hold of something. I wonder just where. She warned you, did she?'

'Yes, but I was not to tell you.'

'Never mind that. I shan't eat her, shall I?' The pale blue eyes became suddenly lost in speculation.

Rowe tried to recall them. 'Where can I go?'

'Oh, just underground,' Hilfe said casually. He seemed in no hurry at all. 'It's the fashion of our decade. Communists are always doing it. Don't you know how?'

'This isn't a joke.'

'Listen,' Hilfe said. 'The end we are working for isn't a joke, but if we are going to keep our nerve we've got to keep our sense of humour. You see, They have none. Give me only a week. Keep out of the way as long as that.'

'The police will be here soon.'

Hilfe said, 'It's only a small drop from this window to the flower-bed. It's nearly dark outside and in ten minutes the sirens will be going. Thank God, one can set one's clock by them.'

'And you?'

'Pull the plug as you open the window. No one will hear you then. Wait till the cistern refills, then pull the plug again and knock me out "good and hard". It's the best alibi you can give me. After all, I'm an enemy alien.'

CHAPTER 5

BETWEEN SLEEPING AND
WAKING

'They came to a great forest, which seemed
to have no path through it.'
The Little Duke

There are dreams which belong only partly to the unconscious; these are the dreams we remember on waking so vividly that we deliberately continue them, and so fall asleep again and wake and sleep and the dream goes on without interruption, with a thread of logic the pure dream doesn't possess.

Rowe was exhausted and frightened; he had made tracks half across London while the nightly raid got under way. It was an empty London with only occasional bursts of noise and activity. An umbrella shop was burning at the corner of Oxford Street; in Wardour Street he walked through a cloud of grit: a man with a grey dusty face leant against a wall and laughed and a warden said sharply, 'That's enough now. It's nothing to laugh about.' None of these things mattered. They were like something written; they didn't belong to his own life and he paid them no attention. But he had to find a bed, and so somewhere south of the river he obeyed Hilfe's advice and at last went underground.

He lay on the upper tier of a canvas bunk and dreamed that he was walking up a long hot road near Trumpington scuffing the white chalk-dust with his shoe caps. Then he was having tea on the lawn at home behind the red brick wall and his mother was lying back in a garden chair eating a cucumber sandwich. A bright blue croquet-ball lay at her feet, and she was smiling and paying him the half-attention a parent pays a child. The summer lay all around them, and evening was coming on. He was saying, 'Mother, I murdered her . . .' and his mother said, 'Don't be silly, dear. Have one of these nice sandwiches.'

'But Mother,' he said, 'I did. I did.' It seemed terribly important to him to convince her; if she were convinced, she could do something about it, she could tell him it didn't matter and it would matter no longer, but he had to convince her first. But she turned away her head and called out in a little vexed voice to someone who wasn't there, 'You *must* remember to dust the piano.'

'Mother, please listen to me,' but he suddenly realized that he was a child, so how could he make her believe? He was not yet eight years old, he could see the nursery window on the second floor with the bars across, and presently the old nurse would put her face to the glass and signal to him to come in. 'Mother,' he said, 'I've killed my wife, and the police want me.' His mother smiled and shook her head and said, 'My little boy couldn't kill anyone.'

Time was short; from the other end of the long peaceful lawn, beyond the croquet hoops and out of the shadow of the great somnolent pine, came the vicar's wife carrying a basket of apples. Before she reached them he must convince his mother, but he had only childish words. 'I have. I have.'

His mother leant back smiling in the deck-chair, and said, 'My little boy wouldn't hurt a beetle.' (It was a way she had, always to get the conventional phrase just wrong.)

'But that's why,' he said. 'That's why,' and his mother waved to the vicar's wife and said, 'It's a dream, dear, a nasty dream.'

He woke up to the dim lurid underground place—somebody had tied a red silk scarf over the bare globe to shield it. All along the walls the bodies lay two deep, while outside the raid rumbled and receded. This was a quiet night: any raid which happened a mile away wasn't a raid at all. An old man snored across the aisle and at the end of the shelter two lovers lay on a mattress with their hands and knees touching.

Rowe thought: this would be a dream, too, to her; she wouldn't believe it. She had died before the first great war, when aeroplanes—strange crates of wood—just staggered across the Channel. She could no more have imagined this than that her small son in his brown corduroy knickers and his blue jersey with his pale serious face—he could see himself like a stranger in the yellowing snapshots of her album—should grow up to be a murderer. Lying on his back he caught the dream and held it— pushed the vicar's wife back into the shadow of the pine—and argued with his mother.

'This isn't real life any more,' he said. 'Tea on the lawn, even-song, croquet, the old ladies calling, the gentle unmalicious gos-sip, the gardener trundling the wheelbarrow full of leaves and grass. People write about it as if it still went on; lady novelists de-scribe it over and over again in books of the month, but it's not there any more.'

His mother smiled at him in a scared way but let him talk; he was the master of the dream now. He said, 'I'm wanted for a mur-der I didn't do. People want to kill me because I know too much. I'm hiding underground, and up above the Germans are method-ically smashing London to bits all round me. You remember St Clement's—the bells of St Clement's. They've smashed that—St James's, Piccadilly, the Burlington Arcade, Garland's Hotel, where we stayed for the pantomime, Maples and John Lewis. It sounds like a thriller, doesn't it, but the thrillers are like life—more like life than you are, this lawn, your sandwiches, that pine. You used to laugh at the books Miss Savage read—about spies, and murders, and violence, and wild motor-car chases, but dear, that's real life: it's what we've all made of the world since you died. I'm your little Arthur who wouldn't hurt a beetle and I'm a murderer too. The world has been remade by William Le Queux.' He couldn't bear the frightened eyes which he had himself printed on the cement wall; he put his mouth to the steel frame of his bunk and kissed the white cold cheek. 'My dear, my dear, my dear. I'm glad you are dead. Only do you know about it? do you know?' He was filled with horror at the thought of what a child becomes, and what the dead must feel watching the change from innocence to guilt and powerless to stop it.

'Why, it's a madhouse,' his mother cried.

'Oh, it's much quieter there,' he said. 'I know. They put me in one for a time. Everybody was very kind there. They made me a li-brarian . . .' He tried to express clearly the difference between the madhouse and this. 'Everybody in the place was very—reasonable.' He said fiercely, as though he hated her instead of loving her, 'Let me lend you the History of Contemporary Society. It's in hun-dreds of volumes, but most of them are sold in cheap editions: *Death in Piccadilly, The Ambassador's Diamonds, The Theft of the Naval Papers, Diplomacy, Seven Days' Leave, The Four Just Men* . . .'

He had worked the dream to suit himself, but now the dream began to regain control. He was no longer on the lawn; he was in the field behind the house where the donkey grazed which used to take their laundry to the other end of the village on Mondays. He was playing in a haystack with the vicar's son and a strange boy with a foreign accent and a dog called Spot. The dog caught a rat and tossed it, and the rat tried to crawl away with a broken back, and the dog made little playful excited rushes. Suddenly he couldn't bear the sight of the rat's pain any more; he picked up a cricket-bat and struck the rat on the head over and over again; he wouldn't stop for fear it was still alive, though he heard his nurse call out, 'Stop it, Arthur. How can you? Stop it,' and all the time Hilfe watched him with exhilaration. When he stopped he wouldn't look at the rat; he ran away across the field and hid. But you always had to come out of hiding some time, and presently his nurse was saying, 'I won't tell your mother, but don't you ever do it again. Why, she thinks you wouldn't hurt a fly. What came over you I don't know.' Not one of them guessed that what had come over him was the horrible and horrifying emotion of pity.

That was partly dream and partly memory, but the next was altogether dream. He lay on his side breathing heavily while the big guns opened up in North London, and his mind wandered again freely in that strange world where the past and future leave equal traces, and the geography may belong to twenty years ago or to next year. He was waiting for someone at a gate in a lane: over a high hedge came the sound of laughter and the dull thud of tennis-balls, and between the leaves he could see moth-like movements of white dresses. It was evening and it would soon be too dark to play, and someone would come out and he waited dumb with love. His heart beat with a boy's excitement, but it was the despair of a grown man that he felt when a stranger touched his shoulder and said, 'Take him away.' He didn't wake; this time he was in the main street of a small country town where he had sometimes, when a boy, stayed with an elder sister of his mother's. He was standing outside the inn yard of the King's Arms, and up the yard he could see the lit windows of the barn in which dances were held on Saturday nights. He had a pair of pumps under his arm and he was waiting for a girl much older than himself who would presently come out of her cloakroom and take his arm and go up the yard with him. All the next few hours were with him in the street: the small crowded hall full of the familiar peaceful faces—the chemist and his wife, the daughters of the headmaster, the bank manager and the dentist with his blue chin and his look of experience, the paper streamers of blue and green and scarlet, the small local orchestra, the sense of a life good and quiet and enduring, with only the gentle tug of impatience and young passion to disturb it for the while and make it doubly dear for ever after. And then without warning the dream twisted towards nightmare; somebody was crying in the dark with terror—not the young woman he was waiting there to meet, whom he hadn't yet dared to kiss and probably never would, but someone whom he knew better even than his parents, who belonged to a different world altogether, to the sad world of shared love. A policeman stood at his elbow and said in a woman's voice, 'You had better join our little group,' and urged him remorselessly towards a urinal where a rat bled to death in the slate trough. The music had stopped, the lights had gone, and he couldn't remember why he had come to this dark vile corner, where even the ground whined when he pressed it, as if it had learnt the trick of suffering. He said, 'Please let me go away from here,' and the policeman said, 'Where do you want to go to, dear?' He said, 'Home,' and the policeman said, 'This is home. There isn't anywhere else at all,' and whenever he tried to move his feet the earth whined back at him: he couldn't move an inch without causing pain.

He woke and the sirens were sounding the All Clear. One or two people in the shelter sat up for a moment to listen, and then lay down again. Nobody moved to go home: this was their home now. They were quite accustomed to sleeping underground; it had become as much part of life as the Saturday night film or the Sunday service had ever been. This was the world *they* knew.

CHAPTER 6
OUT OF TOUCH

'You will find every door guarded.'
The Little Duke

I

Rowe had breakfast in an A.B.C. in Clapham High Street. Boards had taken the place of windows and the top floor had gone; it was like a shack put up in an earthquake town for relief work. For the enemy had done a lot of damage in Clapham. London was no longer one great city: it was a collection of small towns. People went to Hampstead or St John's Wood for a quiet week-end, and if you lived in Holborn you hadn't time between the sirens to visit friends as far away as Kensington. So special characteristics developed, and in Clapham where day raids were frequent there was a hunted look which was absent from Westminster, where the night raids were heavier but the shelters were better. The waitress who brought Rowe's toast and coffee looked jumpy and pallid, as if she had lived too much on the run; she had an air of listening whenever gears shrieked. Gray's Inn and Russell Square were noted for a more reckless spirit, but only because they had the day to recover in.

The night raid, the papers said, had been on a small scale. A number of bombs had been dropped, and there had been a number of casualties, some of them fatal. The morning communiqué was like the closing ritual of a midnight Mass. The sacrifice was complete and the papers pronounced in calm invariable words the 'Ite Missa Est.' Not even in the smallest type under a single headline was there any reference to an 'Alleged Murder at a Séance'; nobody troubled about single deaths. Rowe felt a kind of indignation. He had made the headlines once, but his own disaster, if it had happened now, would have been given no space at all. He had almost a sense of desertion; nobody was troubling to pursue so insignificant a case in the middle of a daily massacre. Perhaps a few elderly men in the C.I.D., who were too old to realize how the world had passed them by, were still allowed by patient and kindly superiors to busy themselves in little rooms with the trivialities of a murder. They probably wrote minutes to each other; they might even be allowed to visit the scene of the 'crime', but he could hardly believe that the results of their inquiries were read with more interest than the scribblings of those eccentric clergymen who were still arguing about evolution in country vicarages. 'Old So-and-So,' he could imagine a senior officer saying, 'poor old thing, we let him have a few murder cases now and then. In his day, you know, we used to pay quite a lot of attention to murder, and it makes him feel that he's still of use. The results—Oh well, of course, he never dreams that we haven't time to read his reports.'

Rowe, sipping his coffee, seeking over and over again for the smallest paragraph, felt a kinship with the detective inspectors, the Big Five, *My Famous Cases*; he was a murderer and old-fashioned, he belonged to their world—and whoever had murdered Cost belonged there too. He felt a slight resentment against Willi Hilfe, who treated murder as a joke with a tang to it. But Hilfe's sister hadn't treated it as a joke; she had warned him, she had talked as if death were still a thing that mattered. Like a lonely animal he scented the companionship of his own kind.

The pale waitress kept an eye on him; he had had no chance of shaving, so that he looked like one of those who leave without paying. It was astonishing what a single night in a public shelter could do to you; he could smell disinfectant on his clothes as though he had spent the night in a workhouse infirmary.

He paid his bill and asked the waitress, 'Have you a telephone?' She indicated one near the cash desk, and he dialled Rennit. It was risky, but something had to be done. Of course, the hour was too early. He could hear the bell ringing uselessly in the empty room and he wondered whether the sausage-roll still lay beside it on the saucer. It was always in these days questionable whether a telephone bell would ring at all, because overnight a building might have ceased to exist. He knew now that part of the world was the same: Orthotex still stood.

He went back to his table and ordered another coffee and some notepaper. The waitress regarded him with increasing suspicion.

Even in a crumbling world the conventions held; to order again after payment was unorthodox, but to ask for notepaper was continental. She could give him a leaf from her order pad, that was all. Conventions were far more rooted than morality; he had himself found that it was easier to allow oneself to be murdered than to break up a social gathering. He began to write carefully in spidery hand an account of everything that had happened. Something had got to be done; he wasn't going to remain permanently in hiding for a crime he hadn't committed, while the real criminals got away with—whatever it was they were trying to get away with. In his account he left out Hilfe's name—you never knew what false ideas the police might get, and he didn't want his only ally put behind bars. He was already deciding to post his narrative straight to Scotland Yard.

When he had finished it, he read it over while the waitress watched; the story was a terribly thin one—a cake, a visitor, a taste he thought he remembered, until you got to Cost's body and all the evidence pointing at himself. Perhaps after all he would do better not to post it to the police, but rather to some friend . . . But he had no friend, unless he counted Hilfe . . . or Rennit. He made for the door and the waitress stopped him. 'You haven't paid for your coffee.'

'I'm sorry. I forgot.'

She took the money with an air of triumph; she had been right all the time. She watched him through the window from between the empty cake-stands making his uncertain way up Clapham High Street.

Promptly at nine o'clock he rang again—from close by Stockwell Station—and again the empty room drummed on his ear. By nine-fifteen, when he rang a third time, Mr Rennit had returned He heard his sharp anxious voice saying, 'Yes. Who's there?'

'This is Rowe.'

'What have you done with Jones?' Mr Rennit accused him.

'I left him yesterday,' Rowe said, 'outside . . .'

'He hasn't come back,' Mr Rennit said.

'Maybe he's shadowing . . .'

'I owe him a week's wages. He said he'd be back last night. It's not natural.' Mr Rennit wailed up the phone, 'Jones wouldn't stay away, not with me owing him money.'

'Worse things have happened than that.'

'Jones is my right arm,' Mr Rennit said. 'What have you done with him?'

'I went and saw Mrs Bellairs . . .'

'That's neither here nor there. I want Jones.'

'And a man was killed.'

'What?'

'And the police think I murdered him.'

There was another wail up the line. The small shifty man was being carried out of his depth; all through his life he had swum safely about among his prickly little adulteries, his compromising letters, but the tide was washing him out to where the bigger fishes hunted. He moaned, 'I never wanted to take up your case.'

'You've got to advise me, Rennit. I'll come and see you.'

'No.' He could hear the breath catch down the line. The voice imperceptibly altered. 'When?'

'At ten o'clock. Rennit, are you still there?' He had to explain to somebody. 'I didn't do it, Rennit. You must believe that. I don't make a habit of murder.' He always bit on the word murder as you bite a sore spot on the tongue; he never used the word without self-accusation. The law had taken a merciful view: himself he took the merciless one. Perhaps if they had hanged him he would have found excuses for himself between the trap-door and the bottom of the drop, but they had given him a lifetime to analyse his motives in.

He analysed now—an unshaven man in dusty clothes sitting in the Tube between Stockwell and Tottenham Court Road. (He had to go a roundabout route because the Tube had been closed at many stations.) The dreams of the previous night had set his mind in reverse. He remembered himself twenty years ago day-dreaming and in love; he remembered without self-pity, as one might watch the development of a biological specimen. He had in those days imagined himself capable of extraordinary heroisms and endurances which would make the girl he loved forget the awkward hands and the spotty chin of adolescence. Everything had seemed possible. One could laugh at day-dreams, but so long as you had the capacity to day-dream, there was a chance that you might develop some of the qualities of which you dreamed. It was like the religious discipline: words however emptily repeated can in time form a habit, a kind of unnoticed sediment at the bottom of the mind—until one day to your own surprise you find yourself acting on the belief you thought you didn't believe in. Since the death of his wife Rowe had never day-dreamed; all through the trial he had never even dreamed of an acquittal. It was as if that side of the brain had been dried up; he was no longer capable of sacrifice, courage, virtue, because he no longer dreamed of them. He was aware of the loss—the world had dropped a dimension and become paper-thin. He wanted to dream, but all he could practise now was despair, and the kind of cunning which warned him to approach Mr Rennit with circumspection.

2

Nearly opposite Mr Rennit's was an auction-room which specialised in books. It was possible from before the shelves nearest the door to keep an eye on the entrance to Mr Rennit's block. The weekly auction was to take place next day, and visitors flowed in with catalogues; an unshaven chin and a wrinkled suit were not out of place here. A man with a ragged moustache and an out-at-elbows jacket, the pockets bulging with sandwiches, looked carefully through a folio volume of landscape gardening: a Bishop—or he might have been a Dean—was examining a set of the Waverley novels: a big white beard brushed the libidinous pages of an illustrated Brantôme. Nobody here was standardized; in tea-shops and theatres people are cut to the pattern of their environment, but in this auction-room the goods were too various to appeal to any one type. Here was pornography—eighteenth-century French with beautiful little steel engravings celebrating the copulations of elegant over-clothed people on Pompadour couches, here were all the Victorian novelists, the memoirs of obscure pig-stickers, the eccentric philosophies and theologies of the seventeenth century—Newton on the geographical position of Hell, and Jeremiah Whiteley on the Path of Perfection. There was a smell of neglected books, of the straw from packing cases and of clothes which had been too often rained upon. Standing by the shelves containing lots one to thirty-five Rowe was able to see anyone who came in or out by the door Mr Rennit used.

Just on the level of his eyes was a Roman missal of no particular value included in Lot 20 with Religious Books Various. A big round clock, which itself had once formed part of an auction, as you could tell from the torn label below the dial, pointed 9.45 above the auctioneer's desk. Rowe opened the missal at random, keeping three-quarters of his attention for the house across the street. The missal was ornamented with ugly coloured capitals; oddly enough, it was the only thing that spoke of war in the old quiet room. Open it where you would, you came on prayers for deliverance, the angry nations, the unjust, the wicked, the adversary like a roaring lion . . . The words stuck out between the decorated borders like cannon out of a flower-bed. 'Let not man prevail,' he read—and the truth of the appeal chimed like music. For in all the world outside that room man had indeed prevailed; he had himself prevailed. It wasn't only evil men who did these things. Courage smashes a cathedral, endurance lets a city starve, pity kills . . . we are trapped and betrayed by our virtues. It might be that whoever killed Cost had for that instant given his goodness rein, and Rennit, perhaps for the first time in his life, was behaving like a good citizen by betraying his client. You couldn't mistake the police officer who had taken his stand behind a newspaper just outside the auction-room.

He was reading the *Daily Mirror*. Rowe could see the print over his shoulder with Zec's cartoon filling most of the page. Once, elusively, from an upper window Mr Rennit peered anxiously out and withdrew. The clock in the auction-room said five minutes to ten. The grey day full of last night's débris and the smell of damp plaster crept on. Even Mr Rennit's desertion made Rowe feel a degree more abandoned.

There had been a time when he had friends, not many because he was not gregarious—but for that very reason in his few friendships he had plunged deeply. At school there had been three: they had shared hopes, biscuits, measureless ambitions, but now he couldn't remember their names or their faces. Once he had been addressed suddenly in Piccadilly Circus by an extraordinary grey-haired man with a flower in his button-hole and a double-breasted waistcoat and an odd finicky manner, an air of uncertain and rather seedy prosperity. 'Why, if it isn't Boojie,' the stranger said, and led the way to the bar of the Piccadilly Hotel, while Rowe sought in vain for some figure in the lower fourth—in black Sunday trousers or football shorts, inky or mud-stained—who might be connected with this over-plausible man who now tried unsuccessfully to borrow a fiver, then slid away to the gents and was no more seen, leaving the bill for Boojie to pay.

More recent friends he had had, of course: perhaps half a dozen. Then he married and his friends became his wife's friends even more than his own. Tom Curtis, Crooks, Perry and Vane . . . Naturally they had faded away after his arrest. Only poor silly Henry Wilcox continued to stand by, because, he said, 'I know you are innocent. You wouldn't hurt a fly'—that ominous phrase which had been said about him too often. He remembered how Wilcox had looked when he said, 'But I'm not innocent. I did kill her.' After that there wasn't even Wilcox or his small domineering wife who played hockey. (Their mantelpiece was crowded with the silver trophies of her prowess.)

The plain-clothes man looked impatient. He had obviously read every word of his paper because it was still open at the same place. The clock said five past ten. Rowe closed his catalogue, after marking a few lots at random, and walked out into the street. The plain-clothes man said, 'Excuse me,' and Rowe's heart missed a beat.

'Yes?'

'I've come out without a match.'

'You can keep the box,' Rowe said.

'I couldn't do that, not in these days.' He looked over Rowe's shoulder, up the street to the ruins of the Safe Deposit, where safes stood about like the above-ground tombs in Latin cemeteries, then followed with his eye a middle-aged clerk trailing his umbrella past Rennit's door.

'Waiting for someone?' Rowe asked.

'Oh, just a friend,' the detective said clumsily. 'He's late.'

'Good morning.'

'Good morning, sir.' The 'sir' was an error in tactics, like the soft hat at too official an angle and the unchanging page of the *Daily Mirror*. They don't trouble to send their best men for mere murder, Rowe thought, touching the little sore again with his tongue.

What next? He found himself, not for the first time, regretting

Henry Wilcox. There were men who lived voluntarily in deserts, but they had their God to commune with. For nearly ten years he had felt no need of friends—one woman could include any number of friends. He wondered where Henry was in wartime. Perry would have joined up and so would Curtis. He imagined Henry as an air-raid warden, fussy and laughed at when all was quiet, a bit scared now during the long exposed vigils on the deserted pavements, but carrying on in dungarees that didn't suit him and a helmet a size too large. God damn it, he thought, coming out on the ruined corner of High Holborn, I've done my best to take part too. It's not my fault I'm not fit enough for the army, and as for the damned heroes of civil defence—the little clerks and prudes and what-have-yous—they didn't want me: not when they found I had done time—even time in an asylum wasn't respectable enough for Post Four or Post Two or Post any number. And now they've thrown me out of their war altogether; they want me for a murder I didn't do. What chance would they give me with my record?

He thought: Why should I bother about that cake any more? It's nothing to do with me: it's their war, not mine. Why shouldn't I just go into hiding until everything's blown over (surely in wartime a murder does blow over). It's not my war; I seem to have stumbled into the firing-line, that's all. I'll get out of London and let the fools scrap it out, and the fools die. . . . There may have been nothing important in the cake; it may have contained only a paper cap, a motto, a lucky sixpence. Perhaps that hunchback hadn't meant a thing: perhaps the taste was imagination: perhaps the whole scene never happened at all as I remember it. Blast often did odd things, and it certainly wasn't beyond its power to shake a brain that had too much to brood about already . . .

As if he were escaping from some bore who walked beside him explaining things he had no interest in, he dived suddenly into a telephone-box and rang a number. A stern dowager voice admonished him down the phone as though he had no right on the line at all, 'This is the Free Mothers. Who is that, please?'

'I want to speak to Miss Hilfe.'

'Who is that?'

'A friend of hers.' A disapproving grunt twanged the wires. He said sharply, 'Put me through, please,' and almost at once he heard the voice which if he had shut his eyes and eliminated the telephone-box and ruined Holborn he could have believed was his wife's. There was really no resemblance, but it was so long since he had spoken to a woman, except his landlady or a girl behind a counter, that any feminine voice took him back . . . 'Please. Who is that?'

'Is that Miss Hilfe?'

'Yes. Who are you?'

He said as if his name were a household word, 'I'm Rowe.'

There was such a long pause that he thought she had put the receiver back. He said, 'Hullo. Are you there?'

'Yes.'

'I wanted to talk to you.'

'You shouldn't ring me.'

'I've nobody else to ring—except your brother. Is he there?'

'No.'

'You heard what happened?'

'He told me.'

'You had expected something, hadn't you?'

'Not that. Something worse.' She explained, 'I didn't know *him.*'

'I brought you some worries, didn't I, when I came in yesterday?'

'Nothing worries my brother.'

'I rang up Rennit.'

'Oh, no, no. You shouldn't have done that.'

'I haven't learnt the technique yet. You can guess what happened.'

'Yes. The police.'

'You know what your brother wants me to do?'

'Yes.'

Their conversation was like a letter which has to pass a censorship. He had an overpowering desire to talk to someone frankly. He said, 'Would you meet me somewhere—for five minutes?'

'No,' she said. 'I can't. I can't get away.'

'Just for two minutes.'

'It's not possible.'

It suddenly became of great importance to him. 'Please,' he said.

'It wouldn't be safe. My brother would be angry.'

He said, 'I'm so alone. I don't know what's happening. I've got nobody to advise me. There are so many questions . . .'

'I'm sorry.'

'Can I write to you . . . or him?'

She said, 'Just send your address here—to me. No need to sign the note—or sign it with any name you like.'

Refugees had such stratagems on the tip of the tongue; it was a familiar way of life. He wondered whether if he were to ask her about money she would have an answer equally ready. He felt like a child who is lost and finds an adult hand to hold, a hand that guides him understandingly homewards . . . He became reckless of the imaginary censor. He said, 'There's nothing in the papers.'

'Nothing.'

'I've written a letter to the police.'

'Oh,' she said, 'you shouldn't have done that. Have you posted it?'

'No.'

'Wait and see,' she said. 'Perhaps there won't be any need. Just wait and see.'

'Do you think it would be safe to go to my bank?'

'You are so helpless,' she said, 'so helpless. Of course you mustn't. They will watch for you there.'

'Then how can I live . . .?'

'Haven't you a friend who would cash you a cheque?'

Suddenly he didn't want to admit to her that there was no one at all. 'Yes,' he said, 'yes. I suppose so.'

'Well then . . . Just keep away,' she said so gently that he had to strain his ears.

'I'll keep away.'

She had rung off. He put the receiver down and moved back into Holborn, keeping away. Just ahead of him, with bulging pockets, went one of the bookworms from the auction-room.

'Haven't you a friend?' she had said. Refugees had always friends; people smuggled letters, arranged passports, bribed officials; in that enormous underground land as wide as a continent there was companionship. In England one hadn't yet learned the technique. Whom could he ask to take one of his cheques? Not a tradesman. Since he began to live alone he had dealt with shops only through his landlady. He thought for the second time that day of his former friends. It hadn't occurred to Anna Hilfe that a refugee might be friendless. A refugee always has a party—or a race.

He thought of Perry and Vane: not a chance even if he had known how to find them. Crooks, Boyle, Curtis . . . Curtis was quite capable of knocking him down. He had simple standards, primitive ways and immense complacency. Simplicity in friends had always attracted Rowe: it was a complement to his own qualities. There remained Henry Wilcox. There was just a chance there . . . if the hockey-playing wife didn't interfere. Their two wives had had nothing in common. Rude health and violent pain were too opposed, but a kind of self-protective instinct would have made Mrs Wilcox hate him. Once a man started killing his wife, she would have ungrammatically thought, you couldn't tell where it would stop.

But what excuse could he give Henry? He was aware of the bulge in his breast pocket where his statement lay, but he couldn't tell Henry the truth: no more than the police would Henry believe that he had been present at a murder as an onlooker. He must wait till after the banks closed—that was early enough in wartime, and then invent some urgent reason.

What? He thought about it all through lunch in an Oxford Street Lyons, and got no clue. Perhaps it was better to leave it to what people called the inspiration of the moment, or, better still, give it up, give himself up. It only occurred to him as he was paying his bill that probably he wouldn't be able to find Henry anyway. Henry had lived in Battersea, and Battersea was not a good district to live in now. He might not even be alive—twenty thousand people were dead already. He looked him up in a telephone book. He was there.

That meant nothing, he told himself; the blitz was newer than the edition. All the same, he dialled the number just to see—it was as if all his contacts now had to be down a telephone line. He was almost afraid to hear the ringing tone, and when it came he put the receiver down quickly and with pain. He had rung Henry up so often—before things happened. Well, he had to make up his mind now: the flat was still there, though Henry mightn't be in it. He couldn't brandish a cheque down a telephone line; this time the contact had got to be physical. And he hadn't seen Henry since the day before the trial.

He would almost have preferred to throw his hand in altogether.

He caught a number 19 bus from Piccadilly. After the ruins of St James's Church one passed at that early date into peaceful country. Knightsbridge and Sloane Street were not at war, but Chelsea was, and Battersea was in the front line. It was an odd front line that twisted like the track of a hurricane and left patches of peace. Battersea, Holborn, the East End, the front line curled in and out of them . . . and yet to a casual eye Poplar High Street had hardly known the enemy, and there were pieces of Battersea where the public house stood at the corner with the dairy and the baker beside it, and as far as you could see there were no ruins anywhere.

It was like that in Wilcox's street; the big middle-class flats stood rectangular and gaunt like railway hotels, completely undamaged, looking out over the park. There were To Let boards up all the way down, and Rowe half hoped he would find one outside No. 63. But there was none. In the hall was a frame in which occupants could show whether they were in or out, but the fact that the Wilcox's was marked In meant nothing at all, even if they still lived there, for Henry had a theory that to mark the board Out was to invite burglary. Henry's caution had always imposed on his friends a long tramp upstairs to the top floor (there were no lifts).

The stairs were at the back of the flats looking towards Chelsea, and as you climbed above the second floor and your view lifted, the war came back into sight. Most of the church spires seemed to have been snapped off two-thirds up like sugar-sticks, and there was an appearance of slum clearance where there hadn't really been any slums.

It was painful to come in sight of the familiar 63. He used to pity Henry because of his masterful wife, his conventional career, the fact that his work—chartered accountancy—seemed to offer no escape; four hundred a year of Rowe's own had seemed like wealth, and he had for Henry some of the feeling a rich man might have for a poor relation. He used to give Henry things. Perhaps that was why Mrs Wilcox hadn't liked him. He smiled

with affection when he saw a little plaque on the door marked
A.R.P. Warden: it was exactly as he had pictured. But his finger
hesitated on the bell.

3

He hadn't had time to ring when the door opened and there was
Henry. An oddly altered Henry. He had always been a neat little
man—his wife had seen to that. Now he was in dirty blue dungarees, and he was unshaven. He walked past Rowe as though he
didn't see him and leant over the well of the staircase. 'They
aren't here,' he said.

A middle-aged woman with red eyes who looked like a cook
followed him out and said, 'It's not time, Henry. It's really not
time.' For a moment—so altered was Henry—Rowe wondered
whether the war had done this to Henry's wife too.

Henry suddenly became aware of him—or half aware of him.
He said, 'Oh, Arthur . . . good of you to come,' as though they'd
met yesterday. Then he dived back into his little dark hall and became a shadowy abstracted figure beside a grandfather clock.

'If you'd come in,' the woman said, 'I don't think they'll be
long now.'

He followed her in and noticed that she left the door open, as
though others were expected; he was getting used now to life
taking him up and planting him down without his own volition
in surroundings where only he was not at home. On the oak
chest—made, he remembered, to Mrs Wilcox's order by the Tu-
dor Manufacturing Company—a pair of dungarees was neatly
folded with a steel hat on top. He was reminded of prison, where
you left your own clothes behind. In the dimness Henry repeated,
'Good of you, Arthur,' and fled again.

The middle-aged woman said, 'Any friend of Henry's is welcome. I am Mrs Wilcox.' She seemed to read his astonishment
even in the dark, and explained, 'Henry's mother.' She said,
'Come and wait inside. I don't suppose they'll be long. It's so dark
here. The blackout, you know. Most of the glass is gone.' She led
the way into what Rowe remembered was the dining-room. There
were glasses laid out as though there was going to be a party. It

seemed an odd time of day . . . too late or too early. Henry was there; he gave the effect of having been driven into a corner, of having fled here. On the mantelpiece behind him were four silver cups with the names of teams engraved in double entry under a date: to have drunk out of one of them would have been like drinking out of an account book.

Rowe, looking at the glasses, said, 'I didn't mean to intrude,' and Henry remarked for the third time, as though it were a phrase he didn't have to use his brain in forming, 'Good of you . . .' He seemed to have no memory left of that prison scene on which their friendship had foundered. Mrs Wilcox said, 'It's so good the way Henry's old friends are all rallying to him.' Then Rowe, who had been on the point of inquiring after Henry's wife, suddenly understood. Death was responsible for the glasses, the unshaven chin, the waiting . . . even for what had puzzled him most of all, the look of youth on Henry's face. People say that sorrow ages, but just as often sorrow makes a man younger—ridding him of responsibility, giving in its place the lost unanchored look of adolescence.

He said, 'I didn't know. I wouldn't have come if I'd known.'

Mrs Wilcox said with gloomy pride, 'It was in all the papers.'

Henry stood in his corner; his teeth chattered while Mrs Wilcox went remorselessly on—she had had a good cry, her son was hers again. 'We are proud of Doris. The whole post is doing her honour. We are going to lay her uniform—her clean uniform—on the coffin, and the clergyman is going to read about "Greater love hath no man".'

'I'm sorry, Henry.'

'She was crazy,' Henry said angrily. 'She had no right . . . I told her the wall would collapse.'

'But we are proud of her, Henry,' his mother said, 'we are proud of her.'

'I should have stopped her,' Henry said. 'I suppose,' his voice went high with rage and grief, 'she thought she'd win another of those blasted pots.'

'She was playing for England, Henry,' Mrs Wilcox said. She turned to Rowe and said, 'I think we ought to lay a hockey-stick beside the uniform, but Henry won't have it.'

'I'll be off,' Rowe said. 'I'd never have come if . . .'

'No,' Henry said, '*you* stay. *You* know how it is . . .' He stopped and looked at Rowe as though he realized him fully for the first time. He said, 'I killed my wife too. I could have held her, knocked her down . . .'

'You don't know what you are saying, Henry,' his mother said. 'What will this gentleman think . . . ?'

'This is Arthur Rowe, mother.'

'Oh,' Mrs Wilcox said, 'oh,' and at that moment up the street came the slow sad sound of wheels and feet.

'How dare he . . .?' Mrs Wilcox said.

'He's my oldest friend, mother,' Henry said. Somebody was coming up the stairs. 'Why *did* you come, Arthur?' Henry said.

'To get you to cash me a cheque.'

'The impudence,' Mrs Wilcox said.

'I didn't know about this . . .'

'How much, old man?'

'Twenty?'

'I've only got fifteen. You can have that.'

'Don't trust him,' Mrs Wilcox said.

'Oh, my cheques are good enough. Henry knows that.'

'There are banks to go to.'

'Not at this time of day, Mrs Wilcox. I'm sorry. It's urgent.'

There was a little trumpery Queen Anne desk in the room: it had obviously belonged to Henry's wife. All the furniture had an air of flimsiness; walking between it was like walking, in the old parlour game, blindfold between bottles. Perhaps in her home the hockey-player had reacted from the toughness of the field. Now moving to get at the desk Henry's shoulder caught a silver cup and set it rolling across the carpet. Suddenly in the open door appeared a very fat man in dungarees carrying a white steel helmet. He picked up the cup and said solemnly, 'The procession's here, Mrs Wilcox.'

Henry dithered by the desk.

'I have the uniform ready,' Mrs Wilcox said, 'in the hall.'

'I couldn't get a Union Jack,' the post warden said, 'not a big one. And those little ones they stick on ruins didn't somehow look respectful.' He was painfully trying to exhibit the bright side of death. 'The whole post's turned out, Mr Wilcox,' he said, 'except those that have to stay on duty. And the A.F.S.—they've sent a contingent. And there's a rescue party and four salvage men—and the police band.'

'I think that's wonderful,' Mrs Wilcox said. 'If only Doris could see it all.'

'But she *can* see it, ma'am,' the post warden said. 'I'm sure of that.'

'And afterwards,' Mrs Wilcox said, gesturing towards the glasses, 'if you'll all come up here . . .'

'There's a good many of us, ma'am. Perhaps we'd better make it just the wardens. The salvage men don't really expect . . .'

'Come along, Henry,' Mrs Wilcox said. 'We can't keep all these brave kind souls waiting. You must carry the uniform down in your arms. Oh dear, I wish you looked more tidy. Everybody will be watching you.'

'I don't see,' Henry said, 'why we shouldn't have buried her quietly.'

'But she's a heroine,' Mrs Wilcox exclaimed.

'I wouldn't be surprised, the post warden said, 'if they gave her the George Medal—posthumously. It's the first in the borough— it would be a grand thing for the post.'

'Why, Henry,' Mrs Wilcox said, 'she's not just your wife any more. She belongs to England.'

Henry moved towards the door: the post warden still held the silver cup awkwardly—he didn't know where to put it. 'Just anywhere,' Henry said to him, 'anywhere.' They all moved into the hall, leaving Rowe. 'You've forgotten your helmet, Henry,' Mrs Wilcox said. He had been a very precise man, and he'd lost his precision; all the things which had made Henry Henry were gone. It was as if his character had consisted of a double-breasted waistcoat, columns of figures, a wife who played hockey. Without these things he was unaccountable, he didn't add up. 'You go,' he said to his mother, 'you go.'

'But Henry . . .'

'It's understandable, ma'am,' the post warden said, 'it's feeling that does it. We've always thought Mr Wilcox a very sensitive gentleman at the post. They'll understand,' he added kindly, meaning, one supposed, the post, the police band, the A.F.S., even the four salvage men. He urged Mrs Wilcox towards the door with a friendly broad hand, then picked up the uniform himself.

Hints of the past penetrated the anonymity of the dungarees—the peaceful past of a manservant, or perhaps of a Commissionaire who ran out into the rain carrying an umbrella. War is very like a bad dream in which familiar people appear in terrible and unlikely disguises. Even Henry . . .

Rowe made an indeterminate motion to follow; he couldn't help hoping it would remind Henry of the cheque. It was his only chance of getting any money: there was nobody else. Henry said, 'We'll just see them go off and then we'll come back here. You do understand don't you, I couldn't bear to watch . . .' They came out together into the road by the park; the procession had already started: it moved like a little dark trickle towards the river. The steel hat on the coffin lay blackened and unreflecting under the winter sun, and the rescue party didn't keep step with the post. It was like a parody of a State funeral—but this *was* a State funeral. The brown leaves from the park were blowing across the road, and the drinkers coming out at closing time from the Duke of Rockingham took off their hats. Henry said, 'I told her not to do it . . .' and the wind blew the sound of footsteps back to them. It was as if they had surrendered her to the people, to whom she had never belonged before.

Henry said suddenly, 'Excuse me, old man,' and started after her. He hadn't got his helmet: his hair was beginning to go grey: he broke into a trot, for fear after all of being left behind. He was rejoining his wife and his post. Arthur Rowe was left alone. He turned his money over in his pocket and found there wasn't much of it.

CHAPTER 7
A LOAD OF BOOKS

'Taken as we are by surprise, our resistance
will little avail.'
The Little Duke

I

Even if a man has been contemplating the advantages of suicide
for two years, he takes time to make his final decision—to move
from theory to practice. Rowe couldn't simply go then and
there and drop into the river—besides, he would have been
pulled out again. And yet watching the procession recede he
could see no other solution. He was wanted by the police for murder, and he had thirty-five shillings in his pocket. He couldn't
go to the bank and he had no friend but Henry; of course, he
could wait till Henry came back, but the cold-blooded egotism
of that act repelled him. It would be simpler and less disgust-
ing to die. A brown leaf settled on his coat—that according to
the old story meant money, but the old story didn't say how
soon.

He walked along the Embankment towards Chelsea Bridge;
the tide was low and the sea-gulls walked delicately on the mud.
One noticed the absence of perambulators and dogs: the only dog
in sight looked stray and uncared for and evasive. A barrage balloon staggered up from behind the park trees: its huge nose bent
above the thin winter foliage, and then it turned its dirty old
backside and climbed.

It wasn't only that he had no money: he had no longer what he
called a home—somewhere to shelter from people who might
know him. He missed Mrs Purvis coming in with the tea; he used
to count the days by her: punctuated by her knock they would
slide smoothly towards the end—annihilation, forgiveness, pun-
ishment or peace. He missed *David Copperfield* and *The Old
Curiosity Shop*; he could no longer direct his sense of pity towards the fictitious sufferings of little Nell—it roamed around

and saw too many objects—too many rats that needed to be killed. And he was one of them.

Leaning over the Embankment in the time-honoured attitude of would-be suicides, he began to go into the details. He wanted as far as possible to be unobtrusive; now that his anger had died it seemed to him a pity that he hadn't drunk that cup of tea—he didn't want to shock any innocent person with the sight of an ugly death. And there were very few suicides which were not ugly. Murder was infinitely more graceful because it was the murderer's object not to shock—a murderer went to infinite pains to make death look quiet, peaceful, happy. Everything, he thought, would be so much easier if he had only a little money.

Of course, he could go to the bank and let the police get him. It seemed probable that then he would be hanged. But the idea of hanging for a crime he hadn't committed still had power to anger him: if he killed himself it would be for a crime of which he was guilty. He was haunted by a primitive idea of Justice. He wanted to conform: he had always wanted to conform.

A murderer is regarded by the conventional world as something almost monstrous, but a murderer to himself is only an ordinary man—a man who takes either tea or coffee for breakfast, a man who likes a good book and perhaps reads biography rather than fiction, a man who at a regular hour goes to bed, who tries to develop good physical habits but possibly suffers from constipation, who prefers either dogs or cats and has certain views about politics.

It is only if the murderer is a good man that he can be regarded as monstrous.

Arthur Rowe was monstrous. His early childhood had been passed before the first world war, and the impressions of childhood are ineffaceable. He was brought up to believe that it was wrong to inflict pain, but he was often ill, his teeth were bad and he suffered agonies from an inefficient dentist he knew as Mr Griggs. He learned before he was seven what pain was like—he wouldn't willingly allow even a rat to suffer it. In childhood we live under the brightness of immortality—heaven is as near and actual as the seaside. Behind the complicated details of the world stand the simplicities: God is good, the grown-up man or woman knows the answer to every question, there is such a thing as

truth, and justice is as measured and faultless as a clock. Our heroes are simple: they are brave, they tell the truth, they are good
swordsmen and they are never in the long run really defeated.
That is why no later books satisfy us like those which were read
to us in childhood—for those promised a world of great simplicity of which we knew the rules, but the later books are complicated and contradictory with experience; they are formed out of
our own disappointing memories—of the V.C. in the police-
court dock, of the faked income tax return, the sins in corners,
and the hollow voice of the man we despised talking to us of
courage and purity. The Little Duke is dead and betrayed and
forgotten; we cannot recognize the villain and we suspect the
hero and the world is a small cramped place. The two great pop-
ular statements of faith are 'What a small place the world is' and
'I'm a stranger here myself.'

But Rowe was a murderer—as other men are poets. The statues
still stood. He was prepared to do anything to save the innocent
or to punish the guilty. He believed against all the experience of
life that somewhere there was justice, and justice condemned
him. He analysed his motives minutely and always summed up
against himself. He told himself, leaning over the wall, as he had
told himself a hundred times, that it was he who had not been
able to bear his wife's pain—and not she. Once, it was true, in
the early days of the disease, she had broken down, said she
wanted to die, not to wait: that was hysteria. Later it was her endurance and her patience which he had found most unbearable.
He was trying to escape his own pain, not hers, and at the end
she had guessed or half-guessed what it was he was offering her.
She was scared and afraid to ask. How could you go on living
with a man if you had once asked him whether he had put poison
into your evening drink? Far easier when you love him and are
tired of pain just to take the hot milk and sleep. But he could
never know whether the fear had been worse than the pain, and
he could never tell whether she might not have preferred any
sort of life to death. He had taken the stick and killed the rat,
and saved himself the agony of watching. . . . He had gone over
the same questions and the same answers daily, ever since the
moment when she took the milk from him and said, 'How queer
it tastes,' and lay back and tried to smile. He would have liked

to stay beside her till she slept, but that would have been unusual, and he must avoid anything unusual, so he had to leave her to die alone. And she would have liked to ask him to stay—he was sure of that—but that would have been unusual too. After all, in an hour he would be coming up to bed. Convention held them at the moment of death. He had in mind the police questions, 'Why did you stay?' and it was quite possible that she too was deliberately playing his game against the police. There were so many things he would never know. But when the police did ask questions he hadn't the heart or the energy to tell them lies. Perhaps if he had lied to them a little they would have hanged him . . .

It was about time now to bring the trial to an end.

2

'They can't spoil Whistler's Thames,' a voice said.

'I'm sorry,' Rowe said, 'I didn't catch . . .'

'It's safe underground. Bomb-proof vaults.'

Somewhere, Rowe thought, he had seen that face before: the thin depressed grey moustache, the bulging pockets, out of which the man now took a piece of bread and threw it towards the mud. Before it had reached the river the gulls had risen: one out-distanced the others, caught it and sailed on, down past the stranded barges and the paper mill, a white scrap blown towards the blackened chimneys of Lots Road.

'Come, my pretties,' the man said, and his hand suddenly became a landing ground for sparrows. 'They know uncle,' he said, 'they know uncle.' He put a bit of bread between his lips and they hovered round his mouth giving little pecks at it as though they were kissing him.

'It must be difficult in wartime,' Rowe said, 'to provide for all your nephews.'

'Yes, indeed,' the man said—and when he opened his mouth you saw his teeth were in a shocking condition, black stumps like the remains of something destroyed by fire. He sprinkled some crumbs over his old brown hat and a new flock of sparrows landed there. 'Strictly illegal,' he said, 'I dare say. If Lord Woolton knew.' He put a foot up on a heavy suitcase, and a sparrow perched on his knee. He was overgrown with birds.

'I've seen you before,' Rowe said.

'I dare say.'

'Twice today now I come to think of it.'

'Come, my pretties,' the elderly man said.

'In the auction-room in Chancery Lane.'

A pair of mild eyes turned on him. 'It's a small world.'

'Do you buy books?' Rowe asked, thinking of the shabby clothes.

'Buy and sell,' the man said. He was acute enough to read Rowe's thoughts. 'Working clothes,' he said. 'Books carry a deal of dust.'

'You go in for old books?'

'Landscape gardening's my speciality. Eighteenth century. Fullove, Fulham Road, Battersea.'

'Do you find enough customers?'

'There are more than you'd think.' He suddenly opened his arms wide and shooed the birds away as though they were children with whom he'd played long enough. 'But everything's depressed,' he said, 'these days. What they want to fight for I don't understand.' He touched the suitcase tenderly with his foot. 'I've got a load of books here,' he said, 'I got from a lord's house. Salvage. The state of some of them would make you weep, but others . . . I don't say it wasn't a good bargain. I'd show them you, only I'm afraid of bird-droppings. First bargain I've had for months. In the old days I'd have treasured them, treasured them. Waited till the Americans came in the summer. Now I'm glad of any chance of a turnover. If I don't deliver these to a customer at Regal Court before five, I lose a sale. He wants to take them down to the country before the raid starts. I haven't a watch, sir. Could you tell me the time?'

'It's only four o'clock.'

'I ought to go on,' Mr Fullove said. 'Books are heavy though and I feel just tired out. It's been a long day. You'll excuse me, sir, if I sit down a moment.' He sat himself down on the suitcase and drew out a ragged packet of Tenners. 'Will you smoke, sir? You look a bit done, if I may say so, yourself.'

'Oh, I'm all right.' The mild exhausted ageing eyes appealed to him. He said, 'Why don't you take a taxi?'

'Well, sir, I work on a very narrow margin these days. If I take a taxi that's a dollar gone. And then when he gets the books to the country, perhaps he won't want one of them.'

'They are landscape gardening?'

'That's right. It's a lost art, sir. There's a lot more to it, you know, than flowers. That's what gardening means today,' he said with contempt, 'flowers.'

'You don't care for flowers?'

'Oh, flowers,' the bookseller said, 'are all right. You've got to have flowers.'

'I'm afraid,' Rowe said, 'I don't know much about gardening— except flowers.'

'It's the tricks they played.' The mild eyes looked up with cunning enthusiasm. 'The machinery.'

'Machinery?'

'They had statues that spurted water at you when you passed, and the grottoes—the things they thought up for grottoes. Why, in a good garden you weren't safe anywhere.'

'I should have thought you were meant to feel safe in a garden.'

'They didn't think so, sir,' the bookseller said, blowing the stale smell of carious teeth enthusiastically in Rowe's direction. Rowe wished he could get away; but automatically with that wish the sense of pity worked and he stayed.

'And then,' the bookseller said, 'there were the tombs.'

'Did they spurt water too?'

'Oh no. They gave the touch of solemnity, sir, the *memento mori*.'

'Black thoughts,' Rowe said, 'in a black shade?'

'It's how you look at it, isn't it, sir?' But there was no doubt that the bookseller looked at it with a kind of gloating. He brushed a little bird-lime off his jacket and said, 'You don't have a taste, sir, for the Sublime—or the Ridiculous?'

'Perhaps,' Rowe said, 'I prefer human nature plain.'

The little man giggled. 'I get your meaning, sir. Oh, they had room for human nature, believe me, in the grottoes. Not one without a comfortable couch. They never forgot the comfortable couch,' and again with sly enthusiasm he blew his carious breath towards his companion.

'Don't you think,' Rowe said, 'you should be getting on? You mustn't let me rob you of a sale,' and immediately he reacted from his own harshness seeing only the mild tired eyes, thinking, poor devil, he's had a weary day, each one to his taste . . . after all, he liked me. That was a claim he could never fail to honour because it astonished him.

'I suppose I ought, sir.' He rose and brushed away some crumbs the birds had left. 'I enjoy a good talk,' he said. 'It's not often you can get a good talk these days. It's a rush between shelters.'

'You sleep in a shelter?'

'To tell you the truth, sir,' he said as if he were confessing to an idiosyncrasy, 'I can't bear the bombs. But you don't sleep as you ought in a shelter.' The weight of the suitcase cramped him: he looked very old under its weight. 'Some people are not considerate. The snores and squabbles . . .'

'Why did you come into the park? It's not your shortest way?'

'I wanted a rest, sir—and the trees invited, and the birds.'

'Here,' Rowe said, 'you'd better let me take that. There's no bus this side of the river.'

'Oh, I couldn't bother you, sir. I really couldn't.' But there was no genuine resistance in him; the suitcase was certainly very heavy: folios of landscape gardening weighed a lot. He excused himself, 'There's nothing so heavy as books, sir—unless it's bricks.'

They came out of the park and Rowe changed the weight from one arm to the other. He said, 'You know it's getting late for your appointment.'

'It's my tongue that did it,' the old bookseller said with distress. 'I think—I really think I shall have to risk the fare.'

'I think you will.'

'If I could give you a lift, sir, it would make it more worth while. Are you going in my direction?'

'Oh, in any,' Rowe said.

They got a taxi at the next corner, and the bookseller leant back with an air of bashful relaxation. He said, 'If you make up your mind to pay for a thing, enjoy it, that's my idea.'

But in the taxi with the windows shut it wasn't easy for another to enjoy it; the smell of dental decay was very strong. Rowe talked for fear of showing his distaste. 'And have you gone in yourself for landscape gardening?'

'Well, not what you would call the garden part.' The man kept peering through the window—it occurred to Rowe that his simple enjoyment rang a little false. He said, 'I wonder, sir, if you'd do me one last favour. The stairs at Regal Court—well, they are a caution to a man of my age. And no one offers somebody like me a hand. I deal in books, but to them, sir, I'm just a tradesman. If you wouldn't mind taking up the bag for me. You needn't stay a moment. Just ask for Mr Travers in number six. He's expecting the bag—there's nothing you have to do but leave it with him.' He took a quick sideways look to catch a refusal on the wing. 'And afterwards, sir, you've been very kind, I'd give you a lift anywhere you wanted to go.'

'You don't know where I want to go,' Rowe said.

'I'll risk that, sir. In for a penny, in for a pound.'

'I might take you at your word and go a very long way.'

'Try me. Just try me, sir,' the other said with forced glee.

'I'd sell you a book and make it even.' Perhaps it was the man's servility—or it may have been only the man's smell—but Rowe felt unwilling to oblige him. 'Why not get the commissionaire to take it up for you?' he asked.

'I'd never trust him to deliver—straightaway.'

'You could see it taken up yourself.'

'It's the stairs, sir, at the end of a long day.' He lay back in his seat and said, 'If you must know, sir, I oughtn't to have been carrying it,' and he made a movement towards his heart, a gesture for which there was no answer.

Well, Rowe thought, I may as well do one good deed before I go away altogether—but all the same he didn't like it. Certainly the man looked sick and tired enough to excuse any artifice, but he had been too successful. Why, Rowe thought, should I be sitting here in a taxi with a stranger promising to drag a case of eighteenth-century folios to the room of another stranger? He felt directed, controlled, moulded, by some agency with a surrealist imagination.

They drew up outside Regal Court—an odd pair, both dusty,

both unshaven. Rowe had agreed to nothing, but he knew there was no choice; he hadn't the hard strength of mind to walk away and leave the little man to drag his own burden. He got out under the suspicious eyes of the commissionaire and lugged the heavy case after him. 'Have you got a room booked,' the commissionaire asked and added dubiously, 'sir?'

'I'm not staying here. I'm leaving this case for Mr Travers.'

'Ask at the desk, please,' the commissionaire said, and leapt to serve a more savoury carload.

The bookseller had been right; it was a hard pull up the long wide stairs of the hotel. You felt they had been built for women in evening-dress to walk slowly down; the architect had been too romantic—he hadn't seen a man with two days' beard dragging a load of books. Rowe counted fifty steps.

The clerk at the counter eyed him carefully. Before Rowe had time to speak he said, 'We are quite full up, I'm afraid.'

'I've brought some books for a Mr Travers in room six.'

'Oh yes,' the clerk said. 'He was expecting you. He's out, but he gave orders'—you could see that he didn't like the orders—'that you were to be allowed in.'

'I don't want to wait. I just want to leave the books.'

'Mr Travers gave orders that you were to wait.'

'I don't care a damn what orders Mr Travers gave.'

'Page,' the clerk called sharply, 'show this man to number six. Mr Travers. Mr Travers has given orders that he's to be allowed in.' He had very few phrases and never varied them. Rowe wondered on how few he could get through life, marry and have children. He followed at the page's heels down interminable corridors lit by concealed lighting; once a woman in pink mules and a dressing gown squealed as they went by. It was like the corridor of a monstrous Cunarder—one expected to see stewards and stewardesses, but instead a small stout man wearing a bowler hat padded to meet them from what seemed a hundred yards away, then suddenly veered aside into the intricacies of the building. 'Do you unreel a thread of cotton?' Rowe asked, swaying under the weight of the case which the page never offered to take, and feeling the strange light-headedness which comes, we are told, to dying men. But the back, the tight little blue trousers and the

bum-freezer jacket, just went on ahead. It seemed to Rowe
that one could be lost here for a lifetime: only the clerk at the
desk would have a clue to one's whereabouts, and it was doubtful
whether he ever penetrated very far in person into the enormous
wilderness. Water would come regularly out of taps, and at dusk
one could emerge and collect tinned foods. He was touched by a
forgotten sense of adventure, watching the numbers go backwards, 49, 48, 47; once they took a short cut which led them
through the 60's to emerge suddenly among the 30's.

A door in the passage was ajar and odd sounds came through it as
though someone were alternately whistling and sighing, but nothing
to the page seemed strange. He just went on: he was a child of this
building. People of every kind came in for a night with or without
luggage and then went away again; a few died here and the bodies
were removed unobtrusively by the service lift. Divorce suits
bloomed at certain seasons; co-respondents gave tips and detectives
out-trumped them with larger tips—because their tips went on the
expense account. The page took everything for granted.

Rowe said, 'You'll lead me back?' At each corner arrows
pointed above the legend AIR RAID SHELTER. Coming on them
every few minutes one got the impression that one was walking
in circles.

'Mr Travers left orders you was to stay.'

'But I don't take orders from Mr Travers,' Rowe said.

This was a modern building; the silence was admirable and disquieting. Instead of bells ringing, lights went off and on. One got
the impression that all the time people were signalling news of
great importance that couldn't wait. This silence—now that they
were out of earshot of the whistle and the sigh—was like that of a
stranded liner; the engines had stopped, and in the sinister silence
you listened for the faint depressing sound of lapping water.

'Here's six,' the boy said.

'It must take a long time to get to a hundred.'

'Third floor,' the boy said, 'but Mr Travers gave orders . . .'

'Never mind,' Rowe said. 'Forget I said it.'

Without the chromium number you could hardly have told
the difference between the door and the wall; it was as if the inhabitants had been walled up. The page put in a master-key and

pushed the wall in. Rowe said, 'I'll just put the case down . . .'
But the door had shut behind him. Mr Travers, who seemed to
be a much-respected man, had given his orders and if he didn't
obey them he would have to find his way back alone. There was
an exhilaration in the absurd episode; he had made up his mind
now about everything—justice as well as the circumstances of
the case demanded that he should kill himself (he had only to decide the method), and now he could enjoy the oddness of existence; regret, anger, hatred, too many emotions had obscured for
too long the silly shape of life. He opened the sitting-room door.

'Well,' he said, 'this beats all.'

It was Anna Hilfe.

He asked, 'Have you come to see Mr Travers too? Are you interested in landscape gardening?'

She said, 'I came to see you.'

It was really his first opportunity to take her in. Very small and
thin, she looked too young for all the things she must have seen,
and now taken out of the office frame she no longer looked
efficient—as though efficiency were an imitative game she could
only play with adult properties, a desk, a telephone, a black
suit. Without them she looked just decorative and breakable,
but he knew that life hadn't been able to break her. All it had
done was to put a few wrinkles round eyes as straightforward
as a child's.

'Do you like the mechanical parts of gardening too?' he asked.
'Statues that spurt water . . .'

His heart beat at the sight of her, as though he were a young
man and this his first assignation outside a cinema, in a Lyons Corner House . . . or in an inn yard in a country town where dances
were held. She was wearing a pair of shabby blue trousers ready
for the night's raid and a wine-coloured jersey. He thought with
melancholy that her thighs were the prettiest he had ever seen.

'I don't understand,' she said.

'How did you know I was going to cart a load of books here
for Mr Travers—whoever Mr Travers is? I didn't know myself
until ten minutes ago.'

'I don't know what excuse they thought up for you,' she said.
'Just go. Please.'

She looked the kind of child you want to torment—in a kindly

way; in the office she had been ten years older. He said, 'They do
people well here, don't they. You get a whole flat for a night. You
can sit down and read a book and cook a dinner.'

A pale brown curtain divided the living-room in half; he drew it
aside and there was the double bed, a telephone on a little table, a
bookcase. He asked, 'What's through here?' and opened a door.
'You see,' he said, 'they throw in a kitchen, stove and all.' He came
back into the sitting-room and said, 'One could live here and forget it wasn't one's home.' He no longer felt care-free; it had been a
mood which had lasted minutes only.

She said, 'Have you noticed anything?'

'How do you mean?'

'You don't notice much for a journalist.'

'You know I was a journalist?'

'My brother checked up on everything.'

'On everything?'

'Yes.' She said again, 'You didn't notice anything?'

'No.'

'Mr Travers doesn't seem to have left behind him so much as a
used piece of soap. Look in the bathroom. The soap's wrapped
up in its paper.'

Rowe went to the front door and bolted it. He said, 'Whoever
he is, he can't get in now till we've finished talking. Miss Hilfe,
will you please tell me slowly—I'm a bit stupid, I think—first
how you knew I was here and secondly why you came?'

She said obstinately, 'I won't tell you how. As to why—I've
asked you to go away quickly. I was right last time, wasn't I,
when I telephoned . . .'

'Yes, you were right. But why worry? You said you knew all
about me, didn't you?'

'There's no harm in you,' she said simply.

'Knowing everything,' he said, 'you wouldn't worry . . .'

'I like justice,' she said, as if she were confessing an eccentricity.

'Yes,' he said, 'it's a good thing if you can get it.'

'But They don't.'

'Do you mean Mrs Bellairs,' he asked, 'and Canon Topling?' It
was too complicated: he hadn't any fight left. He sat down in the
arm-chair—they allowed in the ersatz home one arm-chair and a
couch.

'Canon Topling is quite a good man,' she said and suddenly smiled. 'It's too silly,' she said, 'the things we are saying.'

'You must tell your brother,' Rowe said, 'that he's not to bother about me any more. I'm giving up. Let them murder whom they like—I'm out of it. I'm going away.'

'Where?'

'It's all right,' he said. 'They'll never find me. I know a place . . . But they won't want to. I think all they were really afraid of was that I should find *them*. I'll never know now, I suppose, what it was all about. The cake . . . and Mrs Bellairs. Wonderful Mrs Bellairs.'

'They are bad,' she said, as if that simple phrase disposed of them altogether. 'I'm glad you are going away. It's not your business.' To his amazement she added, 'I don't want you to be hurt any more.'

'Why,' he said, 'you know everything about me. You've checked up.' He used her own childish word. 'I'm bad too.'

'Mr Rowe,' she said, 'I have seen so many bad people where I come from, and you don't fit: you haven't the right marks. You worry too much about what's over and done. People say English justice is good. Well, they didn't hang you. It was a mercy killing, that was what the papers called it.'

'You've read all the papers?'

'All of them. I've even seen the pictures they took. You put your newspaper up to hide your face . . .'

He listened to her with dumb astonishment. No one had ever talked to him openly about it. It was painful, but it was the sort of pain you feel when iodine is splashed on a wound—the sort of pain you can bear. She said, 'Where I come from I have seen a lot of killings, but they were none of them mercy killings. Don't think so much. Give yourself a chance.'

'I think,' he said, 'we'd better decide what to do about Mr Travers.'

'Just go. That's all.'

'And what will you do?'

'Go too. I don't want any trouble either.'

Rowe said, 'If they are your enemies, if they've made you suffer, I'll stay and talk to Mr Travers.'

'Oh, no,' she said. 'They are not mine. This isn't my country.'

He said, 'Who are they? I'm in a fog. Are they your people or my people?'

'They are the same everywhere,' she said. She put out a hand and touched his arm tentatively, as if she wanted to know what he felt like. 'You think you are so bad,' she said, 'but it was only because you couldn't bear the pain. But *they* can bear pain— other people's pain—endlessly. They are the people who don't care.'

He could have gone on listening to her for hours; it seemed a pity that he had to kill himself, but he had no choice in the matter. Unless he left it to the hangman. He said, 'I suppose if I stay till Mr Travers comes, he'll hand me over to the police.'

'I don't know what they'll do.'

'And that little smooth man with the books was in it too. What a lot of them there are.'

'An awful lot. More every day.'

'But why should they think I'd stay—when once I'd left the books?' He took her wrist—a small bony wrist—and said sadly, 'You aren't in it too, are you?'

'No,' she said, not pulling away from him, just stating a fact. He had the impression that she didn't tell lies. She might have a hundred vices, but not the commonest one of all.

'I didn't think you were,' he said, 'but that means—it means they meant us both to be here.'

She said, 'Oh,' as if he'd hit her.

'They knew we'd waste time talking, explaining. They want us both, but the *police* don't want you.' He exclaimed, 'You're coming away with me now.'

'Yes.'

'If we are not too late. They seem to time things well.' He went into the hall and very carefully and softly slid the bolt, opened the door a crack and then very gently shut it again. He said, 'Just now I was thinking how easy it would be to get lost in this hotel, in all these long passages.'

'Yes?'

'We shan't get lost. There's someone at the end of the passage waiting for us. His back's turned. I can't see his face.'

'They do think of everything,' she said.

He found his exhilaration returning. He had thought he was

going to die today—but he wasn't; he was going to live, because he could be of use to someone again. He no longer felt that he was dragging round a valueless and ageing body. He said, 'I don't see how they can starve us out. And they can't get in. Except through the window.'

'No,' Miss Hilfe said. 'I've looked. They can't get in there. There's twelve feet of smooth wall.'

'Then all we have to do is sit and wait. We might ring up the restaurant and order dinner. Lots of courses, and a good wine. Travers can pay. We'll begin with a very dry sherry.'

'Yes,' Miss Hilfe said, 'if we were sure the right waiter would bring it.'

He smiled. 'You think of everything. It's the continental training. What's your advice?'

'Ring up the clerk—we know him by sight. Make trouble about something. Insist that he must come along, and then we'll walk out with him.'

'You're right,' he said. 'Of course that's the way.'

He lifted the curtain and she followed him. 'What are you going to say?'

'I don't know. Leave it to the moment. I'll think of something.' He took up the receiver and listened . . . and listened. He said, 'I think the line's dead.' He waited for nearly two minutes, but there was only silence.

'We *are* besieged,' she said. 'I wonder what they mean to do.' They neither of them noticed that they were holding hands: it was as though they had been overtaken by the dark and had to feel their way . . .

He said, 'We haven't got much in the way of weapons. You don't wear hatpins nowadays, and I suppose the police have got the only knife I've ever had.' They came back hand in hand into the small living-room. 'Let's be warm, any way,' he said, 'and turn on the fire. It's cold enough for a blizzard, and we've got the wolves outside.'

She had let go his hand and was kneeling by the fire. She said, 'It doesn't go on.'

'You haven't put in the sixpence.'

'I've put in a shilling.'

It was cold and the room was darkening. The same thought struck both of them. 'Try the light,' she said, but his hand had already felt the switch. The light didn't go on.

'It's going to be very dark and very cold,' he said. 'Mr Travers is not making us comfortable.'

'Oh,' Miss Hilfe said, putting her hand to her mouth like a child. 'I'm scared. I'm sorry, but I *am* scared. I don't like the dark.'

'They can't do anything,' Rowe said. 'The door's bolted. They can't batter it down, you know. This is a civilized hotel.'

'Are you sure,' Miss Hilfe said, 'that there's no connecting door? In the kitchen . . .'

A memory struck him. He opened the kitchen door. 'Yes,' he said. 'You're right again. The tradesmen's entrance. These are good flats.'

'But you can bolt that too. Please,' Miss Hilfe said.

Rowe came back. He said gently, 'There's only one flaw in this well-furnished flat. The kitchen bolt is broken.' He took her hand again quickly. 'Never mind,' he said. 'We're imagining things. This isn't Vienna, you know. This is London. We are in the majority. This hotel is full of people—on *our* side.' He repeated, 'On our side. They are all round us. We've only to shout.' The world was sliding rapidly towards night; like a torpedoed liner heeling too far over, she would soon take her last dive into darkness. Already they were talking louder because they couldn't clearly see each other's faces.

'In half an hour,' Miss Hilfe said, 'the sirens will go. And then they'll all go down into the basement, and the only ones left will be us—and them.' Her hand felt very cold.

'Then that's our chance,' he said. 'When the sirens go, we go too with the crowd.'

'We are at the end of the passage. Perhaps there won't be a crowd. How do you know there *is* anyone left in this passage? They've thought of so much. Don't you think they'll have thought of that? They've probably booked every room.'

'We'll try,' he said. 'If we had any weapon at all—a stick, a stone.' He stopped and let her hand go. 'If those aren't books,' he said, 'perhaps they are bricks. Bricks.' He felt one of the catches.

'It isn't locked,' he said. 'Now we'll see . . .' But they both looked at the suitcase doubtfully. Efficiency is paralysing. *They* had thought of everything, so wouldn't they have thought of this too?'

'I wouldn't touch it,' she said.

They felt the inertia a bird is supposed to feel before a snake: a snake too knows all the answers.

'They must make a mistake some time,' he said.

The dark was dividing them. Very far away the guns grumbled.

'They'll wait till the sirens,' she said, 'till everybody's down there, out of hearing.'

'What's that?' he said. He was getting jumpy himself.

'What?'

'I think someone tried the handle.'

'How near they are getting,' she said.

'By God,' he said, 'we aren't powerless. Give me a hand with the couch.' They stuck the end of it against the kitchen door. They could hardly see a thing now; they were really in the dark. 'It's lucky,' Miss Hilfe said, 'that the stove's electric.'

'But I don't think it is. Why?'

'We've shut them out of here. But they can turn on the gas.'

He said, 'You ought to be in the game yourself. The things you think of. Here. Give me a hand again. We'll push this couch through into the kitchen.' But they stopped almost before they started. He said, 'It's too late. Somebody's in there.' The tiniest click of a closing door was all they had heard.

'What happens next?' he asked. Memories of *The Little Duke* came incongruously back. He said, 'In the old days they always called on the castle to surrender.'

'Don't,' she whispered. 'Please. They are listening.'

'I'm getting tired of this cat and mouse act,' he said. 'We don't even know he's in there. They are frightening us with squeaking doors and the dark.' He was moved by a slight hysteria. He called out, 'Come in, come in. Don't bother to knock,' but no one replied.

He said angrily, 'They've chosen the wrong man. They think they can get everything by fear. But you've checked up on me. I'm a murderer, aren't I? You know that. I'm not afraid to kill. Give me any weapon. Just give me a brick.' He looked at the suitcase.

Miss Hilfe said, 'You're right. We've got to do something, even if it's the wrong thing. Not just let them do everything. Open it.'

He gave her hand a quick nervous pressure and released it. Then, as the sirens took up their nightly wail, he opened the lid of the suitcase . . .

BOOK TWO
THE HAPPY MAN

CHAPTER I
CONVERSATIONS IN ARCADY

'His guardians would fain have had it supposed that
the castle did not contain any such guest.'

The Little Duke

I

The sun came into the room like pale green underwater light.
That was because the tree outside was just budding. The light
washed over the white clean walls of the room, over the bed with
its primrose yellow cover, over the big arm-chair and the couch,
and the bookcase which was full of advanced reading. There
were some early daffodils in a vase which had been bought in
Sweden, and the only sounds were a fountain dripping somewhere in the cool out-of-doors and the gentle voice of the earnest
young man with rimless glasses.

'The great thing, you see, is not to worry. You've had your
share of the war for the time being, Mr Digby, and you can lie
back with an easy conscience.'

The young man was always strong on the subject of conscience.
His own, he had explained weeks ago, was quite clear. Even if his
views had not inclined to pacifism, his bad eyes would have pre-
vented him from being of any active value—the poor things
peered weakly and trustfully through the huge convex lenses like
bottle-glass; they pleaded all the time for serious conversation.

'Don't think I'm not enjoying myself here. I am. You know it's
a great rest. Only sometimes I try to think—who am I?'

'Well, we know that, Mr Digby. Your identity card . . .'

'Yes, I know my name's Richard Digby, but who is Richard
Digby? What sort of life do you think I led? Do you think I shall
ever have the means to repay you all . . . for this?'

'Now that needn't worry you, Mr Digby. The doctor is repaid
all he wants simply by the interest of your case. You're a very
valuable specimen under his microscope.'

'But he makes life on the slide so very luxurious, doesn't he?'

'He's wonderful,' the young man said. 'This place—he planned it all, you know. He's a very great man. There's not a finer shell-shock clinic in the country. Whatever people may say,' he added darkly.

'I suppose you have worse cases than mine . . . violent cases.'

'We've had a few. That's why the doctor arranged the sick bay for them. A separate wing and a separate staff. He doesn't want even the attendants in this wing to be mentally disturbed . . . You see it's essential that we should be calm too.'

'You're certainly all very calm.'

'When the time's ripe I expect the doctor will give you a course of psycho-analysis, but it's really much better, you know, that the memory should return of itself—gently and naturally. It's like a film in a hypo bath,' he went on, obviously drawing on another man's patter. 'The development will come out in patches.'

'Not if it's a good hypo bath, Johns,' Digby said. He lay back smiling lazily in the arm-chair, lean and bearded and middle-aged. The angry scar on his forehead looked out of place—like duelling cuts on a professor.

'Hold on to that,' Johns said—it was one of his favourite expressions. 'You went in for photography then?'

'Do you think that perhaps I was a fashionable portrait photographer?' Digby asked. 'It doesn't exactly ring a bell, though of course it goes—doesn't it?—with the beard. No, I was thinking of a darkroom on the nursery floor at home. It was a linen cupboard too, and if you forgot to lock the door, a maid would come in with clean pillow slips and bang went the negative. You see, I remember things quite clearly until say, eighteen.'

'You can talk about that time,' Johns said, 'as much as you like. You may get a clue and there's obviously no resistance—from the Freudian censor.'

'I was just wondering in bed this morning which of the people I wanted to become I did in fact choose. I remember I was very fond of books on African exploration—Stanley, Baker, Livingstone, Burton, but there doesn't seem much opportunity for explorers nowadays.'

He brooded without impatience. It was as if his happiness were drawn from an infinite fund of tiredness. He didn't want to exert himself. He was comfortable exactly as he was. Perhaps that was why his memory was slow in returning. He said dutifully, because of course one had to make some effort, 'One might look up the old Colonial Office lists. Perhaps I went in for that. It's odd, isn't it, that knowing my name, you shouldn't have found any acquaintance. You'd think there would have been inquiries. If I had been married, for instance. That does trouble me. Suppose my wife is trying to find me . . .' If only that could be cleared up, he thought, I should be perfectly happy.

'As a matter of fact,' Johns said and stopped.

'Don't tell me you've unearthed a wife?'

'Not exactly, but I think the doctor has something to tell you.'

'Well,' Digby said, 'it *is* the hour of audience, isn't it?'

Each patient saw the doctor in his study for a quarter of an hour a day, except those who were being treated by psychoanalysis—they were given an hour of his time. It was like visiting a benign headmaster out of school hours to have a chat about personal problems. One passed through the commonroom where the patients could read the papers, play chess or draughts, or indulge in the rather unpredictable social intercourse of shell-shocked men. Digby as a rule avoided the place; it was disconcerting, in what might have been the lounge of an exclusive hotel, to see a man quietly weeping in a corner. He felt himself to be so completely normal—except for the gap of he didn't know how many years and an inexplicable happiness as if he had been relieved suddenly of some terrible responsibility—that he was ill at ease in the company of men who all exhibited some obvious sign of an ordeal, the twitch of an eyelid, a shrillness of voice, or a melancholy that fitted as completely and inescapably as the skin.

Johns led the way. He filled with perfect tact a part which combined assistant, secretary and male nurse. He was not qualified, though the doctor occasionally let him loose on the simpler psyches. He had an enormous fund of hero-worship for the doctor, and Digby gathered that some incident in the doctor's past—it might have been the suicide of a patient, but Johns was studiously vague—enabled him to pose before himself as the champion of the great misunderstood. He said, 'The jealousies of medical people—you wouldn't believe it. The malice. The lies.' He would

get quite pink on the subject of what he called the doctor's mar-
tyrdom. There had been an inquiry: the doctor's methods were far
in advance of his time; there had been talk—so Digby gathered—
of taking away the doctor's licence to practice. 'They crucified
him,' he said once with an illustrative gesture and knocked over
the vase of daffodils. But eventually good had come out of evil
(one felt the good included Johns); the doctor in disgust at the
West End world had retired to the country, had opened his private
clinic where he refused to accept any patient without a signed personal request—even the more violent cases had been sane enough
to put themselves voluntarily under the doctor's care.

'But what about me?' Digby had asked.

'Ah, you are the doctor's special case,' Johns said mysteriously.
'One day he'll tell you. You stumbled on salvation all right that
night. And anyway you did sign.'

It never lost its strangeness—to remember nothing of how he
had come here. He had simply woken to the restful room, the
sound of the fountain, and a taste of drugs. It had been winter
then. The trees were black, and sudden squalls of rain broke the
peace. Once very far across the fields came a faint wail like a ship
signalling departure. He would lie for hours, dreaming confusedly.
It was as if then he might have remembered, but he hadn't got the
strength to catch the hints, to fix the sudden pictures, he hadn't the
vitality to connect . . . He would drink his medicines without com-
plaint and go off into deep sleep which was only occasionally broken by strange nightmares in which a woman played a part.

It was a long time before they told him about the war, and that
involved an enormous amount of historical explanation. What
seemed odd to him, he found, was not what seemed odd to other
people. For example, the fact that Paris was in German hands appeared to him quite natural—he remembered how nearly it had
been so before in the period of his life that he could recall, but
the fact that we were at war with Italy shook him like an inexplicable catastrophe of nature.

'Italy,' he exclaimed. Why, Italy was where two of his maiden
aunts went every year to paint. He remembered too the Primi-
tives in the National Gallery and Caporetto and Garibaldi, who
had given a name to a biscuit, and Thomas Cook's. Then Johns
patiently explained about Mussolini.

2

The doctor sat behind a bowl of flowers at his very simple un-
stained desk and he waved Digby in as if this were a favourite
pupil. His elderly face under the snow-white hair was hawk-like
and noble and a little histrionic, like the portrait of a Victorian.
Johns sidled out, he gave the impression of stepping backwards the
few paces to the door, and he stumbled on the edge of the carpet.

'Well, and how are you feeling?' the doctor said. 'You look
more yourself every day.'

'Do I?' Digby asked. 'But who knows really if I do? I don't,
and you don't, Dr Forester. Perhaps I look less myself.'

'That brings me to a piece of important news,' Dr Forester
said. 'I have found somebody who *will* know. Somebody who
knew you in the old days.'

Digby's heart beat violently. He said, 'Who?'

'I'm not going to tell you that. I want you to discover everything for yourself.'

'It's silly of me,' Digby said, 'but I feel a bit faint.'

'That's only natural,' Dr Forester said. 'You aren't very strong
yet.' He unlocked a cupboard and took out a glass and a bottle of
sherry. 'This'll put you to rights,' he said.

'Tio Pepe,' Digby said, draining it.

'You see,' the doctor said, 'things are coming back. Have another glass?'

'No, it's blasphemy to drink this as medicine.'

The news had been a shock. He wasn't sure that he was glad.
He couldn't tell what responsibility might descend on him when
his memory returned. Life is broken as a rule to every man gently;
duties accumulate so slowly that we hardly know they are there.
Even a happy marriage is a thing of slow growth; love helps to
make imperceptible the imprisonment of a man, but in a moment,
by order, would it be possible to love a stranger who entered bearing twenty years of emotional claims? Now, with no memories
nearer than his boyhood, he was entirely free. It wasn't that he
feared to face himself; he knew what he was and he believed he
knew the kind of man the boy he remembered would have become. It wasn't failure he feared nearly so much as the enormous
tasks that success might confront him with.

Dr Forester said, 'I have waited till now, till I felt you were strong enough.'

'Yes,' Digby said.

'You won't disappoint us, I'm sure,' the doctor said. He was more than ever the headmaster, and Digby a pupil who had been entered for a university scholarship; he carried the prestige of the school as well as his own future with him to the examination. Johns would be waiting with anxiety for his return—the form-master. Of course, they would be very kind if he failed. They would even blame the examiners . . .

'I'll leave the two of you alone,' the doctor said.

'He's here now?'

'*She* is here,' the doctor said.

3

It was an immense relief to see a stranger come in. He had been afraid that a whole generation of his life would walk through the door, but it was only a thin pretty girl with reddish hair, a small girl—perhaps too small to be remembered. She wasn't, he felt certain, anybody he needed to fear.

He rose; politeness seemed the wrong thing; he didn't know whether he ought to shake hands—or kiss her. He did neither. They looked at each other from a distance, and his heart beat heavily.

'How you've changed,' she said.

'They are always telling me,' he said, 'that I'm looking quite myself.'

'Your hair is much greyer. And that scar. And yet you look so much younger . . . happier.'

'I lead a very pleasant easy life here.'

'They've been good to you?' she asked with anxiety.

'Very good.'

He felt as though he had taken a stranger out to dinner and now couldn't hit on the right conversational move. He said, 'Excuse me. It sounds so abrupt. But I don't know your name.'

'You don't remember me at all?'

'No.'

He had occasionally had dreams about a woman, but it wasn't this woman. He couldn't remember any details of the dream except the woman's face, and that they had been filled with pain. He was glad that this was not the one. He looked at her again. 'No,' he said. 'I'm sorry. I wish I could.'

'Don't be sorry,' she said with strange ferocity. 'Never be sorry again.'

'I just meant—this silly brain of mine.'

She said, 'My name's Anna.' She watched him carefully, 'Hilfe.'

'That sounds foreign.'

'I am Austrian.'

He said, 'All this is so new to me. We are at war with Germany. Isn't Austria . . .?'

'I'm a refugee.'

'Oh, yes,' he said. 'I've read about them.'

'You have even forgotten the war?' she asked.

'I have a terrible lot to learn,' he said.

'Yes, terrible. But need they teach it you?' She repeated, 'You look so much happier . . .'

'One wouldn't be happy, not knowing anything.' He hesitated and again said, 'You must excuse me. There are so many questions. Were we simply friends?'

'Just friends. Why?'

'You are very pretty. I couldn't tell . . .'

'You saved my life.'

'How did I do that?'

'When the bomb went off—just before it went off—you knocked me down and fell on me. I wasn't hurt.'

'I'm very glad. I mean,' he laughed nervously, 'there might be all sorts of discreditable things to learn. I'm glad there's one good one.'

'It seems so strange,' she said. 'All these terrible years since 1933—you've just read about them, that's all. They are history to you. You're fresh. You aren't tired like all the rest of us everywhere.'

'1933,' he said. '1933. Now 1066, I can give you that easily. And all the kings of England—at least—I'm not sure . . . perhaps not all.'

'1933 was when Hitler came to power.'

'Of course. I remember now. I've read it all over and over again, but the dates don't stick.'

'And I suppose the hate doesn't either.'

'I haven't any right to talk about these things,' he said. 'I haven't lived them. They taught me at school that William Rufus was a wicked king with red hair—but you couldn't expect us to hate him. People like yourself have a right to hate. I haven't. You see I'm untouched.'

'Your poor face,' she said.

'Oh, the scar. That might have been anything—a motor-car accident. And after all they were not meaning to kill *me*.'

'No?'

'I'm not important.' He had been talking foolishly, at random. He had assumed something, and after all there was nothing he could safely assume. He said anxiously, 'I'm not important, am I? I can't be, or it would have been in the papers.'

'They let you see the papers?'

'Oh yes, this isn't a prison, you know.' He repeated, 'I'm not important?'

She said evasively, 'You are not famous.'

'I suppose the doctor won't let you tell me anything. He says he wants it all to come through my memory, slowly and gently. But I wish you'd break the rule about just one thing. It's the only thing that worries me. I'm not married, am I?'

She said slowly, as if she wanted to be very accurate and not to tell him more than was necessary, 'No, you are not married.'

'It was an awful idea that I might suddenly have to take up an old relationship which would mean a lot to someone else and nothing to me. Just something I had been told about, like Hitler. Of course, a new one's different.' He added with a shyness that looked awkward with grey hair, 'You are a new one.'

'And now there's nothing left to worry you?' she asked.

'Nothing,' he said. 'Or only one thing—that you might go out of that door and not come back.' He was always making advances and then hurriedly retreating like a boy who hasn't learned the technique. He said, 'You see, I've suddenly lost all my friends except you.'

She said rather sadly, 'Did you have a great many?'

'I suppose—by my age—one would have collected a good many.' He said cheerfully, 'Or was I such a monster?'

She wouldn't be cheered up. She said, 'Oh, I'll come back. They want me to come back. They want to know, you see, as soon as you begin to remember . . .'

'Of course they do. And you are the only clue they can give me. But have I got to stay here till I remember?'

'You wouldn't be much good, would you, without a memory—outside?'

'I don't see why not. There's plenty of work for me. If the army won't have me, there's munitions . . .'

'Do you want to be in it all again?'

He said, 'This is lovely and peaceful. But it's only a holiday after all. One's got to be of use.' He went on, 'Of course, it would be much easier if I knew what I'd been, what I could do best. I can't have been a man of leisure. There wasn't enough money in my family.' He watched her face carefully while he guessed. 'There aren't so many professions. Army, Navy, Church . . . I wasn't wearing the right clothes . . . if these are my clothes.' There was so much room for doubt. 'Law? Was it law, Anna? I don't believe it. I can't see myself in a wig getting some poor devil hanged.'

Anna said, 'No.'

'It doesn't connect. After all, the child does make the man. I never wanted to be a lawyer. I did want to be an explorer—but that's unlikely. Even with this beard. They tell me the beard really does belong. I wouldn't know. Oh,' he went on, 'I had enormous dreams of discovering unknown tribes in Central Africa. Medicine? No, I never liked doctoring. Too much pain. I hated pain.' He was troubled by a slight dizziness. He said, 'It made me feel ill, sick, hearing of pain. I remember—something about a rat.'

'Don't strain,' she said. 'It's not good to try too hard. There's no hurry.'

'Oh, that was neither here nor there. I was a child then. Where did I get to? Medicine . . . Trade. I wouldn't like to remember suddenly that I was the general manager of a chain store. That wouldn't connect either. I never particularly wanted to be rich. I suppose in a way I wanted to lead—a good life.'

Any prolonged effort made his head ache. But there were things he had to remember. He could let old friendships and enmities remain in oblivion, but if he were to make something of what was left of life he had to know of what he was capable. He looked at his hand and flexed the fingers: they didn't feel useful.

'People don't always become what they want to be,' Anna said.

'Of course not; a boy always wants to be a hero. A great explorer. A great writer . . . But there's usually a thin disappointing connection. The boy who wants to be rich goes into a bank. The explorer becomes—oh, well, some underpaid colonial officer making minutes in the heat. The writer joins the staff of a penny paper . . .' He said, 'I'm sorry. I'm not as strong as I thought. I've gone a bit giddy. I'll have to stop—work—for the day.'

Again she asked with odd anxiety, 'They are good to you here?'

'I'm a prize patient,' he said. 'An interesting case.'

'And Dr Forester—you like Dr Forester?'

'He fills one with awe,' he said.

'You've changed so much.' She made a remark he couldn't understand. 'This is how you should have been.' They shook hands like strangers. He said, 'And you'll come back often?'

'It's my job,' she said, 'Arthur.' It was only after she had gone that he wondered at the name.

4

In the mornings a servant brought him breakfast in bed: coffee, toast, a boiled egg. The Home was nearly self-supporting; it had its own hens and pigs and a good many acres of rough shooting. The doctor did not shoot himself; he did not approve, Johns said, of taking animal life, but he was not a doctrinaire. His patients needed meat, and therefore shoots were held, though the doctor took no personal part. 'It's really the idea of making it a sport,' Johns explained, 'which is against the grain. I think he'd really rather trap . . .'

On the tray lay always the morning paper. Digby had not been allowed this privilege for some weeks, until the war had been gently broken to him. Now he could lie late in bed, propped comfortably on three pillows, take a look at the news: 'Air Raid Casualties this Week are Down to 255', sip his coffee and tap the shell of his boiled egg: then back to the paper—'The Battle of the Atlantic'. The eggs were always done exactly right: the white set and the yolk liquid and thick. Back to the paper: 'The Admiralty regret to announce . . . lost with all hands.' There was always enough butter to put a little in the egg, for the doctor kept his own cows.

This morning as he was reading Johns came in for a chat, and Digby looking up from the paper asked, 'What's a Fifth Column?'

There was nothing Johns liked better than giving information. He talked for quite a while, bringing in Napoleon.

'In other words people in enemy pay?' Digby said. 'That's nothing new.'

'There's this difference,' Johns said. 'In the last war—except for Irishmen like Casement—the pay was always cash. Only a certain class was attracted. In this war there are all sorts of ideologies. The man who thinks gold is evil. . . . He's naturally attracted to the German economic system. And the men who for years have talked against nationalism . . . well, they are seeing all the old national boundaries obliterated. Pan-Europe. Perhaps not quite in the way they meant. Napoleon too appealed to idealists.' His glasses twinkled in the morning sun with the joys of instruction. 'When you come to think of it, Napoleon was beaten by the little men, the materialists. Shopkeepers and peasants. People who couldn't see beyond their counter or their field. They'd eaten their lunch under that hedge all their life and they meant to go on doing it. So Napoleon went to St Helena.'

'You don't sound a convinced patriot yourself,' Digby said.

'Oh, but I am,' Johns said earnestly. 'I'm a little man too. My father's a chemist, and how he hates all these German medicines that were flooding the market. I'm like him. I'd rather stick to Burroughs and Wellcome than all the Bayers. . . .' He went on, 'All the same, the other does represent a mood. It's we who are the materialists. The scrapping of all the old boundaries, the new economic ideas . . . the hugeness of the dream. It *is* attractive to men who are not tied—to a particular village or town they don't want to see scrapped. People with unhappy childhoods, progressive people who learn Esperanto, vegetarians who don't like shedding blood.'

'But Hitler seems to be shedding plenty.'

'Yes, but the idealists don't see blood like you and I do. They aren't materialists. It's all statistics to them.'

'What about Dr Forester?' Digby asked. 'He seems to fit the picture.'

'Oh,' Johns said enthusiastically, 'he's sound as a bell. He's written a pamphlet for the Ministry of Information, "The Psycho-Analysis of Nazidom". But there was a time,' he added, 'when there was—talk. You can't avoid witch-hunting in wartime, and, of course, there were rivals to hollo on the pack. You see, Dr Forester—well, he's so alive to everything. He likes to know. For instance, spiritualism—he's very interested in spiritualism, as an investigator.'

'I was just reading the questions in Parliament,' Digby said. 'They suggest there's another kind of Fifth Column. People who are blackmailed.'

'The Germans are wonderfully thorough,' Johns said. 'They did that in their own country. Card-indexed all the so-called leaders, Socialites, diplomats, politicians, labour leaders, priests—and then presented the ultimatum. Everything forgiven and forgotten, or the Public Prosecutor. It wouldn't surprise me if they'd done the same thing over here. They formed, you know, a kind of Ministry of Fear—with the most efficient under-secretaries. It isn't only that they get a hold on certain people. It's the general atmosphere they spread, so that you can't depend on a soul.'

'Apparently,' Digby said, 'this M.P. has got the idea that important plans were stolen from the Ministry of Home Security. They had been brought over from a Service Ministry for a consultation and lodged overnight. He claims that next morning they were found to be missing.'

'There must be an explanation,' Johns said.

'There is. The Minister says that the honourable member was misinformed. The plans were not required for the morning conference, and at the afternoon conference they were produced, fully discussed and returned to the Service Ministry.'

'These M.P.s get hold of odd stories,' Johns said.

'Do you think,' Digby asked, 'that by any chance I was a detective before this happened? That might fit the ambition to be an explorer, mightn't it? Because there seem to me to be so many holes in the statement.'

'It seems quite clear to me.'

'The M.P. who asked the question must have been briefed by someone who knew about those plans. Somebody at the conference—or somebody who was concerned in sending or receiving the plans. Nobody else could have known about them. Their existence is admitted by the Minister.'

'Yes, yes. That's true.'

'It's strange that anyone in that position should spread a canard. And do you notice that in that smooth elusive way politicians have the Minister doesn't, in fact, deny that the plans were missing? He says that they weren't wanted, and that when they were wanted they were there.'

'You mean there was time to photograph them?' Johns said excitedly. 'Would you mind if I smoked a cigarette? Here, let me take your tray.' He spilt some coffee on the bedsheet. 'Do you know,' he said, 'there was a suggestion of that kind made nearly three months ago? It was just after your arrival. I'll look it out for you. Dr Forester keeps a file of *The Times*. Some papers were missing then for several hours. They tried to hush that up—said it was just a case of carelessness and that the papers had never been out of the Ministry. An M.P. made a fuss—talked about photographs, and they came down on him like a sledge-hammer. Trying to undermine public confidence. The papers had never left the possession—I can't remember whose possession. Somebody whose word you had to take or else one of you would go to Brixton, and you could feel sure that it wouldn't be he. The papers shut down on it right away.'

'It would be strange, wouldn't it, if the same thing had happened again.'

Johns said excitedly, 'Nobody outside would know. And the others wouldn't say.'

'Perhaps the first time was a failure. Perhaps the photos didn't come out properly. Someone bungled. And of course they couldn't use the same man twice. They had to wait until they got their hands on a second man. Until they had him carded and filed in the Ministry of Fear.' He thought aloud, 'I suppose the only men they couldn't blackmail for something shabby would be saints—or outcasts with nothing to lose.'

'You weren't a detective,' Johns exclaimed, 'you were a detective writer.'

Digby said, 'You know, I feel quite tired. The brain begins to tick and then suddenly I feel so tired I could lie down and sleep. Perhaps I will.' He closed his eyes and then opened them again. 'The thing to do,' he said, 'would be to follow up the first case . . . the bungle done, to find the point of failure.' Then he slept.

5

It was a fine afternoon, and Digby went for a solitary walk in the garden. Several days had passed since Anna Hilfe's visit, and he felt restless and moody like a boy in love. He wanted an opportunity to show that he was no invalid, that his mind could work as well as another man's. There was no satisfaction in shining before Johns . . . He dreamed wildly between the box-hedges.

The garden was of a rambling kind which should have belonged to childhood and only belonged to childish men. The apple trees were old apple trees and gave the effect of growing wild; they sprang unexpectedly up in the middle of a rose-bed, trespassed on a tennis-court, shaded the window of a little outside lavatory like a potting-shed which was used by the gardener—an old man who could always be located from far away by the sound of a scythe or the trundle of a wheelbarrow. A high red brick wall divided the flower-garden from the kitchen-garden and the orchard, but flowers and fruit could not be imprisoned by a wall. Flowers broke among the artichokes and sprang up like flames under the trees. Beyond the orchard the garden faded gradually out into paddocks and a stream and a big untidy pond with an island the size of a billiard-table.

It was by the pond that Digby found Major Stone. He heard him first: a succession of angry grunts like a dog dreaming. Digby scrambled down a bank to the black edge of the water and Major Stone turned his very clear blue military eyes on him and said, 'The job's got to be done.' There was mud all over his tweed suit and mud on his hands; he had been throwing large stones into the water and now he was dragging a plank he must have found in the potting-shed along the edge of the water.

'It's sheer treachery,' Major Stone said, 'to leave a place like that unoccupied. You could command the whole house. . . .' He slid the plank forward so that one end rested on a large stone. 'Steady does it,' he said. He advanced the plank inch by inch to-wards the next stone. 'Here,' he said, 'you ease it along. I'll take the other end.'

'Surely you aren't going in?'

'No depth at this side,' Major Stone said, and walked straight into the pond. The black mud closed over his shoes and the turn-ups of his trousers. 'Now,' he said, 'push. Steady does it.' Digby pushed, but pushed too hard: the plank toppled sideways into the mud. 'Damnation,' said Major Stone. He bent and heaved and brought the plank up: scattering mud up to his waist, he lugged it ashore.

'Apologize,' he said. 'My temper's damned short. You aren't a trained man. Good of you to help.'

'I'm afraid I wasn't much good.'

'Just give me half a dozen sappers,' Major Stone said, 'and you'd see . . .' He stared wistfully across at the little bushy island. 'But it's no good asking for the impossible. We've just got to make do. We'd manage all right if it wasn't for all this treachery.' He looked Digby in the eyes as though he were sizing him up. 'I've seen you about here a lot,' he said. 'Never spoke to you before. Liked the look of you, if you don't mind my saying so. I suppose you've been sick like the rest of us. Thank God, I'll be leaving here soon. Able to be of use again. What's been your trouble?'

'Loss of memory,' Digby said.

'Been out there?' the major asked, jerking his head in the di-rection of the island.

'No, it was a bomb. In London.'

'A bad war, this,' the major said. 'Civilians with shell-shock.' It was uncertain whether he disapproved of the civilians or the shell-shock. His stiff fair hair was grizzled over the ears, and his very blue eyes peered out from under a yellow thatch. The whites were beautifully clear; he was a man who had always kept him-self fit and ready to be of use. Now that he wasn't fit and wasn't of use, an awful confusion ruled the poor brain. He said, 'There was treachery somewhere or it would never have happened,' and turning his back abruptly on the island and the muddy remnants of his causeway, he scrambled up the bank and walked briskly towards the house.

Digby strolled on. At the tennis-court a furious game was in progress—a really furious game. The two men leapt and sweated and scowled; their immense concentration was the only thing that looked abnormal about Still and Fishguard, but when the set was over, they would grow shrill and quarrelsome and a little hysterical. The same climax would be reached at chess . . .

The rose-garden was sheltered by two walls: one the wall of the vegetable-garden, the other the high wall that cut communication—except for one small door—with what Dr Forester and Johns called euphemistically 'the sick bay'. Nobody cared to talk about the sick bay—grim things were assumed, a padded room, strait-jackets. You could see only the top windows from the garden, and they were barred. Not one man in the sanatorium was ignorant of how close he lived to that quiet wing. Hysteria over a game, a sense of treachery, in the case of Davis tears that came too easily—they knew those things meant sickness just as much as violence did. They had signed away their freedom to Dr Forester in the hope of escaping worse, but if worse happened the building was there on the spot—'the sick bay'—there would be no need to travel to a strange asylum. Only Digby felt quite free from its shadow; the sick bay was not there for a happy man. Behind him the voices rose shrilly from the tennis-court: Fishguard's 'I tell you it was inside'. 'Out.' 'Are you accusing me of cheating?' 'You ought to have your eyes seen to'—that was Still. The voices sounded so irreconcilable that you would have said such a quarrel could have no other end than blows—but no blow was ever struck. Fear of the sick bay perhaps. The voices went suddenly off the air like an unpopular turn. When the dusk fell Still and Fishguard would be in the lounge playing chess together.

How far was the sick bay, Digby sometimes wondered, a fantasy of disordered minds? It was there, of course, the brick wing and the barred windows and the high wall; there was even a segregated staff whom other patients had certainly met at the monthly social evening which he had not yet attended. (The doctor believed that these occasions on which strangers were present—the local clergyman, a sprinkling of elderly ladies, a retired architect—helped the shell-shocked brains to adapt themselves to society and the conventions of good behaviour.) But was anybody certain that the sick bay was occupied? Sometimes it occurred to Digby that the wing had no more reality than the conception of Hell presented by sympathetic theologians— a place without inhabitants which existed simply as a warning.

Suddenly Major Stone appeared again, walking rapidly. He saw Digby and veered towards him down one of the paths. Little beads of sweat stood on his forehead. He said to Digby, 'You haven't seen me, do you hear? You haven't seen me,' and brushed by. He seemed to be making for the paddock and the pond. In another moment he was out of sight among the shrubberies, and Digby walked on. It seemed to him that the time had come for him to leave. He wasn't in place here: he was normal. A faint uneasiness touched him when he remembered that Major Stone, too, had considered himself cured.

As he came in front of the house Johns emerged. He looked ruffled and anxious. He said, 'Have you seen Major Stone?' Digby hesitated for a second only. Then he said, 'No.'

Johns said, 'The doctor wants him. He's had a relapse.'

The cameraderie of a fellow-patient weakened. Digby said, 'I did see him earlier . . .'

'The doctor's very anxious. He may do himself an injury—or someone else.' The rimless glasses seemed to be heliographing a warning—do *you* wish to be responsible?

Digby said uneasily, 'You might have a look round the pond.'

'Thanks,' Johns said, and called out, 'Poole. Poole.'

'I'm coming,' a voice said.

A sense of apprehension moved like a heavy curtain in Digby's mind; it was as though someone had whispered faintly to him so that he couldn't be sure of the words, 'Take care.' A man stood at the gate from the sick bay wearing the same kind of white coat that Johns wore on duty, but not so clean. He was a dwarfish man with huge twisted shoulders and an arrogant face. 'The pond,' Johns said.

The man blinked and made no movement, staring at Digby with impertinent curiosity. He had obviously come from the sick bay; he didn't belong in the garden. His coat and fingers were stained with what looked like iodine.

'We've got to hurry,' Johns said. 'The doctor's anxious . . .'

'Haven't I met you,' Poole said, 'somewhere before?' He watched Digby with a kind of enjoyment. 'Oh yes I'm sure I have.'

'No,' Digby said. 'No.'

'Well, we know each other now,' Poole said. He grinned at Digby and said with relish, 'I'm the keeper,' swinging a long simian arm towards the sick bay.

Digby said loudly, 'I don't know you from Adam. I don't want to know you,' and had time to see Johns' look of amazement before he turned his back and listened to their footsteps hurrying towards the pond.

It was true: he didn't know the man, but the whole obscurity of his past had seemed to shake—something at any moment might emerge from behind the curtain. He had been frightened and so he had been vehement, but he felt sure that a black mark would be made on his chart of progress and he was apprehensive . . . Why should he fear to remember anything? He whispered to himself, 'After all, I'm not a criminal.'

6

At the front door a servant met him. 'Mr Digby,' she told him, 'there's a visitor for you,' and his heart beat with hope.

'Where?'

'In the lounge.'

She was there looking at a *Tatler,* and he had no idea what to say to her. She stood there as he seemed to remember her from very far back, small, tense, on guard, and yet she was part of a whole world of experience of which he was innocent.

'It's good of you,' he began and stopped. He was afraid if he once began making the small talk of a stranger, they would be condemned for life to that shadowy relationship. The weather would lie heavily on their tongues, and they would meet occasionally and talk about the theatre. When they passed in the street he would raise his hat, and something which was only just alive would be safely and hopelessly dead.

He said slowly, 'I have been longing for this ever since you came. The days have been very long with nothing to do in them but think and wonder. This is such a strange life . . .'

'Strange and horrible,' she said.

'Not so horrible,' he said, but then he remembered Poole. He said, 'How did we talk before my memory went? We didn't stand stiffly, did we, like this—you holding a paper and I—we were good friends, weren't we?'

'Yes.'

He said, 'We've got to get back. This isn't right. Sit down here and we'll both shut our eyes. Pretend it's the old days before the bomb went off. What were you saying to me then?' She sat in miserable silence and he said with astonishment, 'You shouldn't cry.'

'You said shut your eyes.'

'They are shut now.'

The bright artificial lounge where he felt a stranger, the glossy magazines and the glass ash-trays were no longer visible: there was just darkness. He put out his hand and touched her. He said, 'Is this strange?'

After a long time a dried-up voice said, 'No.'

He said, 'Of course I loved you, didn't I?' When she didn't answer, he said, 'I must have loved you. Because directly you came in the other day—there was such a sense of relief, of peace, as if I'd been expecting someone different. How could I have helped loving you?'

'It doesn't seem likely,' she said.

'Why not?'

'We'd only known each other a few days.'

'Too short, of course, for you to care about me.'

Again there was a long silence. Then she said, 'Yes, I did.'

'Why? I'm so much older. I'm not much to look at. What sort of a person was I?'

She replied at once as though this were easy: this was part of the lesson she had really learnt: she had turned this over in her mind again and again. 'You had a great sense of pity. You didn't like people to suffer.'

'Is that unusual?' he asked, genuinely seeking information; he knew nothing of how people lived and thought outside.

'It was unusual,' she said, 'where I came from. My brother . . .' She caught her breath sharply.

'Of course,' he said quickly, snatching at a memory before it went again, 'you had a brother, hadn't you? He was a friend of mine too.'

'Let's stop playing this game,' she said. 'Please.' They opened their eyes simultaneously on the suave room.

He said, 'I want to leave here.'

'No,' she said, 'stay. Please.'

'Why?'

'You are safe here.'

He smiled. 'From more bombs?'

'From a lot of things. You are happy here, aren't you?'

'In a way.'

'There'—she seemed to indicate the whole external world beyond the garden wall—'you weren't happy.' She added slowly, 'I would do anything to keep you happy. This is how you should be. This is how I like you.'

'You didn't like me out there?' He tried to catch her humorously in a contradiction, but she wouldn't play. She said, 'You can't go on seeing someone unhappy all day every day without breaking.'

'I wish I could remember.'

'Why bother to remember?'

He said simply—it was one of the few things of which he was certain, 'Oh, of course, one's got to remember . . .'

She watched him with intensity, as though she were making up her mind to some course of action. He went on, 'If only to remember you, how I talked to you . . .'

'Oh, don't,' she said, 'don't,' and added harshly like a declaration of war, 'Dear heart.'

He said triumphantly, 'That was how we talked.'

She nodded, keeping her eyes on him. He said, 'My dear . . .'

Her voice was dry like an old portrait: the social varnish was cracking. She said, 'You once said you'd do impossible things for me.'

'Yes?'

'Do a possible one. Just be quiet. Stay here a few more weeks till your memory comes back . . .'

'If you'll come often . . .'

'I'll come.'

He put his mouth against hers: the action had all the uncertainty of an adolescent kiss. 'My dear, my dear,' he said. 'Why did you say we were only friends . . .?'

'I wasn't going to bind you.'

'You've bound me now.'

She said slowly, as though she were astonished, 'And I'm glad.'

All the way upstairs to his room, he could smell her. He could have gone into any chemist's shop and picked out her powder, and he could have told in the dark the texture of her skin. The experience was as new to him as adolescent love: he had the blind passionate innocence of a boy: like a boy he was driven relentlessly towards inevitable suffering, loss and despair, and called it happiness.

<h1 style="text-align:center">7</h1>

Next morning there was no paper on his tray. He asked the woman who brought his breakfast where it was, but all she could tell him was that she supposed it hadn't been delivered. He was touched again by the faint fear he had felt the previous afternoon when Poole came out of the sick bay, and he waited impatiently for Johns to arrive for his morning chat and smoke. But Johns didn't come. He lay in bed and brooded for half an hour and then rang his bell. It was time for his clothes to be laid out, but when the maid came she said she had no orders.

'But you don't need orders,' he said. 'You do it every day.'

'I has to have my orders,' she said.

'Tell Mr Johns I'd like to see him.'

'Yes, sir'—but Johns didn't come. It was as if a *cordon sanitaire* had been drawn around his room.

For another half an hour he waited doing nothing. Then he got out of bed and went to the bookcase, but there was little that promised him distraction—only the iron rations of learned old men. Tolstoy's *What I Believe,* Freud's *The Psycho-Analysis of Everyday Life,* a biography of Rudolph Steiner. He took the Tolstoy back with him, and opening it found faint indentations in the margin where pencil marks had been rubbed out. It is always of interest to know what strikes another human being as remarkable and he read:

'Remembering all the evil I have done, suffered and seen, resulting from the enmity of nations, it is clear to me that the cause of it all lay in the gross fraud called patriotism and love of one's country . . .'

There was a kind of nobility in the blind shattering dogma, just as there was something ignoble in the attempt to rub out the pencil-mark. This was an opinion to be held openly if at all. He looked farther up the page: 'Christ showed me that the fifth snare depriving me of welfare is the separation we make of our own from other nations. I cannot but believe this, and therefore if in a moment of forgetfulness feelings of enmity towards a man of another nation may rise within me . . .'

But that wasn't the point, he thought; he felt no enmity towards any individual across the frontier: if he wanted to take part again, it was love which drove him and not hate. He thought: Like Johns, I am one of the little men, not interested in ideologies, tied to a flat Cambridgeshire landscape, a chalk quarry, a line of willows across the featureless fields, a market town . . . his thoughts scrabbled at the curtain . . . where he used to dance at the Saturday hops. His thoughts fell back on one face with a sense of relief: he could rest there. Ah, he thought, Tolstoy should have lived in a small country—not in Russia, which was a continent rather than a country. And why does he write as if the worst thing we can do to our fellow-man is to kill him? Everybody has to die and everybody fears death, but when we kill a man we save him from his fear which would otherwise grow year by year. . . . One doesn't necessarily kill because one hates: one may kill because one loves . . . and again the old dizziness came back as though he had been struck over the heart.

He lay back on his pillow, and the brave old man with the long beard seemed to buzz at him: 'I cannot acknowledge any States or nations . . . I cannot take part . . . I cannot take part.' A kind of waking dream came to him of a man—perhaps a friend, he couldn't see his face—who hadn't been able to take part; some private grief had isolated him and hidden him like a beard—what was it? he couldn't remember. The war and all that happened round him had seemed to belong to other people. The old man in the beard, he felt convinced, was wrong. He was too busy saving his own soul. Wasn't it better to take part even in the crimes of people you loved, if it was necessary hate as they did, and if that were the end of everything suffer damnation with them, rather than be saved alone?

But that reasoning, it could be argued, excused your enemy. And why not? he thought. It excused anyone who loved enough to kill or be killed. Why shouldn't you excuse your enemy? That didn't mean you must stand in lonely superiority, refuse to kill, and turn the intolerable cheek. 'If a man offend *thee* . . .' there was the point—not to kill for one's own sake. But for the sake of people you loved, and in the company of people you loved, it was right to risk damnation.

His mind returned to Anna Hilfe. When he thought of her it was with an absurd breathlessness. It was as if he were waiting again years ago outside—wasn't it the King's Arms?—and the girl he loved was coming down the street, and the night was full of pain and beauty and despair because one knew one was too young for anything to come of this . . .

He couldn't be bothered with Tolstoy any longer. It was unbearable to be treated as an invalid. What woman outside a Victorian novel could care for an invalid? It was all very well for Tolstoy to preach non-resistance: he had had his heroic violent hour at Sebastopol. Digby got out of bed and saw in the long narrow mirror his thin body and his grey hair and his beard . . .

The door opened: it was Dr Forester. Behind him, eyes lowered, subdued like someone found out, came Johns. Dr Forester shook his head and, 'It won't do, Digby,' he said, 'it won't do. I'm disappointed.'

Digby was still watching the sad grotesque figure in the mirror. He said, 'I want my clothes. And a razor.'

'Why a razor?'

'To shave. I'm certain this beard doesn't belong . . .'

'That only shows your memory isn't returning yet.'

'And I had no paper this morning,' he went weakly on.

Dr Forester said, 'I gave orders that the paper was to be stopped. Johns has been acting unwisely. These long conversations about the war . . . You've excited yourself. Poole has told me how excited you were yesterday.'

Digby, with his eyes on his own ageing figure in the striped pyjamas, said, 'I won't be treated like an invalid or a child.'

'You seem to have got it into your head,' Dr Forester said, 'that you have a talent for detection, that you were a detective perhaps in your previous life . . .'

'That was a joke,' Digby said.

'I can assure you you were something quite different. Quite different,' Dr Forester repeated.

'What was I?'

'It may be necessary one day to tell you,' Dr Forester said, as though he were uttering a threat. 'If it will prevent foolish mistakes . . .' Johns stood behind the doctor looking at the floor.

'I'm leaving here,' Digby said.

The calm noble old face of Dr Forester suddenly crumpled into lines of dislike. He said sharply, 'And paying your bill, I hope?'

'I hope so too.'

The features reformed, but they were less convincing now. 'My dear Digby,' Dr Forester said, 'you must be reasonable. You are a very sick man. A very sick man indeed. Twenty years of your life have been wiped out. That's not health . . . and yesterday and just now you showed an excitement which I've feared and hoped to avoid.' He put his hand gently on the pyjama sleeve and said, 'I don't want to have to restrain you, to have you certified . . .'

Digby said, 'But I'm as sane as you are. You must know that.'

'Major Stone thought so too. But I've had to transfer him to the sick bay . . . He had an obsession which might at any time have led to violence.'

'But I . . .'

'Your symptoms are very much the same. This excitement. . . .' The doctor raised his hand from the sleeve to the shoulder: a warm, soft, moist hand. He said, 'Don't worry. We won't let it come to that, but for a little we must be very quiet . . . plenty of food, plenty of sleep . . . some very gentle bromides . . . no visitors for a while, not even our friend Johns . . . no more of these exciting intellectual conversations.'

'Miss Hilfe?' Digby said.

'I made a mistake there,' Dr Forester said. 'We are not strong enough yet. I have told Miss Hilfe not to come again.'

CHAPTER 2
THE SICK BAY

'Wherefore shrink from me? What have I done
that you should fear me?
You have been listening to evil tales, my child.'
The Little Duke

I

When a man rubs out a pencil-mark he should be careful to see that the line is quite obliterated. For if a secret is to be kept, no precautions are too great. If Dr Forester had not so inefficiently rubbed out the pencil-marks in the margins of Tolstoy's *What I Believe,* Mr Rennit might never have learnt what had happened to Jones, Johns would have remained a hero-worshipper, and it is possible that Major Stone would have slowly wilted into further depths of insanity between the padded hygienic walls of his room in the sick bay. And Digby? Digby might have remained Digby.

For it was the rubbed-out pencil-marks which kept Digby awake and brooding at the end of a day of loneliness and boredom. You couldn't respect a man who dared not hold his opinions openly, and when respect for Dr Forester was gone, a great deal went with it. The noble old face became less convincing: even his qualifications became questionable. What right had he to forbid the newspapers—above all, what right had he to forbid the visits of Anna Hilfe?

Digby still felt like a schoolboy, but he now knew that his headmaster had secrets of which he was ashamed: he was no longer austere and self-sufficient. And so the schoolboy planned rebellion. At about half-past nine in the evening he heard the sound of a car, and watching between the curtains he saw the doctor drive away. Or rather Poole drove and the doctor sat beside him.

Until Digby saw Poole he had planned only a petty rebellion— a secret visit to Johns' room; he felt sure he could persuade that young man to talk. Now he became bolder; he would visit the sick bay itself and speak to Stone. The patients must combine against tyranny, and an old memory slipped back of a deputation he had once led to his real headmaster because his form against all precedent—for it was a classical form—had been expected by a new master to learn trigonometry. The strange thing about a memory like that was that it seemed young as well as old: so little had happened since that he could remember. He had lost all his mature experience.

A bubble of excited merriment impeded his breath as he opened the door of his room and took a quick look down the corridor. He was afraid of undefined punishments, and for that reason he felt his action was heroic and worthy of someone in love. There was an innocent sensuality in his thought; he was like a boy who boasts of a beating he has risked to a girl, sitting in the sunshine by the cricket-ground, drinking ginger-beer, hearing the pad-pad of wood and leather, under the spell, day-dreaming and in love . . .

There was a graduated curfew for patients according to their health, but by half-past nine all were supposed to be in bed and asleep. But you couldn't enforce sleep. Passing Davis's door he could hear the strange uncontrollable whine of a man weeping . . . Farther down the passage Johns' door was open and the light was on. Taking off his bedroom slippers, he passed quickly across the door-way, but Johns wasn't there. Incurably sociable he was probably chatting with the housekeeper. On his desk was a pile of newspapers; he had obviously picked them out for Digby before the doctor had laid his ban. It was a temptation to stay and read them, but the small temptation didn't suit the mood of high adventure. Tonight he would do something no patient had ever voluntarily done before—enter the sick bay. He moved carefully and silently—the words 'Pathfinder' and 'Indian' came to his mind—downstairs.

In the lounge the lights were off, but the curtains were undrawn and the moonlight welled in with the sound of the splashing fountain and the shadow of silver leaves. The *Tatler*s had been tidied on the tables, the ash-trays taken away, and the cushions shaken on the chairs—it looked now like a room in an exhibition where nobody crosses the ropes. The next door brought him into the passage by Dr Forester's study. As he quietly closed each door behind him he felt as though he were cutting off his own retreat. His ribs seemed to vibrate to the beat-beat of his heart. Ahead of him was the green baize door he had never seen opened, and beyond that door lay the sick bay. He was back in his own childhood, breaking out of dormitory, daring more than he really wanted to dare, proving himself. He hoped the door would be bolted on the other side; then there would be nothing he could do but creep back to bed, honour satisfied . . .

The door pulled easily open. It was only the cover for another door, to deaden sound and leave the doctor in his study undisturbed. But that door, too, had been left unlocked, unbolted. As he passed into the passage beyond, the green baize swung to behind him with a long sigh.

2

He stood stone still and listened. Somewhere a clock ticked with a cheap tinny sound, and a tap had been left driping. This must once have been the servants' quarters: the floor was stone, and his bedroom slippers pushed up a little smoke of dust. Everything spoke of neglect; the woodwork when he reached the stairs had not been polished for a very long time and the thin drugget had been worn threadbare. It was an odd contrast to the spruce nursing home beyond the door; everything around him shrugged its shoulders and said, 'We are not important. Nobody sees us here. Our only duty is to be quiet and not disturb the doctor.' And what could be quieter than dust? If it had not been for the clock ticking he would have doubted whether anyone really lived in this part of the house—the clock and the faintest tang of stale cigarette smoke, of Caporal, that set his heart beating again with apprehension.

Where the clock ticked Poole must live. Whenever he thought of Poole he was aware of something unhappy, something imprisoned at the bottom of the brain trying to climb out. It frightened him in the same way as birds frightened him when they beat up and down in closed rooms. There was only one way to escape— the fear of another creature's pain. That was to lash out until the bird was stunned and quiet or dead. For the moment he forgot Major Stone, and smelt his way towards Poole's room.

It was at the end of the passage where the tap dripped, a large square, comfortless room with a stone floor divided in half by a curtain—it had probably once been a kitchen. Its new owner had lent it an aggressive and squalid masculinity as if he had something to prove; there were ends of cigarettes upon the floor, and nothing was used for its right purpose. A clock and a cheap brown teapot served as book-ends on a wardrobe to prop up a shabby collection—Carlyle's *Heroes and Hero-Worship*, lives of Napoleon and Cromwell, and numbers of little paper-covered books about what to do with Youth, Labour, Europe, God. The windows were all shut, and when Digby lifted the drab curtain he could see the bed had not been properly made—or else Poole had flung himself down for a rest and hadn't bothered to tidy it afterwards. The tap dripped into a fixed basin and a sponge-bag dangled from a bedpost. A used tin which once held lobster paste now held old razor-blades. The place was as comfortless as a transit camp; the owner might have been someone who was just passing on and couldn't be bothered to change so much as a stain on the wall. An open suitcase full of soiled underclothes gave the impression that he hadn't even troubled to unpack.

It was like the underside of a stone: you turned up the bright polished nursing home and found beneath it this.

Everywhere there was the smell of Caporal, and on the beds there were crumbs, as though Poole took food to bed with him. Digby stared at the crumbs a long while: a feeling of sadness and disquiet and dangers he couldn't place haunted him—as though something were disappointing his expectations—as though the cricket match were a frost, nobody had come to the half-term holiday, and he waited and waited outside the King's Arms for a girl who would never turn up. He had nothing to compare this place with. The nursing home was something artificial, hidden in a garden. Was it possible that ordinary life was like this? He remembered a lawn and afternoon tea and a drawing-room with water-colours and little tables, a piano no one played and the smell of eau-de-Cologne; but was *this* the real adult life to which we came in time? had he, too, belonged to this world? He was saddened by a sense of familiarity. It was not of this last he had dreamed a few years back at school, but he remembered that the years since then were not few but many.

At last the sense of danger reminded him of poor imprisoned Stone. He might not have long before the doctor and Poole returned, and though he could not believe they had any power over him, he was yet afraid of sanctions he couldn't picture. His slippers padded again up the passage and up the dingy stairs to the first floor. There was no sound here at all: the tick of the clock didn't reach as far: large bells on rusty wires hung outside what might have been the butler's pantry. They were marked Study, Drawing-Room, 1st Spare Bedroom, 2nd Spare Bedroom, Day Nursery . . . The wires sagged with disuse and a spider had laid its scaffolding across the bell marked Dining-Room.

The barred windows he had seen over the garden wall had been on the second floor, and he mounted unwillingly higher. He was endangering his own retreat with every step, but he had dared himself to speak to Stone, and if it were only one syllable he must speak it. He went down a passage calling softly, 'Stone. Stone.'

There was no reply and the old cracked linoleum creaked under his feet and sometimes caught his toes. Again he felt a familiarity—as if this cautious walking, this solitary passage, belonged more to this world than the sleek bedroom in the other wing. 'Stone,' he called, 'Stone,' and heard a voice answer, 'Barnes. Is that you, Barnes?' coming startlingly from the door beside him.

'Hush,' he said, and putting his lips close to the key-hole, 'It's not Barnes. It's Digby.'

He heard Stone sigh. 'Of course,' the voice said, 'Barnes is dead. I was screaming . . .'

'Are you all right, Stone?'

'I've had an awful time,' Stone said, so low that Digby could hardly hear him, 'an awful time. I didn't really mean I wouldn't eat . . .'

'Come to the door so that I can hear you better.'

Stone said, 'They've got me in one of these strait-jackets. They said I was violent: I don't think I was violent. It's just the treachery . . .' He must have got nearer the door, because his voice was much clearer. He said, 'Old man, I know I've been a bit touched. We all are in this place, aren't we? But I'm not *mad*. It just isn't right.'

'What did you do?'

'I wanted to find a room to enfilade that island from. They'd begun to dig, you see, months ago. I saw them one evening after dark. One couldn't leave it at that. The Hun doesn't let the grass grow. So I came through into this wing and went to Poole's room . . .'

'Yes?'

'I didn't mean to make them jump. I just wanted to explain what I was after.'

'Jump?'

'The doctor was there with Poole. They were doing something in the dark . . .' The voice broke: it was horrible hearing a middle-aged man sobbing invisibly behind a locked door.

'But the digging?' Digby asked. 'You must have dreamed . . .'

'That tube . . . It was awful, old man. I hadn't really meant I wouldn't eat. I was just afraid of poison.'

'Poison?'

'Treachery,' the voice said. 'Listen, Barnes . . .'

'I'm not Barnes.'

Again there was a long sigh. 'Of course. I'm sorry. It's getting me down. I *am* touched, you know. Perhaps they are right.'

'Who's Barnes?'

'He was a good man. They got him on the beach. It's no good, Digby. I'm mad. Every day in every way I get worse and worse.'

Somewhere from far away, through an open window on the floor below, came the sound of a car. Digby put his lips to the door and said, 'I can't stay, Stone. Listen. You are not mad. You've got ideas into your head, that's all. It's not right putting you here. Somehow I'll get you out. Just stick it.'

'You're a good chap, Digby.'

'They've threatened me with this too.'

'You,' Stone whispered back. 'But you're sane enough. By God, perhaps I'm not so touched after all. If they want to put you here, it must be treachery.'

'Stick it.'

'I'll stick it, old man. It was the uncertainty. I thought perhaps they were right.'

The sound of the car faded.

'Haven't you any relations?'

'Not a soul,' the voice said. 'I had a wife, but she went away. She was quite right, old chap, quite right. There was a lot of treachery.'

'I'll get you out. I don't know how, but I'll get you out.'

'That island, Digby . . . you've got to watch it, old man. I can't do anything here, and I don't matter, anyway. But if I could just have fifty of the old bunch . . .'

Digby reassured him gently, 'I'll watch the island.'

'I thought the Hun had got hold of it. They don't let the grass grow . . . But I'm sometimes a bit confused, old man.'

'I must go now. Just stick it.'

'I'll stick it, old man. Been in worse places. But I wish you didn't have to go.'

'I'll come back for you.'

But he hadn't the faintest idea of how. A terrible sense of pity moved him; he felt capable of murder for the release of that gentle tormented creature. He could see him walking into the muddy pond . . . the very clear blue eyes and the bristly military moustache and the lines of care and responsibility. That was a thing you learned in this place: that a man kept his character even when he was insane. No madness would ever dim that military sense of duty to others.

His reconnaissance had proved easier than he had any right to expect: the doctor must be taking a long ride. He reached the green baize door safely, and when it sighed behind him, it was like Stone's weary patience asking him to come back. He passed quickly through the lounge and then more carefully up the stairs until he came again within sight of Johns' open door. Johns wasn't there: the clock on his desk had only moved on twelve minutes: the papers lay in the lamplight. He felt as though he had explored a strange country and returned home to find it all a dream—not a single page of the calendar turned during all his wanderings.

3

He wasn't afraid of Johns. He went in and picked up one of the offending papers. Johns had arranged them in order and marked the passages. He must have been bitten by the passion for detection. The Ministry of Home Security, Digby read, had replied months ago to a question about a missing document in much the same terms as in the later case. It had never been missing. There had been at most a slight indiscretion, but the document had never left the personal possession of—and there was the great staid respected name which Johns had forgotten. In the face of such a statement how could anyone continue to suggest that the document had been photographed? That was to accuse the great staid name not of an indiscretion but of treason. It was perhaps a mistake not to have left the document in the office safe overnight, but the great name had given his personal assurance to the Minister that not for one second had the document been out of his possession. He had slept with it literally under his pillow . . . *The Times* hinted that it would be interesting to investigate how the calumny had started. Was the enemy trying to sap our confidence in our hereditary lead ers by a whisper campaign? After two or three issues there was silence.

A rather frightening fascination lay in these months-old news-papers. Digby had slowly had to relearn most of the household names, but he could hardly turn the page of any newspaper without encountering some great man of whom he had never heard, and occasionally there would crop up a name he did recognize— someone who had been a figure twenty years ago. He felt like a Rip Van Winkle returning after a quarter of a century's sleep; the people of whom he had heard hardly connected better than he did with his youth. Men of brilliant promise had lapsed into the Board of Trade, and of course in one great case a man who had been considered too brilliant and too reckless ever to be trusted with major office was the leader of his country. One of Digby's last memories was of hearing him hissed by ex-servicemen from the public gallery of a law court because he had told an abrupt unpalatable truth about an old campaign. Now he had taught the country to love his unpalatable truths.

He turned a page and read casually under a photograph: 'Arthur Rowe whom the police are anxious to interview in con- nection . . .' He wasn't interested in crime. The photograph showed a lean shabby clean-shaven man. All photographs of crim- inals looked much alike—perhaps it was the spots, the pointilliste technique of the newspaper photograph. There was so much of the past he had to learn that he couldn't be bothered to learn the crim- inals, at any rate of the domestic kind.

A board creaked and he turned. Johns hovered and blinked in the doorway. 'Good evening, Johns,' Digby said.

'What are you doing here?'

'Reading the papers,' Digby said.

'But you heard the doctor say . . .'

'This isn't a prison, Johns,' Digby said, 'except for poor Stone. It's a very charming nursing home and I'm a private patient with nothing wrong except loss of memory due to a bomb . . .' He realized that Johns was listening to him with intensity. 'Isn't that about it?' he asked.

'It must be, mustn't it,' Johns said.

'So we must keep a sense of proportion, and there's no earthly reason why, if I don't feel like sleep, I shouldn't stroll down the passage to your room for a chat and to read . . .'

'When you put it like that,' Johns said, 'it sounds so simple.'

'The doctor makes you see it differently, doesn't he?'

'All the same a patient ought to follow the treatment . . .'

'Or change his doctor. You know I've decided to change my doctor.'

'To leave?' Johns asked. There was fear in his voice.

'To leave.'

'Please don't do anything rash,' Johns said. 'The doctor's a great man. He's suffered a lot . . . and that may have made him a bit . . . eccentric. But you can't do better than stay here, really you can't.'

'I'm going, Johns.'

'Just another month,' Johns entreated. 'You've been doing so well. Until that girl came. Just a month. I'll speak to the doctor. He'll let you have the papers again. Perhaps he'll even let *her* come. Only let me put it to him. I know the way. He's so sensitive: he takes offence.'

'Johns,' Digby asked gently, 'why should you be afraid of my going?'

The unrimmed glasses caught the light and set it flickering along the wall. Johns said uncontrollably, 'I'm not afraid of your going. I'm afraid—I'm afraid of his not letting you go.' Very far away they both heard the purr-purr of a car.

'What's wrong with the doctor?' Johns shook his head and the reflection danced again upon the wall. 'There's something wrong,'

Digby pressed him. 'Poor Stone saw something odd and so he's put away . . .'

'For his own good,' Johns said imploringly. 'Dr Forester knows. He's such a great man, Digby.'

'For his own good be damned. I've been to the sick bay and talked to him . . .'

'You've been *there*?' Johns said.

'Haven't you—ever?'

'It's forbidden,' Johns said.

'Do you always do exactly what Dr Forester tells you?'

'He's a great doctor, Digby. You don't understand: brains are the most delicate mechanisms. The least thing to upset the equilibrium and everything goes wrong. You have to trust the doctor.'

'I don't trust him.'

'You mustn't say that. If you knew how skilful he is, the endless care he takes. He's trying to shelter you until you are really strong enough . . .'

'Stone saw something odd and Stone's put away.'

'No, no.' Johns put out a weak hand and laid it on the newspapers like a badgered politician gaining confidence from the dispatch box. 'If you only knew, Digby. They've made him suffer so with their jealousies and misunderstandings, but he's so great and good and kind . . .'

'Ask Stone about that.'

'If you only knew . . .'

A soft savage voice said, 'I think he'll have to know.' It was Dr Forester, and again that sense of possible and yet inconceivable sanctions set Digby's heart beating.

Johns said, 'Dr Forester, I didn't give him leave . . .'

'That's all right Johns,' Dr Forester said, 'you are very loyal, I know. I like loyalty.' He began to take off the gloves he had been wearing in the car; he drew them slowly off the long beautiful fingers. 'I remember after Conway's suicide how you stood by me. I don't forget a friend. Have you ever told Digby about Conway's suicide?'

'Never,' Johns protested.

'But he should know, Johns. It's a case in point. Conway also suffered from loss of memory. Life, you see, had become too much for him—and loss of memory was his escape. I tried to make him strong, to stiffen his resistance, so that when his memory came back, he would be able to meet his very difficult situation. The time I spent, wasted on Conway. Johns will tell you I was very patient—he was unbearably impertinent. But I'm human, Digby, and one day I lost my temper. I do lose my temper—very seldom, but sometimes. I told Conway everything, and he killed himself that night. You see, his mind hadn't been given time to heal. There was a lot of trouble, but Johns stood by me. He realizes that to be a good psychologist you sometimes have to share the mental weaknesses of the patient: one cannot be quite sane all the time. That's what gives one sympathy—and the other thing.'

He spoke gently and calmly, as though he were lecturing on an abstract subject, but the long surgical fingers had taken up one of the newspapers and was tearing it in long strips.

Digby said, 'But my case is different, Dr Forester. It was only a bomb that destroyed my memory. Not trouble.'

'Do you really believe that?' Dr Forester said. 'And I suppose you think it was just gunfire, concussion, which drove Stone out of his mind? That isn't how the mind works. We make our own insanity. Stone failed—shamefully, so now he explains everything by treachery. But it wasn't anybody else's treachery that left his friend Barnes . . .'

'And you have a revelation up your sleeve for me too, Dr Forester?' He remembered the pencil-marks in the Tolstoy rubbed out by a man without the courage of his opinions and that heartened him. He asked, 'What were you doing with Poole in the dark when Stone found you?' He had meant it only as a piece of impertinent defiance; he had believed that the scene existed only in Stone's persecuted imagination—like the enemy digging on the island. He hadn't expected to halt Dr Forester in the middle of his soft tirade. The silence was disagreeable. He tailed weakly off, 'And digging . . .'

The noble old face watched him, the mouth a little open: a tiny dribble ran down the chin.

Johns said, 'Please go to bed, Digby. Let's talk in the morning.'

'I'm quite ready to go to bed,' Digby said. He felt suddenly ridiculous in his trailing dressing-gown and his heelless slippers; he was apprehensive too—it was like turning his back on a man with a gun.

'Wait,' Dr Forester said. 'I haven't told you yet. When you know you can choose between Conway's method and Stone's method. There's room in the sick bay . . .'

'You ought to be there yourself, Dr Forester.'

'You're a fool,' Dr Forester said. 'A fool in love . . . I watch my patients. I know. What's the good of you being in love? You don't even know your real name.' He tore a piece out of one of the papers and held it out to Digby. 'There you are. That's you. A murderer. Go and think about that.'

It was the photograph he hadn't bothered to examine. The thing was absurd. He said, 'That's not me.'

'Go and look in the glass then,' Dr Forester said. 'And then begin to remember. You've got a lot to remember.'

Johns protested. 'Doctor, that's not the way . . .'

'He asked for it,' Dr Forester said, 'just like Conway did.'

But Digby heard no more of what Johns had to say: he was running down the pasage towards his room; half-way he tripped on his dressing-gown cord and fell. He hardly felt the shock. He got to his feet a little giddy—that was all. He wanted a looking-glass.

The lean bearded face looked out at him in the familiar room. There was a smell of cut flowers. This was where he had been happy. How could he believe what the doctor had said? There must be a mistake. It didn't connect. . . . At first he could hardly see the photograph; his heart beat and his head was confused. This isn't me, he thought, as that lean shaven other face with the unhappy eyes and the shabby suit came into focus. They didn't fit; the memories he had of twenty years ago and Arthur Rowe whom the police wanted to interview in connection with—but Dr Forester had torn the paper too carelessly. In those twenty years he couldn't have gone astray as far as this. He thought: Whatever they say, this man standing here is me. I'm not changed because I lose my memory. This photograph and Anna Hilfe didn't fit, he protested, and suddenly he remembered what had puzzled him and he had quite forgotten, Anna's voice saying, 'It's my job, Arthur.' He put his hand up to his chin and hid the beard; the long twisted nose told its tale, and the eyes which were unhappy enough now. He steadied himself with his hands on the dressing-table and thought: Yes, I'm Arthur Rowe. He began to

talk to himself under his breath, But I'm not Conway. I shan't kill
myself.

He was Arthur Rowe with a difference. He was next door to
his own youth; he had started again from there. He said, In a moment it's going to come back, but I'm not Conway—and I won't
be Stone. I've escaped for long enough: my brain will stand it. It
wasn't all fear that he felt; he felt also the untired courage and
the chivalry of adolescence. He was no longer too old and too
habit-ridden to start again. He shut his eyes and thought of
Poole, and an odd medley of impressions fought at the gateway
of his unconsciousness to be let out: a book called *The Little
Duke* and the word Naples—see Naples and die—and Poole
again, Poole sitting crouched in a chair in a little dark dingy
room eating cake, and Dr Forester, Dr Forester stooping over
something dark and bleeding. . . . The memories thickened—
a woman's face came up for a moment with immense sadness and
then sank again like someone drowned, out of sight; his head was
racked with pain as other memories struggled to get out like a
child out of its mother's body. He put his hands on the dressing-
table and held to it; he said to himself over and over again, 'I must
stand up. I must stand up,' as though there were some healing
virtue in simply remaining on his feet while his brain reeled with
the horror of returning life.

BOOK THREE

BITS AND PIECES

CHAPTER I

THE ROMAN DEATH

'A business that could scarcely have been pleasant.'
The Little Duke

I

Rowe followed the man in the blue uniform up the stone stairs and along a corridor lined with doors; some of them were open, and he could see that they led into little rooms all the same shape and size like confessionals. A table and three chairs: there was never anything else, and the chairs were hard and upright. The man opened one door—but there seemed no reason why he should not have opened any of the others—and said, 'Wait here, sir.'

It was early in the morning; the steel rim of the window enclosed a grey cold sky. The last stars had only just gone out. He sat with his hands between his knees in a dull tired patience; he wasn't important, he hadn't become an explorer; he was just a criminal. The effect of reaching this place had exhausted him; he couldn't even remember with any clearness what he had done—only the long walk through the dark countryside to the station, trembling when the cows coughed behind the hedgerows and an owl shrieked, pacing up and down upon the platform till the train came, the smell of grass and steam. The collector had wanted his ticket and he had none nor had he any money to pay with He knew his name or thought he knew his name, but he had no address to give. The man had been very kind and gentle; perhaps he looked sick. He had asked him if he had no friends to whom he was going, and he replied that he had no friends . . . 'I want to see the police,' he said, and the collector rebuked him mildly, 'You don't have to go all the way to London for that, sir.'

There was a moment of dreadful suspense when he thought he would be returned like a truant child. The collector said, 'You are one of Dr Forester's patients, aren't you, sir? Now if you get out at the next station, they'll telephone for a car. It won't take more than thirty minutes.'

'No.'

'You lost your way, sir, I expect, but you don't need to worry with a gentleman like Dr Forester.'

He gathered all the energy of which he was capable and said, 'I am going to Scotland Yard. I'm wanted there. If you stop me, it's your responsibility.'

At the next stop—which was only a halt, a few feet of platform and a wooden shed among dark level fields—he saw Johns; they must have gone to his room and found it empty and Johns had driven over. Johns saw him at once and came with strained naturalness to the door of the compartment; the guard hovered in the background.

'Hullo, old man,' Johns said uneasily, 'just hop out. I've got the car here—it won't take a moment to get home.'

'I'm not coming.'

'The doctor's very distressed. He'd had a long day and he lost his temper. He didn't mean half of what he said.'

'I'm not coming.'

The guard came nearer to show that he was willing to lend a hand if force were necessary. Rowe said furiously, 'You haven't certified me yet. You can't drag me out of the train,' and the guard edged up. He said softly to Johns, 'The gentleman hasn't got a ticket.'

'It's all right,' Johns said surprisingly, 'there's nothing wrong.' He leant forward and said in a whisper, 'Good luck, old man.' The train drew away, laying its steam like a screen across the car, the shed, the figure which didn't dare to wave.

Now all the trouble was over; all that was left was a trial for murder.

Rowe sat on; the steely sky paled and a few taxis hooted. A small fat distrait man in a double-breasted waistcoat opened the door once, took a look at him and said, 'Where's Beale?' but didn't wait for an answer. The long wounded cry of a boat came up from the Pool. Somebody went whistling down the corridor outside, once there was the chink-chink of tea-cups, and a faint smell of kipper blew in from a distance.

The little stout man came briskly in again; he had a round

over-sized face and a small fair moustache. He carried the slip
Rowe had filled in down below. 'So you are Mr Rowe,' he said
sternly. 'We are glad you've come to see us at last.' He rang a bell
and a uniformed constable answered it. He said, 'Is Beavis on
duty? Tell him to come along.'

He sat down and crossed his neat plump thighs and looked at
his nails. They were very well kept. He looked at them from every
angle and seemed worried about the cuticle of his left thumb. He
said nothing. It was obvious that he wouldn't talk without a wit-
ness. Then a big man in a ready-to-wear suit came with a pad
and a pencil and took the third chair. His ears were enormous
and stuck out straight from his skull and he had an odd air of
muted shame like a bull who has begun to realize that he is out of
place in a china shop. When he held the pencil to the pad you expected one or the other to suffer in his awkward grasp, and you
felt too that he knew and feared the event.

'Well,' the dapper man said, sighed, and tucked his nails away
for preservation under his thighs. He said, 'You've come here, Mr
Rowe, of your own accord to volunteer a statement?'

Rowe said, 'I saw a photograph in the paper . . .'

'We've been asking you to come forward for months.'

'I knew it for the first time last night.'

'You seem to have lived a bit out the world.'

'I've been in a nursing home. You see . . .'

Every time he spoke the pencil squeaked on the paper, making
a stiff consecutive narrative out of his haphazard sentences.

'What nursing home?'

'It was kept by a Dr Forester.' He gave the name of the railway
station. He knew no other name. He explained, 'Apparently there
was a raid.' He touched the scar on his forehead. 'I lost my mem
ory. I found myself at this place knowing nothing—except bits of
my childhood. They told me my name was Richard Digby. I didn't
even recognize the photograph at first. You see, this beard . . .'

'And your memory has come back now, I hope?' the little man
asked sharply, with a touch—a very faint touch—of sarcasm.

'I can remember something, but not much.'

'A very convenient sort of memory.'

'I am trying,' Rowe said with a flash of anger, 'to tell you all I
know . . . In English law isn't a man supposed to be innocent until

you prove him guilty? I'm ready to tell you everything I can remember about the murder, but I'm not a murderer.'

The plump man began to smile. He drew out his hands and
looked at his nails and tucked them back again. 'That's interesting, Mr Rowe,' he said. 'You mentioned murder, but I have said
nothing about murder to you, and no paper has mentioned the
word murder . . . yet.'

'I don't understand.'

'We play strictly fair. Read out his statement so far, Beavis.'

Beavis obeyed, blushing nervously, as though he were an overgrown schoolboy at a lectern reading Deuteronomy. 'I Arthur
Rowe, have made this statement voluntarily. Last night, when I
saw a photograph of myself in a newspaper, I knew for the first
time that the police wanted to interview me. I have been in a
nursing home kept by a Dr Forester for the last four months, suffering from loss of memory due to an air-raid. My memory is not
fully restored, but I wish to tell everything I know in connection
with the murder of . . .'

The detective stopped Beavis. He said, 'That's quite fair,
isn't it?'

'I suppose it is.'

'You'll be asked to sign it presently. Now tell us the name of
the murdered man.'

'I don't remember it.'

'I see. Who told you we wanted to talk to you about a murder?'

'Dr Forester.'

The promptness of the reply seemed to take the detective by
surprise. Even Beavis hesitated before the pencil bore down again
upon the pad. 'Dr Forester told you?'

'Yes.'

'How did he know?'

'I suppose he read it in the papers.'

'We have never mentioned murder in the papers.'

Rowe leant his head wearily on his hand. Again his brain felt
the pressure of associations. He said, 'Perhaps. . . .' The horrible
memory, stirred, crystallized, dissolved . . . 'I don't know.'

It seemed to him that the detective's manner was a little more
sympathetic. He said, 'Just tell us—in any order—in your own
words—what you do remember.'

'It will have to be in any order. First there's Poole. He's an attendant in Dr Forester's sick bay—where the violent cases go,
only I don't think they are always violent. I know that I met him
in the old days—before my memory went. I can remember a little shabby room with a picture of the Bay of Naples. I seemed to
be living there—I don't know why. It's not the sort of place I'd
choose. So much of what's come back is just feelings, emotion—
not fact.'

'Never mind,' the detective said.

'It's the way you remember a dream when most of it has gone.
I remember great sadness—and fear, and, yes, a sense of danger,
and an odd taste.'

'Of what?'

'We were drinking tea. He wanted me to give him something.'

'What?'

'I can't remember. What I do remember is absurd. A cake.'

'A cake?'

'It was made with real eggs. And then something happened. . . .'
He felt terribly tired. The sun was coming out. People all over the
city were going to work. He felt like a man in mortal sin who
watches other people go to receive the sacrament—abandoned. If
only he knew what *his* work was.

'Would you like a cup of tea?'

'Yes. I'm a bit tired.'

'Go and find some tea, Beavis, and some biscuits—or cake.'

He asked no more questions until Beavis had returned, but
suddenly as Rowe put out his hand to take a piece of cake, he
said, 'There are no real eggs in that, I'm afraid. Yours must have
been home-made. You couldn't have bought it.'

Without considering his reply, Rowe said: 'Oh no, I didn't buy
it, I won it . . .' and stopped. 'That's absurd. I wasn't thinking . . .'
The tea made him feel stronger. He said, 'You don't treat your
murderers too badly.'

The detective said, 'Just go on remembering.'

'I remember a lot of people sitting round a room and the lights
going out. And I was afraid that someone was going to come up
behind me and stab me or strangle me. And a voice speaking.
That's worse than anything—a hopeless pain, but I can't remember a word. And then all the lights are on, and a man's dead, and

I suppose that's what you say I've done. But I don't think it's true.'

'Would you remember the man's face?'

'I think I would.'

'File, Beavis.'

It was growing hot in the small room. The detective's forehead was beaded and the little fair moustache damp. He said, 'You can take off your coat if you like,' and took his own off, and sat in a pearl-grey shirt with silvered armlets to keep the cuffs exactly right. He looked doll-like as though only the coat were made to come off.

Beavis brought a paper-covered file and laid it on the table. The detective said, 'Just look through these—you'll find a few loose photographs too—and see if you can find the murdered man.'

A police photograph is like a passport photograph; the intelligence which casts a veil over the crude common shape is never recorded by the cheap lens. No one can deny the contours of the flesh, the shape of nose and mouth, and yet we protest: This isn't me . . .

The turning of the pages became mechanical. Rowe couldn't believe that it was among people like these that his life had been cast. Only once he hesitated for a moment: something in his memory stirred at sight of a loose photograph of a man with a lick of hair plastered back, a pencil on a clip in the lower left-hand corner, and wrinkled evasive eyes that seemed to be trying to escape too bright a photographer's lamp.

'Know him?' the detective asked.

'No. How could I? Or is he a shopkeeper? I thought for a moment, but no, I don't know him.' He turned on. Looking up once he saw that the detective had got his hand out from under his thigh; he seemed to have lost interest. There were not many more pages to turn—and then unexpectedly there the face was: the broad anonymous brow, the dark city suit, and with him came a whole throng of faces bursting through the gate of the unconscious, rioting horribly into the memory. He said, 'There,' and lay back in his chair giddy, feeling the world turn around him . . .

'Nonsense,' the detective said. The harsh voice hardly penetrated. 'You had me guessing for a moment . . . a good actor . . . waste any more time . . .'

'They did it with my knife.'

'Stop play-acting,' the detective said. 'That man hasn't been murdered. He's just as alive as you are.'

2

'Alive?'

'Of course he's alive. I don't know why you picked on him.'

'But in that case'—all his tiredness went: he began to notice the fine day outside—'I'm not a murderer. Was he badly hurt?'

'Do you really mean . . .?' the detective began incredulously; Beavis had given up the attempt at writing. He said, 'I don't know what you are talking about. Where did this happen? when? what was it you think you saw?'

As Rowe looked at the photograph it came back in vivid patches: he said, 'Wonderful Mrs—Mrs Bellairs. It was her house. A séance.' Suddenly he saw a thin beautiful hand blood-stained. He said, 'Why . . . Dr Forester was there. He told us the man was dead. They sent for the police.'

'The same Dr Forester?'

'The same one.'

'And they let you go?'

'No, I escaped.'

'Somebody helped you?'

'Yes.'

'Who?'

The past was swimming back to him, as though now that there was nothing to fear the guard had been removed from the gate. Anna's brother had helped him; he saw the exhilarated young face and felt the blow on his knuckles. He wasn't going to betray him. He said, 'I don't remember that.'

The little plump man sighed. 'This isn't for us, Beavis,' he said, 'we'd better take him across to 59.' He put a call through to someone called Prentice. 'We turn 'em in to you,' he complained, 'but how often do you turn them in to us?' Then they accompanied Rowe across the big collegiate court-yard under the high grey block; the trams twanged on the Embankment, and pigeons' droppings gave a farm-yard air to the sandbags stacked around.

He didn't care a damn that they walked on either side of him, an obvious escort; he was a free man still and he hadn't committed murder, and his memory was coming back at every step. He said suddenly, 'It was the cake he wanted,' and laughed.

'Keep your cake for Prentice,' the little man said sourly. 'He's the surrealist round here.'

They came to an almost identical room in another block, where a man in a tweed suit with a drooping grey Edwardian moustache sat on the edge of a chair as though it were a shooting-stick. 'This is Mr Arthur Rowe we've been advertising for,' the detective said and laid the file on the table. 'At least he says he is. No identity card. Says he's been in a nursing home with loss of memory. We are the lucky fellows who've set his memory going again. Such a memory. We ought to set up a clinic. You'll be interested to hear he saw Cost murdered.'

'Now that is interesting,' Mr Prentice said with middle-aged courtesy. 'Not *my* Mr Cost?'

'Yes. And a Dr Forester attended the death.'

'*My* Dr Forester.'

'It seems likely. This gentleman has been a patient of his.'

'Take a chair, Mr Rowe . . . and you, Graves.'

'Not me. You like the fantastic. I don't. I'll leave you Beavis, in case you want any notes taken.' He turned at the door and said, 'Pleasant nightmares to you.'

'Nice chap, Graves,' Mr Prentice said. He leant forward as though he were going to offer a hip flask. The smell of good tweeds came across the table. 'Now would you say it was a good nursing home?'

'So long as you didn't quarrel with the doctor.'

'Ha, ha . . . exactly. And then?'

'You might find yourself in the sick bay for violent cases.'

'Wonderful,' Mr Prentice said, stroking his long moustache. 'One can't help admiring . . . You wouldn't have any complaints to make?'

'They treated me very well.'

'Yes, I was afraid so. You see, if only someone would complain—they are all voluntary patients—one might be able to have a look at the place. I've been wanting to for a long time.'

'When you get in the sick bay it's too late. If you aren't mad,

they can soon make you mad.' In his blind fight he had tem-
porarily forgotten Stone. He felt a sense of guilt, remembering
the tired voice behind the door. He said, 'They've got a man in
there now. He's not violent.'

'A difference of opinion with our Dr Forester?'

'He said he saw the doctor and Poole—he's the attendant—doing something in the dark in Poole's room. He told them he was
looking for a window from which he could enfilade—' Rowe
broke off. 'He *is* a little mad, but quite gentle, not violent.'

'Go on,' Mr Prentice said.

'He thought the Germans were in occupation of a little island
in a pond. He said he'd seen them digging in.'

'And he told the doctor that?'

'Yes.' Rowe implored him, 'Can't you get him out? They've
put him in a strait-jacket, but he wouldn't hurt a soul . . .'

'Well,' Mr Prentice said, 'we must think carefully.' He stroked
his moustache with a milking movement. 'We must look all
round the subject, mustn't we?'

'He'll go really mad . . .'

'Poor fellow,' Mr Prentice said unconvincingly. There was a
merciless quality in his gentleness. He switched, 'And Poole?'

'He came to me once—I don't know how long ago—and
wanted a cake I'd won. There was an air-raid on. I have an idea
that he tried to kill me because I wouldn't give him the cake. It
was made with real eggs. Do you think I'm mad too?' he asked
with anxiety.

Mr Prentice said thoughtfully, 'I wouldn't say so. Life can be
very odd. Oh, very odd. You should read more history. Silk-
worms, you know, were smuggled out of China in a hollow
walking-stick. One can't really mention the places diamond-
smugglers use. And at this very moment I'm looking—oh, most
anxiously—for something which may not be much bigger than
a diamond. A cake . . . very good, why not? But he didn't kill
you.'

'There are so many blanks,' Rowe said.

'Where was it he came to see you?'

'I don't remember. There are years and years of my life I still
can't remember.'

'We forget very easily,' Mr Prentice said, 'what gives us pain.'

'I almost wish I *were* a criminal, so that there could be a record of me here.'

Mr Prentice said gently, 'We are doing very well, very well. Now let's go back to the murder of—Cost. Of course that might have been staged to send you into hiding, to stop you coming to us. But what came next? Apparently you didn't go into hiding and you didn't come to us. And what was it you knew . . . or we knew?' He put his hands flat on the table and said, 'It's a beautiful problem. One could almost put it into algebraic terms. Just tell me all you told Graves.'

He described again what he could remember: the crowded room and the light going out and a voice talking and fear . . .

'Graves didn't appreciate all that, I dare say,' Mr Prentice said, clasping his bony knees and rocking slightly. 'Poor Graves—the passionate crimes of railway porters are his spiritual province. In this branch our interests have to be rather more bizarre. And so he distrusts us—really distrusts us.'

He began turning the pages of the file rather as he might have turned over a family album, quizzically. 'Are you a student of human nature, Mr Rowe?'

'I don't know what I am.'

'This face for instance . . .'

It was the photograph over which Rowe had hesitated: he hesitated again.

'What profession do you think *he* followed?' Mr Prentice asked.

The pencil clipped in the breast-pocket: the depressed suit: the air of a man always expecting a rebuff: the little lines of knowledge round the eyes—when he examined it closely he felt no doubt at all. 'A private detective,' he said.

'Right the first time. And this little anonymous man had his little anonymous name . . .'

Rowe smiled. 'Jones I should imagine.'

'You wouldn't think it, Mr Rowe, but you and he—let's call him Jones—had something in common. You both disappeared. But you've come back. What was the name of the agency which employed him, Beavis?'

'I don't remember, sir. I could go and look it up.'

'It doesn't matter. The only one I can remember is the Clifford. It wasn't that.'

'Not the Orthotex?' Rowe asked. 'I once had a friend . . .' and stopped.

'It comes back, doesn't it, Mr Rowe. His name was Jones, you see. And he did belong to the Orthotex. What made you go there? We can tell you even if you don't remember. You thought that someone had tried to murder you—about a cake. You had won the cake unfairly at a fair (what a pun!) because a certain Mrs Bellairs had told you the weight. You went to find out where Mrs Bellairs lived—from the offices of the Fund for the Mothers of the Free Nations (if I've got the outlandish name correct) and Jones followed, just to keep an eye on them—and you. But you must have given him the slip somehow, Mr Rowe, because Jones never came back, and when you telephoned next day to Mr Rennit you said you were wanted for murder.'

Rowe sat with his hand over his eyes—trying to remember? trying not to remember?—while the voice drove carefully and precisely on.

'And yet no murder had been committed in London during the previous twenty-four hours—so far as we knew—unless poor Jones had gone that way. You obviously knew something, perhaps you knew everything: we advertised for you and you didn't come forward. Until today, when you arrive in a beard you certainly used not to wear, saying you had lost your memory, but remembering at least that you had been accused of murder—only you picked out a man we know is alive. How does it all strike you, Mr Rowe?'

Rowe said, 'I'm waiting for the handcuffs,' and smiled unhappily.

'You can hardly blame our friend Graves,' Mr Prentice said.

'Is life really like this?' Rowe asked. Mr Prentice leant forward with an interested air, as though he were always ready to abandon the particular in favour of the general argument. He said, 'This is life, so I suppose one can say it's like life.'

'It isn't how I had imagined it,' Rowe said. He went on, 'You see, I'm a learner. I'm right at the beginning, trying to find my way about. I thought life was much simpler and—grander. I suppose that's how it strikes a boy. I was brought up on stories of Captain Scott writing his last letters home. Oates walking into the blizzard, I've forgotten who losing his hands from his experiments with radium, Damien among the lepers . . .' The memories which are overlaid by the life one lives came freshly back in the little stuffy office in the great grey Yard. It was a relief to talk. 'There was a book called the *Book of Golden Deeds* by a woman called Yonge . . . *The Little Duke* . . .' He said, 'If you were suddenly taken from that world into this job you are doing now you'd feel bewildered. Jones and the cake, the sick bay, poor Stone . . . all this talk of a man called Hitler . . . your files of wretched faces, the cruelty and meaninglessness . . . It's as if one had been sent on a journey with the wrong map. I'm ready to do everything you want, but remember I don't know my way about. Everybody else has changed gradually and learnt. This whole business of war and hate—even that's strange. I haven't been worked up to it. I expect much the best thing would be to hang me.'

'Yes,' Mr Prentice said eagerly, 'yes, it's a most interesting case. I can see that to you,' he became startlingly colloquial, 'this is rather a dingy hole. We've come to terms with it of course.'

'What frightens me,' Rowe said, 'is knowing how I came to terms with it before my memory went. When I came in to London today I hadn't realized there would be so many ruins. Nothing will seem as strange as that. God knows what kind of a ruin I am myself. Perhaps I *am* a murderer?'

Mr Prentice reopened the file and said rapidly, 'Oh, we no longer think you killed Jones.' He was like a man who has looked over a wall, seen something disagreeable and now walks rapidly, purposefully, away, talking as he goes. 'The question is—what made you lose your memory? What do you know about that?'

'Only what I've been told.'

'And what have you been told?'

'That it was a bomb. It gave me this scar.'

'Were you alone?'

Before he could brake his tongue he said, 'No.'

'Who was with you?'

'A girl.' It was too late now; he had to bring her in, and after all if he were not a murderer, why should it matter that her brother had aided his escape? 'Anna Hilfe.' The plain words were sweet on the tongue.

'Why were you with her?'

'I think we were lovers.'

'You think?'

'I don't remember.'

'What does she say about it?'

'She says I saved her life.'

'The Free Mothers,' Mr Prentice brooded. 'Has she explained how you got to Dr Forester's?'

'She was forbidden to.' Mr Prentice raised an eyebrow. 'They wanted—so they told us—my memory to come back naturally and slowly of itself. No hypnotism, no psycho-analysis.'

Mr Prentice beamed at him and swayed a little on his shooting-stick; you felt he was taking a well-earned rest in the middle of a successful shoot. 'Yes, it wouldn't have done, would it, if it had come back too quickly . . . Although of course there was always the sick bay.'

'If only you'd tell me what it's all about.'

Mr Prentice stroked his moustache; he had the *fainéant* air of Arthur Balfour, but you felt that he knew it. He had stylized himself—life was easier that way. He had chosen a physical mould just as a writer chooses a technical form. 'Now were you ever a habitué of the Regal Court?'

'It's a hotel?'

'You remember that much.'

'Well, it's an easy guess.'

Mr Prentice closed his eyes; it was perhaps an affectation, but who could live without affectations?

'Why do you ask about the Regal Court?'

'It's a shot in the dark,' Mr Prentice said. 'We have so little time.'

'Time for what?'

'To find a needle in a haystack.'

3

One wouldn't have said that Mr Prentice was capable of much exertion; rough shooting, you would have said, was beyond him. From the house to the brake and from the brake to the butts was about as far as you could expect him to walk in a day. And yet during the next few hours he showed himself capable of great exertion, and the shooting was indubitably rough . . .

He had dropped his enigmatic statement into the air and was out of the room almost before the complete phrase had formed, his long legs moving stiffly, like stilts. Rowe was left alone with Beavis and the day wore slowly on. The sun's early promise had been false; a cold unseasonable drizzle fell like dust outside the window. After a long time they brought him some cold pie and tea on a tray.

Beavis was not inclined to conversation. It was as though *his* words might be used in evidence, and Rowe only once attempted to break the silence. He said, 'I wish I knew what it was all about' and watched Beavis's long-toothed mouth open and clap to like a rabbit snare. 'Official secrets,' Beavis said and stared with flat eyes at the blank wall.

Then suddenly Mr Prentice was with them again, rushing into the room in his stiff casual stride, followed by a man in black who held a bowler hat in front of him with both hands like a basin of water and panted a little in the trail of Mr Prentice. He came to a stop inside the door and glared at Rowe. He said, 'That's the scoundrel. I haven't a doubt of it. I can see through the beard. It's a disguise.'

Mr Prentice gave a giggle. 'That's excellent,' he said. 'The pieces are really fitting.'

The man with the bowler said, 'He carried in the suitcase and he wanted just to leave it. But I had my instructions. I told him he must wait for Mr Travers. He didn't want to wait. Of course he didn't want to, knowing what was inside . . . Something must have gone wrong. He didn't get Mr Travers, but he nearly got the poor girl . . . and when the confusion was over, he'd gone.'

'I don't remember ever seeing him before,' Rowe said.

The man gesticulated passionately with his bowler, 'I'll swear to him in any court of law.'

Beavis watched with his mouth a little open and Mr Prentice giggled again. 'No time,' he said. 'No time for squabbles. You two can get to know each other later. I need you both now.'

'If you'd tell me a little,' Rowe pleaded. To have come all this way, he thought, to meet a charge of murder and to find only a deeper confusion . . .

'In the taxi,' Mr Prentice said. 'I'll explain in the taxi.' He made for the door.

'Aren't you going to charge him?' the man asked, panting in pursuit.

Mr Prentice without looking round said, 'Presently, presently, perhaps . . .' and then darkly, 'Who?'

They swept into the court-yard and out into broad stony Northumberland Avenue, policemen saluting: into a taxi and off along the ruined front of the Strand: the empty eyes of an insurance building: boarded windows: sweet-shops with one dish of mauve cachous in the window.

Mr Prentice said in a low voice, 'I just want you two gentlemen to behave naturally. We are going to a city tailor's where I'm being measured for a suit. I shall go in first and after a few minutes you, Rowe, and last you, Mr Davis,' and he touched the bowler hat with the tip of a finger where it balanced on the stranger's lap.

'But what's it all about, sir?' Davis asked. He had edged away from Rowe, and Mr Prentice curled his long legs across the taxi, sitting opposite them in a tip-up.

'Never mind. Just keep your eyes open and see if there's anyone in the shop you recognize.' The mischief faded from his eyes as the taxi looped round the gutted shell of St Clement Danes. He said, 'The place will be surrounded. You needn't be afraid . . .'

Rowe said, 'I'm not afraid. I only want to know . . .' staring out at odd devastated boarded-up London.

'It's really serious,' Mr Prentice said. 'I don't know quite how serious. But you might say that we all depend on it.' He shuddered away from what was almost an emotional statement, giggled, touched doubtfully the silky ends of his moustache and said, with sadness in his voice, 'You know there are always weaknesses that have to be covered up. If the Germans had known after Dunkirk just how weak . . . There are still weaknesses of which if they knew the exact facts . . .' The ruins around St Paul's unfolded; the obliterated acres of Paternoster Row. He said, 'This would be nothing to it. Nothing.' He went slowly on, 'Perhaps I was wrong to say there was no danger. If we are on the right track, of course, there must be danger, mustn't there? It's worth—oh, a thousand lives to them.'

'If I can be of any use,' Rowe said. 'This is so strange to me. I didn't imagine war was this,' staring out at desolation. Jerusalem must have looked something like this in the mind's eye of Christ when he wept . . .

'I'm not scared,' the man with the bowler said sharply, defensively.

'We are looking,' Mr Prentice said, clasping his bony knees and vibrating with the taxi, 'for a little roll of film—probably a good deal smaller than a cotton reel. Smaller than those little rolls you put in Leica cameras. You must have read the questions in Parliament about certain papers which were missing for an hour. It was hushed up publicly. It doesn't help anybody to ruin confidence in a big name—and it doesn't help us to have the public and the press muddying up the trail. I tell you two only because—well, we could have you put quietly away for the duration if there was any leakage. It happened twice—the first time the roll was hidden in a cake and the cake was to be fetched from a certain fête. But you won it,' Mr Prentice nodded at Rowe, 'the password as it were was given to the wrong man.'

'Mrs Bellairs?' Rowe said.

'She's being looked after at this minute.' He went on explaining with vague gestures of his thin useless-looking hands, 'That attempt failed. A bomb that hit your house destroyed the cake and everything—and probably saved your life. But they didn't like the way you followed the case up. They tried to frighten you into hiding—but for some reason that was not enough. Of course they meant to blow you into pieces, but when they found you'd lost your memory, that was good enough. It was better than killing you, because by disappearing you took the blame for the bomb—as well as for Jones.'

'But why the girl?'

'We'll leave out the mysteries,' Mr Prentice said. 'Perhaps because her brother helped you. They aren't above revenge. There isn't time for all that now.' They were at the Mansion House. 'What we know is this—they had to wait until the next chance came. Another big name and another fool. He had this in common with the first fool—he went to the same tailor.' The taxi drew up at the corner of a city street.

'We foot it from here,' Mr Prentice said. A man on the opposite kerb began to walk up the street as they alighted.

'Do you carry a revolver?' the man in the bowler hat asked nervously.

'I wouldn't know how to use it,' Mr Prentice said. 'If there's trouble of that kind just lie flat.'

'You had no right to bring me into this.'

Mr Prentice turned sharply. 'Oh yes,' he said, 'every right. Nobody's got a right to his life these days. My dear chap, you are conscripted for your country.' They stood grouped on the pavement: bank messengers with chained boxes went by in top hats: stenographers and clerks hurried past returning late from their lunch. There were no ruins to be seen; it was like peace. Mr Prentice said, 'If those photographs leave the country, there'll be a lot of suicides . . . at least that's what happened in France.'

'How do you know they haven't left?' Rowe asked.

'We don't. We just hope, that's all. We'll know the worst soon enough.' He said, 'Watch when I go in. Give me five minutes with our man in the fitting-room, and then you, Rowe, come in and ask for me. I want to have him where I can watch him—in all the mirrors. Then, Davis, you count a hundred and follow. *You* are going to be too much of a coincidence. You are going to be the last straw.'

They watched the stiff old-fashioned figure make his way up the street; he was just the kind of man to have a city tailor—somebody reliable and not expensive whom he could recommend to his son. Presently about fifty yards along he turned in: a man stood at the next corner and lit a cigarette. A motor-car drew up next door and a woman got out to do some shopping, leaving a man at the wheel.

Rowe said, 'It's time for me to be moving.' His pulse beat with excitement; it was as if he had come to this adventure unsaddened, with the freshness of a boy. He looked suspiciously at Davis, who stood there with a nerve twitching at his cheek. He said, 'A hundred and you follow.' Davis said nothing. 'You understand. You count a hundred.'

'Oh,' Davis said furiously, 'this play-acting. I'm a plain man.'

'Those were his orders.'

'Who's he to give me orders?'

Rowe couldn't stay to argue: time was up.

War had hit the tailoring business hard. A few rolls of grey inferior cloth lay on the counter; the shelves were nearly empty. A man in a frock-coat with a tired, lined, anxious face said, 'What can we do for you, sir?'

'I came here,' Rowe said, 'to meet a friend.' He looked down the narrow aisle between the little mirrored cubicles. 'I expect he's being fitted now.'

'Will you take a chair, sir?' and 'Mr Ford,' he called, 'Mr Ford.' Out from one of the cubicles, a tape measure slung round his neck, a little bouquet of pins in his lapel, solid, city-like, came Cost, whom he had last seen dead in his chair when the lights went out. Like a piece of a jig-saw puzzle which clicks into place and makes sense of a whole confusing block, that solid figure took up its place in his memory with the man from Welwyn and the proletarian poet and Anna's brother. What had Mrs Bellairs called him? He remembered the whole phrase 'Our business man'.

Rowe stood up as though this were someone of great importance who must be greeted punctiliously, but there seemed to be no recognition in the stolid respectable eyes. 'Yes, Mr Bridges?' Those were the first words he had ever heard him speak; his whole function before had been one of death.

'This gentleman has come to meet the other gentleman.'

The eyes swivelled slowly and rested; no sign of recognition broke their large grey calm—or did they rest a shade longer than was absolutely necessary? 'I have nearly taken the gentleman's measurements. If you would not mind waiting two minutes . . .' Two minutes Rowe thought, and then the other, the straw which will really break you down.

Mr Ford—if this was now to be his name—walked slowly up to the counter; everything he did, you felt, was carefully pondered; his suits must always be well-built. There was no room in that precision for the eccentricity, the wayward act, and yet what a wild oddity lay hidden under the skin. He saw Dr Forester dabbling his fingers in what looked like blood.

A telephone stood on the counter; Mr Ford picked up the receiver and dialled. The dial faced Rowe. He watched with care each time where the finger fitted. B. A. T. He felt sure of the letters; but one number he missed, suddenly wavering and catching

the serene ponderous gaze of Mr Ford as he dialled. He was un-
sure of himself; he wished Mr Prentice would appear.

'Hullo,' Mr Ford said, 'hullo. This is Pauling and Crosthwaite.'

Along the length of the window towards the door dragged the
unwilling form of the man with the bowler hat: Rowe's hands
tightened in his lap. Mr Bridges was sadly straightening the mea-
gre rolls of cloth, his back turned. His listless hands were like a
poignant criticism in the *Tailor and Cutter*.

'The suit was dispatched this morning, sir,' Mr Ford was saying, 'I trust in time for your journey.' He clucked his satisfaction
calmly and inhumanly down the telephone, 'Thank you very
much, sir. I felt very satisfied myself at the last fitting.' His eyes
shifted to the clanging door as Davis looked in with a kind of
wretched swagger. 'Oh, yes, sir. I think when you've worn it
once, you'll find the shoulders will settle . . .' Mr Prentice's
whole elaborate plot was a failure: that nerve had not broken.

'Mr Travers,' Davis exclaimed with astonishment.

Carefully putting his hand over the mouthpiece of the telephone Mr Ford said, 'I beg your pardon, sir?'

'You are Mr Travers.' Then Davis, meeting those clear calm
eyes, added weakly, 'Aren't you?'

'No, sir.'

'I thought . . .'

'Mr Bridges, would you mind attending to this gentleman?'

'Certainly, Mr Ford.'

The hand left the receiver and Mr Ford quietly, firmly, author-
itatively continued to speak up the wire. 'No, sir. I find at the last
moment that we shall not be able to repeat the trousers. It's not a
matter of coupons, no. We can obtain no more of that pattern
from the manufacturers—no more at all.' Again his eyes met
Rowe's and wandered like a blind man's hand delicately along
the contours of his face. 'Personally, sir, I have no hope. No hope
at all.' He put the receiver down and moved a little way along
the counter. 'If you can spare these a moment, Mr Bridges . . .'
He picked up a pair of cutting-shears.

'Certainly, Mr Ford.'

Without another word he passed Rowe, not looking at him
again, and moved down the aisle, without hurry, serious, professional, as heavy as stone. Rowe quickly rose: something, he felt,

must be done, be said, if the whole plan were not to end in fiasco. 'Cost,' he called after the figure, 'Cost.' It was only then that the extreme calm and deliberation of the figure with the shears struck him as strange. He called out 'Prentice' sharply in warning as the fitter turned aside into a cubicle.

But it was not the cubicle from which Mr Prentice emerged. He came bewilderedly out in his silk shirt-sleeves from the opposite end of the aisle. 'What is it?' he asked, but Rowe was already at the other door straining to get in. Over his shoulder he could see the shocked face of Mr Bridges, Davis's goggling eyes. 'Quick,' he said, 'your hat,' and grabbed the bowler and crashed it through the glass of the door.

Under the icicles of splintered glass he could see Cost— Travers—Ford. He sat in the arm-chair for clients opposite the tall triple mirror, leaning forward, his throat transfixed, with the cutting-shears held firmly upright between his knees. It was a Roman death.

Rowe thought: this time I *have* killed him, and heard that quiet respectful but authoritative voice speaking down the telephone. 'Personally I have no hope. No hope at all.'

CHAPTER 2
MOPPING UP

'You had best yield.'
The Little Duke

I

Mrs Bellairs had less dignity.

They had driven straight to Campden Hill, leaving Davis with his wrecked bowler. Mr Prentice was worried and depressed. 'It does no good,' he said. 'We want them alive and talking.'

Rowe said, 'He must have had great courage. I don't know why that's so surprising. One doesn't associate it with tailors . . . except for that one in the story who killed a giant. I suppose you'd say this one was on the side of the giants. I wonder why.'

Mr Prentice burst suddenly out as they drove up through the Park in the thin windy rain. 'Pity is a terrible thing. People talk about the passion of love. Pity is the worst passion of all: we don't outlive it like sex.'

'After all, it's war,' Rowe said with a kind of exhilaration. The old fake truism like a piece of common pyrites in the hands of a child split open and showed its sparkling core to him. He was taking part . . .

Mr Prentice looked at him oddly, with curiosity. 'You don't feel it, do you? Adolescents don't feel pity. It's a mature passion.'

'I expect,' Rowe said, 'that I led a dull humdrum sober life, and so all this excites me. Now that I know I'm not a murderer I can enjoy . . .' He broke off at sight of the dimly remembered house like the scene of a dream: that unweeded little garden with the grey fallen piece of statuary and the small iron gate that creaked. All the blinds were down as though somebody had died, and the door stood open; you expected to see auction tickets on the furniture. 'We pulled her in,' Mr Prentice said, 'simultaneously.'

There was silence about the place; a man in a dark suit who might have been an undertaker stood in the hall. He opened a door for Mr Prentice and they went in. It wasn't the drawing-room that Rowe vaguely remembered, but a small dining-room crammed full with ugly chairs and a too-large table and a desk. Mrs Bellairs sat in an arm-chair at the head of the table with a pasty grey closed face, wearing a black turban; the man at the door said, 'She won't say a thing.'

'Well, ma'am,' Mr Prentice greeted her with a kind of gallant jauntiness.

Mrs Bellairs said nothing.

'I've brought you a visitor, ma'am,' Mr Prentice said and stepping to one side allowed her to see Rowe.

It is a disquieting experience to find yourself an object of terror: no wonder the novelty of it intoxicates some men. To Rowe it was horrible—as though he had suddenly found himself capable of an atrocity. Mrs Bellairs began to choke, sitting grotesquely at the table-head; it was as if she had swallowed a fish-bone at a select dinner-party. She must have been holding herself in with a great effort, and the shock had upset the muscles of her throat.

Mr Prentice was the only one equal to the occasion. He wormed round the table and slapped her jovially on the back. 'Choke up, ma'am,' he said, 'choke up. You'll be all right.'

'I've never seen the man,' she moaned, 'never.'

'Why, you told his fortune,' Mr Prentice said. 'Don't you remember that?'

A glint of desperate hope slid across the old congested eyes. She said, 'If all this fuss is about a little fortune-telling . . . I only do it for charity.'

'Of course, we understand that,' Mr Prentice said.

'And I never tell the future.'

'Ah, if we could see into the future . . .'

'Only character.'

'And the weight of cakes,' Mr Prentice said, and all the hope went suddenly out. It was too late now for silence.

'And your little séances,' Mr Prentice went cheerily on, as though they shared a joke between them.

'In the interests of science,' Mrs Bellairs said.

'Does your little group still meet?'

'On Wednesdays.'

'Many absentees?'

'They are all personal friends,' Mrs Bellairs said vaguely; now that the questions seemed again on safer ground, she put up one plump powdered hand and adjusted the turban.

'Mr Cost now . . . he can hardly attend any longer.'

Mrs Bellairs said carefully, 'Of course, I recognize this gentleman now. The beard confused me. That was a silly joke of Mr Cost's. I knew nothing about it. I was far, far away.'

'Far away?'

'Where the Blessed are.'

'Oh yes, yes. Mr Cost won't play such jokes again.'

'It was meant quite innocently, I'm sure. Perhaps he resented two strangers . . . We are a very compact little group. And Mr Cost was never a real believer.'

'Let's hope he is now.' Mr Prentice did not seem worried at the moment by what he had called the terrible passion of pity. He said, 'You must try to get into touch with him, Mrs Bellairs, and ask him why he cut his throat this morning.'

Into the goggle-eyed awful silence broke the ringing of the telephone. It rang and rang on the desk, and there were too many people in the little crowded room to get to it quickly. A memory shifted like an uneasy sleeper . . . this had happened before.

'Wait a moment,' Mr Prentice said. 'You answer it, ma'am.'

She repeated, 'Cut his throat . . .'

'It was all he had left to do. Except live and hang.'

The telephone cried on. It was as though someone far away had his mind fixed on that room, working out the reason for that silence.

'Answer it, ma'am,' Mr Prentice said again.

Mrs Bellairs was not made of the same stuff as the tailor. She heaved herself obediently up, jangling a little as she moved. She got momentarily stuck between the table and the wall, and the turban slipped over one eye. She said, 'Hullo. Who's there?'

The three men in the room stayed motionless, holding their breaths. Suddenly Mrs Bellairs seemed to recover; it was as if she felt her power—the only one there who could speak. She said, 'It's Dr Forester. What shall I say to him?' speaking over her shoulder with her mouth close to the receiver. She glinted at them, maliciously, intelligently, with her stupidity strung up like a piece of camouflage she couldn't be bothered to perfect.

Mr Prentice took the receiver from her hand and rang off. He said, 'This isn't going to help you.'

She bridled, 'I was only asking . . .'

Mr Prentice said, 'Get a fast car from the Yard. God knows what those local police are doing. They should have been at the house by this time.' He told a second man, 'See that this lady doesn't cut her throat. We've got other uses for it.'

He proceeded to go through the house from room to room as destructively as a tornado; he was white and angry. He said to Rowe, 'I'm worried about your friend—what's his name?—Stone.' He said, 'The old bitch,' and the word sounded odd on the Edwardian lips. In Mrs Bellairs' bedroom he didn't leave a pot of cream unchurned—and there were a great many. He tore open her pillows himself with vicious pleasure. There was a little lubricious book called *Love in the Orient* on a bed-table by a pink-shaded lamp— he tore off the binding and broke the china base of the lamp. Only the sound of a car's horn stopped the destruction. He said, 'I'll want you with me—for identifications,' and took the stairs in three strides and a jump. Mrs Bellairs was weeping now in the drawing-room, and one of the detectives had made her a cup of tea.

'Stop that nonsense,' Mr Prentice said. It was as if he were determined to give an example of thoroughness to weak assistants. 'There's nothing wrong with her. If she won't talk, skin this house alive.' He seemed consumed by a passion of hatred and perhaps despair. He took up the cup from which Mrs Bellairs had been about to drink and emptied the contents on the carpet. Mrs Bellairs wailed at him, 'You've got no right . . .'

He said sharply, 'Is this your best tea-service, ma'am?' wincing ever so slightly at the gaudy Prussian blue.

'Put it down,' Mrs Bellairs implored, but he had already smashed the cup against the wall. He explained to his man, 'The handles are hollow. We don't know how small these films are. You've got to skin the place.'

'You'll suffer for this,' Mrs Bellairs said tritely.

'Oh no, ma'am, it's you who'll suffer. Giving information to the enemy is a hanging offence.'

'They don't hang women. Not in this war.'

'We may hang more people, ma'am,' Mr Prentice said, speaking back at her from the passage, 'than the papers tell you about.'

2

It was a long and gloomy ride. A sense of failure and apprehension must have oppressed Mr Prentice; he sat curled in the corner of the car humming lugubriously. It became evening before they had unwound themselves from the dirty edge of London, and night before they reached the first hedge. Looking back, one could see only an illuminated sky—bright lanes and blobs of light like city squares, as though the inhabited world were up above and down below only the dark unlighted heavens.

It was a long and gloomy ride, but all the time Rowe repressed for the sake of his companion a sense of exhilaration: he was happily drunk with danger and action. This was more like the life he had imagined years ago. He was helping in a great struggle, and when he saw Anna again he could claim to have played a part against her enemies. He didn't worry very much about Stone; none of the books of adventure one read as a boy had an unhappy ending. And none of them was disturbed by a sense of pity for the beaten side. The ruins from which they emerged were only a heroic back-cloth to his personal adventure; they had no more reality than the photographs in a propaganda album: the remains of an iron bedstead on the third floor of a smashed tenement only said, 'They shall not pass,' not 'We shall never sleep in this room, in this home, again.' He didn't understand suffering because he had forgotten that he had ever suffered.

Rowe said, 'After all, nothing can have happened there. The local police . . .'

Mr Prentice observed bitterly, 'England is a very beautiful country. The Norman churches, the old graves, the village green and the public-house, the policeman's home with his patch of garden. He wins a prize every year for his cabbages . . .'

'But the county police . . .'

'The Chief Constable served twenty years ago in the Indian Army. A fine fellow. Has a good palate for port. Talks too much about his regiment, but you can depend on him for a subscription to any good cause. The superintendent . . . he was a good man once, but they'd have retired him from the Metropolitan Police after a few years' service without a pension, so the first chance he got he transferred to the county. You see, being an honest man, he didn't want to lay by in bribes from bookmakers for his old age. Only, of course, in a small county there's not much to keep a man sharp. Running in drunks. Petty pilfering. The judge at the assizes compliments the county on its clean record.'

'You know the men?'

'I don't know *these* men, but if you know England you can guess it all. And then suddenly into this peace—even in wartime it's still peace—comes the clever, the warped, the completely unscrupulous, ambitious, educated criminal. Not a criminal at all, as the county knows crime. He doesn't steal and he doesn't get drunk—and if he murders, they haven't had a murder for fifty years and can't recognize it.'

'What do you expect to find?' Rowe asked.

'Almost anything except what we are looking for. A small roll of film.'

'They may have got innumerable copies by this time.'

'They may have, but they haven't innumerable ways of getting them out of the country. Find the man who's going to do the smuggling—and the organizer. It doesn't matter about the rest.'

'Do you think Dr Forester . . .?'

'Dr Forester,' Mr Prentice said, 'is a victim—oh, a dangerous victim, no doubt, but he's not the victimizer. He's one of the used, the blackmailed. That doesn't mean, of course, that he isn't the courier. If he is, we are in luck. He couldn't get away . . . unless these country police . . .' Again the gloom of defeat descended on him.

'He might pass it on.'

'It isn't so easy,' Mr Prentice said. 'There are not many of these people at large. Remember, to get out of the country now you must have a very good excuse. If only the country police . . .'

'Is it so desperately important?'

Mr Prentice thought gloomily, 'We've made so many mistakes since this war began, and they've made so few. Perhaps this one will be the last we'll make. To trust a man like Dunwoody with anything secret . . .'

'Dunwoody?'

'I shouldn't have let it out, but one gets impatient. Have you heard the name? They hushed it up because he's the son of the grand old man.'

'No, I've never heard of him . . . I think I've never heard of him.'

A screech owl cried over the dark flat fields; their dimmed headlights just touched the near hedge and penetrated no farther into the wide region of night: it was like the coloured fringe along the unexplored spaces of a map. Over there among the unknown tribes a woman was giving birth, rats were nosing among sacks of meal, an old man was dying, two people were seeing each other for the first time by the light of a lamp; everything in that darkness was of such deep importance that their errand could not equal it—this violent superficial chase, this cardboard adventure hurtling at seventy miles an hour along the edge of the profound natural common experiences of men. Rowe felt a longing to get back into that world: into the world of homes and children and quiet love and the ordinary unspecified fears and anxieties the neighbour shared; he carried the thought of Anna like a concealed letter promising just that: the longing was like the first stirring of maturity when the rare experience suddenly ceases to be desirable.

'We shall know the worst soon,' Mr Prentice said. 'If we don't find it here' his hunched hopeless figure expressed the weariness of giving up.

Somebody a long way ahead was waving a torch up and down, up and down. 'What the hell are they playing at?' Mr Prentice said. 'Advertising . . . They can't trust a stranger to find his way through their country without a compass.'

They drew slowly along a high wall and halted outside big heraldic gates. It was unfamiliar to Rowe; he was looking from the outside at something he had only seen from within. The top of a cedar against the sky was not the same cedar that cast a shadow round the bole. A policeman stood at the car door and said, 'What name, sir?'

Mr Prentice showed a card, 'Everything all right?'

'Not exactly, sir. You'll find the superintendent inside.'

They left the car and trailed, a little secretive dubious group, between the great gates. They had no air of authority; they were stiff with the long ride and subdued in spirit: they looked like a party of awed sightseers taken by the butler round the family seat. The policeman kept on saying, 'This way, sir,' and flashing his torch, but there was only one way.

It seemed odd to Rowe, returning like this. The big house was silent—and the fountain was silent too. Somebody must have turned off the switch which regulated the flow. There were lights on in only two of the rooms. This was the place where for months he had lain happily in an extraordinary peace; this scene had been grafted by the odd operation of a bomb on to his childhood. Half his remembered life lay here. Now that he came back like an enemy, he felt a sense of shame. He said, 'If you don't mind, I'd rather not see Dr Forester . . .'

The policeman with the torch said, 'You needn't be afraid, sir, he's quite tidy.'

Mr Prentice had not been listening. 'That car,' he said, 'who does it belong to?'

A Ford V8 stood in the drive—that wasn't the one he meant, but an old tattered car with cracked and stained windscreen—one of those cars that stand with a hundred others in lonely spoilt fields along the highway—yours for five pounds if you can get it to move away.

'That, sir—that's the reverend's.'

Mr Prentice said sharply, 'Are you holding a party?'

'Oh no, sir. But as one of them was still alive, we thought it only right to let the vicar know.'

'Things seem to have happened,' Mr Prentice said gloomily. It had been raining and the constable tried to guide them with his torch between the puddles in the churned-up gravel and up the stone steps to the hall door.

In the lounge where the illustrated papers had lain in glossy stacks, where Davis had been accustomed to weep in a corner and the two nervous men had fumed over the chess pieces, Johns sat in an arm-chair with his head in his hands. Rowe went to him; he said, 'Johns', and Johns looked up. He said, 'He was such a great man . . . such a great man . . .'

'Was?'

'I killed him.'

3

It had been a massacre on an Elizabethan scale. Rowe was the
only untroubled man there—until he saw Stone. The bodies lay
where they had been discovered: Stone bound in his strait-
waistcoat with the sponge of anaesthetic on the floor beside him
and the body twisted in a hopeless attempt to use his hands. 'He
hadn't a chance,' Rowe said. This was the passage he had crept
up excited like a boy breaking a school rule; in the same passage,
looking in through the open door, he grew up—learned that adventure didn't follow the literary pattern, that there weren't always happy endings, felt the awful stirring of pity that told him
something had got to be done, that you couldn't let things stay as
they were, with the innocent struggling in fear for breath and dying pointlessly. He said slowly, 'I'd like . . . how I'd like . . .' and
felt cruelty waking beside pity, its old and tried companion.

'We must be thankful,' an unfamiliar voice said, 'that he felt
no pain.' The stupid complacent and inaccurate phrase stroked
at their raw nerves.

Mr Prentice said, 'Who the hell are you?' He apologized reluctantly, 'I'm sorry. I suppose you are the vicar.'

'Yes. My name's Sinclair.'

'You've got no business here.'

'I *had* business,' Mr Sinclair corrected him. 'Dr Forester was
still alive when they called me. He was one of my parishioners.'
He added in a tone of gentle remonstrance, 'You know—we are
allowed on a battlefield.'

'Yes, yes, I daresay. But there are no inquests on those bodies.
Is that your car at the door?'

'Yes.'

'Well, if you wouldn't mind going back to the vicarage and
staying there till we are through with this . . . '

'Certainly. I wouldn't want to be in the way.'

Rowe watched him: the cylindrical black figure, the round collar glinting under the electric light, the hearty intellectual face.
Mr Sinclair said to him slowly, 'Haven't we met . . .?' con-
fronting him with an odd bold stare.

'No,' Rowe said.

'Perhaps you were one of the patients here?'

'I was.'

Mr Sinclair said with nervous enthusiasm, 'There. That must be it. I felt sure that somewhere . . . On one of the doctor's social evenings, I dare say. Good night.'

Rowe turned away and considered again the man who had felt no pain. He remembered him stepping into the mud, desperately anxious, then fleeing like a scared child towards the vegetable garden. He had always believed in treachery. He hadn't been so mad after all.

They had had to step over Dr Forester's body; it lay at the bottom of the stairs. A sixth snare had entangled the doctor: not love of country but love of one's fellow-man, a love which had astonishingly flamed into action in the heart of respectable, hero-worshipping Johns. The doctor had been too sure of Johns: he had not realized that respect is really less reliable than fear: a man may be more ready to kill one he respects than to betray him to the police. When Johns shut his eyes and pulled the trigger of the revolver which had once been confiscated from Davis and had lain locked away for months in a drawer, he was not ruining the man he respected—he was saving him from the interminable proceedings of the law courts, from the crudities of prosecuting counsel, the unfathomable ignorances of the judge, and the indignity of depending on the shallow opinion of twelve men picked at random. If love of his fellow-man refused to allow him to be a sleeping partner in the elimination of Stone, love also dictated the form of his refusal.

Dr Forester had shown himself disturbed from the moment of Rowe's escape. He had been inexplicably reluctant to call in the police, and he seemed worried about the fate of Stone. There were consultations with Poole from which Johns was excluded, and during the afternoon there was a trunk call to London . . . Johns took a letter to the post and couldn't help noticing the watcher outside the gate. In the village he saw a police car from the country town. He began to wonder . . .

He met Poole on the way back. Poole, too, must have seen. All the fancies and resentments of the last few days came back to Johns. Sitting in a passion of remorse in the lounge, he couldn't explain how all these indications had crystallized into the belief that the doctor was planning Stone's death. He remembered theoretical conversations he had often had with the doctor on the subject of euthanasia: arguments with the doctor, who was quite unmoved by the story of the Nazi elimination of old people and incurables. The doctor had once said, 'It's what any State medical service has sooner or later got to face. If you are going to be kept alive in institutions run by and paid for by the State, you must accept the State's right to economize when necessary . . .' He intruded on a colloquy between Poole and Forester, which was abruptly broken off, he became more and more restless and uneasy, it was as if the house were infected by the future: fear was already present in the passages. At tea Dr Forester made some remark about 'poor Stone'.

'Why poor Stone?' Johns asked sharply and accusingly.

'He's in great pain,' Dr Forester said. 'A tumour . . . Death is the greatest mercy we can ask for him.'

He went restlessly out into the garden in the dusk; in the moonlight the sundial was like a small sheeted figure of someone already dead at the entrance to the rose garden. Suddenly he heard Stone crying out . . . His account became more confused than ever. Apparently he ran straight to his room and got out the gun. It was just like Johns, that he had mislaid the key and found it at last in his pocket. He heard Stone cry out again. He ran through the lounge, into the other wing, made for the stairs—the sickly confected smell of chloroform was in the passage, and Dr Forester stood on guard at the foot of the stairs. He said crossly and nervously, 'What do you want, Johns?' and Johns, who still believed in the misguided purity of the doctor's fanaticism, saw only one solution: he shot the doctor. Poole, with his twisted shoulder and his malign conceited face, backed away from the top of the stairs—and he shot him, too, in a rage because he guessed he was too late.

Then, of course, the police were at the door. He went to meet them, for apparently the servants had all been given the evening off, and it was that small banal fact of which he had read in so many murder stories that brought the squalid truth home to him. Dr Forester was still alive, and the local police thought it only right to send for the parson . . . That was all. It was extraordinary the devastation that could be worked in one evening in what had once seemed a kind of earthy paradise. A fight of bombers could not have eliminated peace more thoroughly than had three men.

The search was then begun. The house was ransacked. More police were sent for. Lights were switched on and off restlessly through the early morning hours in upstairs rooms. Mr Prentice said, 'If we could find even a single print . . .' but there was nothing. At one point of the long night watch Rowe found himself back in the room where Digby had slept. He thought of Digby now as a stranger—a rather gross, complacent, parasitic stranger whose happiness had lain in too great an ignorance. Happiness should always be qualified by a knowledge of misery. There on the book-shelf stood the Tolstoy with the pencil-marks rubbed out. Knowledge was the great thing . . . not abstract knowledge in which Dr Forester had been so rich, the theories which lead one enticingly on with their appearance of nobility, of transcendent virtue, but detailed passionate trivial human knowledge. He opened the Tolstoy again: 'What seemed to me good and lofty—love of fatherland, of one's own people—became to me repulsive and pitiable. What seemed to me bad and shameful—rejection of fatherland and cosmopolitanism—now appeared to me on the contrary good and noble.' Idealism had ended up with a bullet in the stomach at the foot of the stairs; the idealist had been caught out in treachery and murder. Rowe didn't believe they had had to blackmail him much. They had only to appeal to his virtues, his intellectual pride, his abstract love of humanity. One can't love humanity. One can only love people.

'Nothing,' Mr Prentice said. He drooped disconsolately across the room on his stiff lean legs and drew the curtain a little aside. Only one star was visible now: the others had faded into the lightening sky. 'So much time wasted,' Mr Prentice said.

'Three dead and one in prison.'

'They can find a dozen to take their place. I want the films: the top man.' He said, 'They've been using photographic chemicals in the basin in Poole's room. That's where they developed the film, probably. I don't suppose they'd print more than one at a time. They'd want to trust as few people as possible, and so long as they have the negative . . .' He added sadly, 'Poole was a first-class photographer. He specialized in the life history of the bee. Wonderful studies. I've seen some of them. I want you to come

over now to the island. I'm afraid we may find something un-
pleasant there for you to identify . . .'

They stood where Stone had stood; three little red lights ahead
across the pond gave it in the three-quarter dark an illimitable air
as of a harbour just before dawn with the riding lamps of steamers
gathering for a convoy. Mr Prentice waded out and Rowe followed
him; there was a thin skin of water over nine inches of mud. The
red lights were lanterns—the kind of lanterns which are strung at
night where roads are broken. Three policemen were digging in
the centre of the tiny island. There was hardly a foothold for two
more men. 'This was what Stone saw,' Rowe said. 'Men digging.'

'Yes.'

'What do you expect . . . ?' He stopped; there was something
strained in the attitude of the diggers. They put in their spades
carefully as though they might break something fragile, and they
seemed to turn up the earth with reluctance. The dark scene reminded him of something: something distant and sombre. Then
he remembered a dark Victorian engraving in a book his mother
had taken away from him: men in cloaks digging at night in a
graveyard with the moonlight glinting on a spade.

Mr Prentice said, 'There's somebody you've forgotten—
unaccounted for.'

Now as each spade cut down he waited himself with apprehension: he was held by the fear of disgust.

'How do you know where to dig?'

'They left marks. They were amateurs at this. I suppose that
was why they were scared of what Stone saw.'

One spade made an ugly scrunching sound in the soft earth.

'Careful,' Mr Prentice said. The man wielding it stopped and
wiped sweat off his face, although the night was cold. Then he
drew the tool slowly out of the earth and looked at the blade.
'Start again on this side,' Mr Prentice said. 'Take it gently. Don't
go deep.' The other men stopped digging and watched, but you
could tell they didn't want to watch.

The man digging said, 'Here it is.' He left the spade standing in
the ground and began to move the earth with his fingers, gently
as though he were planting seedlings. He said with relief, 'Its
only a box.'

He took his spade again, and with one strong effort lifted the box out of its bed. It was the kind of wooden box which holds groceries, and the lid was loosely nailed down. He prised it open with the edge of the blade and another man brought a lamp nearer. Then one by one an odd sad assortment of objects was lifted out: they were like the relics a company commander sends home when one of his men has been killed. But there was this difference: there were no letters or photographs.

'Nothing they could burn,' Mr Prentice said.

These were what an ordinary fire would reject: a fountain-pen clip, another clip which had probably held a pencil.

'It's not easy to burn things,' Mr Prentice said, 'in an all-electric house.'

A pocket-watch. He nicked open the heavy back and read aloud: 'F.G.J., from N.L.J. on our silver wedding, 3.8.15.' Below was added: 'To my dear son in memory of his father, 1919.'

'A good regular time-piece,' Mr Prentice said.

Two plaited metal arm-bands came next. Then the metal buckles off a pair of sock-suspenders. And then a whole collection of buttons—like pearl buttons off a vest, large ugly brown buttons off a suit, brace buttons, pants buttons, trouser buttons—one could never have believed that one man's single change of clothes required so much holding together. Waist-coat buttons. Shirt buttons. Cuff buttons. Then the metal parts of a pair of braces. So is a poor human creature joined respectably together like a doll: take him apart and you are left with a grocery box full of assorted catches and buckles and buttons.

At the bottom there was a pair of heavy old-fashioned boots with big nails worn with so much pavement tramping, so much standing at street corners.

'I wonder,' Mr Prentice said, 'what they did with the rest of him.'

'Who was he?'

'He was Jones.'

CHAPTER 3
WRONG NUMBERS

'A very slippery, tremendous, quaking road it was.'
The Little Duke

Rowe was growing up; every hour was bringing him nearer to hailing distance of his real age. Little patches of memory returned; he could hear Mr Rennit's voice saying, 'I agree with Jones,' and he saw again a saucer with a sausage-roll upon it beside a telephone. Pity stirred, but immaturity fought hard; the sense of adventure struggled with common sense as though it were on the side of happiness, and common sense were allied to possible miseries, disappointments, disclosures . . .

It was immaturity which made him keep back the secret of the telephone number, the number he had so nearly made out in Cost's shop. He knew the exchange was B A T, and he knew the first three numbers were 271: only the last had escaped him. The information might be valueless—or invaluable. Whichever it was, he hugged it to himself. Mr Prentice had had his chance and failed; now it was his turn. He wanted to boast like a boy to Anna—'I did it.'

About four-thirty in the morning they had been joined by a young man called Brothers. With his umbrella and his moustache and his black hat he had obviously modelled himself upon Mr Prentice. Perhaps in twenty years the portrait would have been adequately copied; it lacked at present the patina of age—the cracks of sadness, disappointment, resignation. Mr Prentice wearily surrendered the picked bones of investigation to Brothers and offered Rowe a seat in the car going back to London. He pulled his hat over his eyes, sank deep into the seat and said, 'We are beaten,' as they splashed down a country lane with the moonlight flat on the puddles.

'What are you going to do about it?'

'Go to sleep.' Perhaps to his fine palate the sentence sounded over-conscious, for without opening his eyes he added, 'One must avoid self-importance, you see. In five hundred years' time, to the historian writing the Decline and Fall of the British Empire, this little episode would not exist. There will be plenty of other causes. You and me and poor Jones will not even figure in a foot-note. It will be all economics, politics, battles.'

'What do you think they did to Jones?'

'I don't suppose we shall ever know. In time of war, so many bodies are unidentifiable. So many bodies,' he said sleepily, 'wait-ing for a convenient blitz.' Suddenly, surprisingly and rather shockingly, he began to snore.

They came into London with the early workers; along the in-dustrial roads men and women were emerging from underground; neat elderly men carrying attaché-cases and rolled umbrellas ap-peared from public shelters. In Gower Street they were sweeping up glass, and a building smoked into the new day like a candle which some late reveller has forgotten to snuff. It was odd to think that the usual battle had been going on while they stood on the island in the pond and heard only the scrape of the spade. A notice turned them from their course, and on a rope strung across the road already flapped a few hand-written labels. 'Bar-clay's Bank. Please inquire at. . . .' 'The Cornwallis Dairy. New address . . .' 'Marquis's Fish Saloon . . .' On a long, quiet, empty expanse of pavement a policeman and a warden strolled in lazy proprietory conversation like gamekeepers on their estate—a no-tice read, 'Unexploded Bomb'. This was the same route they had taken last night, but it had been elaborately and trivially changed. What a lot of activity, Rowe thought, there had been in a few hours—the sticking up of notices, the altering of traffic, the getting to know a slightly different London. He noticed the briskness, the cheerfulness on the faces; you got the impression that this was an early hour of a national holiday. It was simply, he supposed, the effect of finding oneself alive.

Mr Prentice muttered and woke. He told the driver the address of a small hotel near Hyde Park Corner—'if it's still there,' and insisted punctiliously on arranging Rowe's room with the man-ager. It was only after he had waved his hand from the car—'I'll ring you later, dear fellow'—that Rowe realized his courtesy, of course, had an object. He had been lodged where they could reach him; he had been thrust securely into the right pigeon-hole, and would presently, when they required him, be pulled out again. If he tried to leave it would be reported at once. Mr Prentice had even lent him five pounds—you couldn't go far on five pounds.

Rowe had a small early breakfast. The gas-main apparently had been hit, and the gas wouldn't light properly. It wasn't hardly more than a smell, the waitress told him—not enough to boil a kettle or make toast. But there was milk and post-toasties and bread and marmalade—quite an Arcadian meal, and afterwards he walked across the Park in the cool early sun and noticed, looking back over the long empty plain, that he was not followed. He began to whistle the only tune he knew; he felt a kind of serene excitement and well-being, for he was not a murderer. The forgotten years hardly troubled him more than they had done in the first weeks at Dr Forester's home. How good it was, he thought, to play an adult part in life again, and veered with his boy's secret into Bayswater towards a telephone-box.

He had collected at the hotel a store of pennies. He was filled with exhilaration, pressing in the first pair and dialling. A voice said briskly, 'The Hygienic Baking Company at your service,' and he rang off. It was only then he began to realize the difficulties ahead: he couldn't expect to know Cost's customer by a sixth sense. He dialled again and an old voice said, 'Hullo.' He said, 'Excuse me. Who is that, please?'

'Who do you want?' the voice said obstinately—it was so old that it had lost sexual character and you couldn't tell whether it was a man's or a woman's.

'This is Exchange,' Rowe said; the idea came to him at the moment of perplexity, as though his brain had kept it in readiness all the while. 'We are checking up on all subscribers since last night's raid.'

'Why?'

'The automatic system has been disarranged. A bomb on the district exchange. Is that Mr Isaacs of Prince of Wales Road?'

'No, it isn't. This is Wilson.'

'Ah, you see, according to our dialling you should be Mr Isaacs.'

He rang off again; he wasn't any the wiser; after all, even a Hygienic Bakery might conceal Mr Cost's customer—it was even possible that his conversation had been a genuine one. But no, that he did not believe, hearing again the sad stoical voice of the tailor, 'Personally I have no hope. No hope at all.' Personally—the emphasis had lain there. He had conveyed as clearly as he dared that it was for him alone the battle was over.

He went on pressing in his pennies; reason told him that it was useless, that the only course was to let Mr Prentice into his secret—and yet he couldn't believe that somehow over the wire some sense would not be conveyed to him, the vocal impression of a will and violence sufficient to cause so many deaths—poor Stone asphyxiated in the sick bay, Forester and Poole shot down upon the stairs, Cost with the shears through his neck, Jones . . . The cause was surely too vast to come up the wire only as a commonplace voice saying, 'Westminster Bank speaking.'

Suddenly he remembered that Mr Cost had not asked for any individual. He had simply dialled a number and had begun to speak as soon as he heard a voice reply. That meant he could not be speaking to a business address—where some employee would have to be brought to the phone.

'Hullo.'

A voice took any possible question out of his mouth. 'Oh, Ernest,' a torrential voice said, 'I knew you'd ring. You dear sympathetic thing. I suppose David's told you Minny's gone. Last night in the raid, it was awful. We heard her voice calling to us from outside, but, of course there was nothing we could do. We couldn't leave our shelter. And then a landmine dropped—it must have been a land-mine. Three houses went, a huge hole. And this morning not a sign of Minny. David still hopes of course, but I knew at the time, Ernest, there was something elegiac in her mew . . .'

It was fascinating, but he had work to do. He rang off.

The telephone-box was getting stiflingly hot. He had already used up a shillingsworth of coppers; surely among these last four numbers a voice would speak and he would know. 'Police Station, Mafeking Road.' Back on to the rest with the receiver. Three numbers left. Against all reason he was convinced that one of these days three . . . His face was damp with sweat. He wiped it dry, and immediately the beads formed again. He felt suddenly an apprehension; the dryness of his throat, his heavily beating heart warned him that this voice might present too terrible an issue. There had been five deaths already . . . His head swam with relief when a voice said 'Gas Light and Coke Company.' He could still walk out and leave it to Mr Prentice. After all, how did he know that the voice he was seeking was not that of the operator at the Hygienic Baking Company—or even Ernest's friend?

But if he went to Mr Prentice he would find it hard to explain his silence all these invaluable hours. He was not, after all, a boy: he was a middle-aged man. He had started something and he must go on. And yet he still hesitated while the sweat got into his eyes. Two numbers left: a fifty per cent chance. He would try one, and if that number conveyed nothing at all, he would walk out of the box and wash his hands of the whole business. Perhaps his eyes and his wits had deceived him in Mr Cost's shop. His finger went reluctantly through the familiar acts: BAT 271: which number now? He put his sleeve against his face and wiped, then dialled.

BOOK FOUR
THE WHOLE MAN

CHAPTER I
JOURNEY'S END

'Must I—and all alone.'
The Little Duke

I

The telephone rang and rang; he could imagine the empty rooms spreading round the small vexed instrument. Perhaps the rooms of a girl who went to business in the city, or a tradesman who was now at his shop: of a man who left early to read at the British Museum: innocent rooms. He held the welcome sound of an unanswered bell to his ear. He had done his best. Let it ring.

Or were the rooms perhaps guilty rooms? The rooms of a man who had disposed in a few hours of so many human existences. What would a guilty room be like? A room, like a dog, takes on some of the characteristics of its master. A room is trained for certain ends—comfort, beauty, convenience. This room would surely be trained to anonymity. It would be a room which would reveal no secrets if the police should ever call; there would be no Tolstoys with pencilled lines imperfectly erased, no personal touches; the common mean of taste would furnish it—a wireless set, a few detective novels, a reproduction of Van Gogh's sunflower. He imagined it all quite happily while the bell rang and rang. There would be nothing significant in the cupboards: no love-letters concealed below the handkerchiefs, no cheque-book in a drawer: would the linen be marked? There would be no presents from anyone at all—a lonely room: everything in it had been bought at a standard store.

Suddenly a voice he knew said a little breathlessly, 'Hullo. Who's that?' If only, he thought, putting the receiver down, she had been quite out of hearing when the bell rang, at the bottom of the stairs, or in the street. If only he hadn't let his fancy play so long, he need never have known that this was Anna Hilfe's number.

He came blindly out into Bayswater; he had three choices—the sensible and the honest choice was to tell the police. The second was to say nothing. The third was to see for himself. He had no doubt at all that this was the number Cost had rung; he remembered how she had known his real name all along, how she had said—it was a curious phrase—that it was her 'job' to visit him at the home. And yet he didn't doubt that there was an answer, an answer he couldn't trust the police to find. He went back to his hotel and up to his room, carrying the telephone directory with him from the lounge—he had a long job to do. In fact, it was several hours before he reached the number. His eyes were swimming and he nearly missed it. 16, Prince Consort Mansions, Battersea—a name which meant nothing at all. He thought wryly: of course, a guilty room would be taken furnished. He lay down on his bed and closed his eyes.

It was past five o'clock in the afternoon before he could bring himself to act, and then he acted mechanically. He wouldn't think any more: what was the good of thinking before he heard her speak? A 19 bus took him to the top of Oakley Street, and a 49 to Albert Bridge. He walked across the bridge, not thinking. It was low tide and the mud lay up under the warehouses. Somebody on the Embankment was feeding the gulls; the sight obscurely distressed him and he hurried on, not thinking. The waning sunlight lay in a wash of rose over the ugly bricks, and a solitary dog went nosing and brooding into the park. A voice said, 'Why, Arthur,' and he stopped. A man wearing a beret on untidy grey hair and warden's dungarees stood at the entrance to a block of flats. He said doubtfully, 'It is Arthur, isn't it?'

Since Rowe's return to London many memories had slipped into place—this church and that shop, the way Piccadilly ran into Knightsbridge. He hardly noticed when they took up their places as part of the knowledge of a lifetime. But there were other memories which had to fight painfully for admission; somewhere in his mind they had an enemy who wished to keep them out and often succeeded. Cafés and street corners and shops would turn on him a suddenly familiar face, and he would look away and hurry on as though they were the scenes of a road accident. The man who spoke to him belonged to these, but you can't hurry away from a human being as you can hurry away from a shop.

'The last time you hadn't got the beard. You are Arthur, aren't you?'

'Yes. Arthur Rowe.'

The man looked puzzled and hurt. He said, 'It was good of you to call that time.'

'I don't remember.'

The look of pain darkened like a bruise. 'The day of the funeral.'

Rowe said, 'I'm sorry. I had an accident: my memory went. It's only beginning to come back in parts. Who are you?'

'I'm Henry—Henry Wilcox.'

'And I came here—to a funeral?'

'My wife got killed. I expect you read about it in the papers. They gave her a medal. I was a bit worried afterwards because you'd wanted me to cash a cheque for you and I forgot. You know how it is at a funeral: so many things to think about. I expect I was upset too.'

'Why did I bother you then?'

'Oh, it must have been important. It went right out of my head—and then I thought, I'll see him afterwards. But I never saw you.'

Rowe looked up at the flats above them. 'Was it here?'

'Yes.'

He looked across the road to the gate of the park: a man feeding gulls: an office worker carrying a suitcase; the road reeled a little under his feet. He said, 'Was there a procession?'

'The post turned out. And the police and the rescue party.'

Rowe said, 'Yes. I couldn't go to the bank to cash the cheque. I thought the police thought I was a murderer. But I had to find money if I was going to get away. So I came here. I didn't know about the funeral. I thought all the time about this murder.'

'You brood too much,' Henry said. 'A thing that's done is done,' and he looked quite brightly up the road the procession had taken.

'But this was never done, you see. I know that now. I'm not a murderer,' he explained.

'Of course you aren't, Arthur. No friend of yours—no proper friend—ever believed you were.'

'Was there so much talk?'

'Well, naturally . . .'

'I didn't know.' He turned his mind into another track: along the Embankment wall—the sense of misery and then the little man feeding birds, the suitcase . . . he lost the thread until he remembered the face of the hotel clerk, and then he was walking down interminable corridors, a door opened and Anna was there. They shared the danger—he clung to that idea. There was always an explanation. He remembered how she had told him he had saved her life. He said stiffly, 'Well, good-bye. I must be getting on.'

'It's no use mourning someone all your life,' Henry said. 'That's morbid.'

'Yes. Good-bye.'

'Good-bye.'

2

The flat was on the third floor. He wished the stairs would never end, and when he rang the bell he hoped the flat would be deserted. An empty milk bottle stood outside the door on the small dark landing; there was a note stuck in it; he picked it out and read it—'Only half a pint to-morrow, please.' The door opened while he still held it in his hand, and Anna said hopelessly, 'It's you.'

'Yes, me.'

'Every time the bell rang, I've been afraid it would be you.'

'How did you think I'd find you?'

She said, 'There's always the police. They are watching the office now.' He followed her in.

It wasn't the way he had at one time—under the sway of the strange adventure—imagined that he would meet her again. There was a heavy constraint between them. When the door closed they didn't feel alone. It was as if all sorts of people they both knew were with them. They spoke in low voices so as not to intrude. He said, 'I got your address by watching Cost's fingers on the dial—he telephoned you just before he killed himself.'

'It's so horrible,' she said. 'I didn't know you were there.'

' "I've no hope at all." That's what he said. "Personally I've no hope." '

They stood in a little ugly crowded hall as though it wasn't worth the bother of going any farther. It was more like a parting than a reunion—a parting too sorrowful to have any grace. She wore the same blue trousers she had worn at the hotel; he had forgotten how small she was. With the scarf knotted at her neck she looked heart-breakingly impromptu. All around them were brass trays, warming-pans, knick-knacks, an old oak chest, a Swiss cuckoo clock carved with heavy trailing creeper. He said, 'Last night was not good either. I was there too. Did you know that Dr Forester was dead—and Poole?'

'No.'

He said, 'Aren't you sorry—such a massacre of your friends?'

'No,' she said, 'I'm glad.' It was then that he began to hope. She said gently, 'My dear, you have everything mixed up in your head, your poor head. You don't know who are your friends and who are your enemies. That's the way they always work, isn't it?'

'They used you to watch me, didn't they, down there at Dr Forester's, to see when my memory would begin to return? Then they'd have put me in the sick bay like poor Stone.'

'You're so right and so wrong,' she said wearily. 'I don't suppose we'll ever get it straight now. It's true I watched you for them. I didn't want your memory to return any more than they did. I didn't want you hurt.' She said with sharp anxiety, 'Do you remember everything now?'

'I remember a lot and I've learned a lot. Enough to know I'm not a murderer.'

She said, "Thank God.'

'But you knew I wasn't?'

'Yes,' she said, 'of course. I knew it. I just meant—oh, that I'm glad *you* know.' She said slowly, 'I like you happy. It's how you ought to be.'

He said as gently as be could, 'I love you. You know that. I want to believe you are my friend. Where are the photographs?'

A painted bird burst raspingly out of the hideous carved clock case and cuckooed the half-hour. He had time to think between the cuckoos that another night would soon be on them. Would that contain horror too? The door clicked shut and she said simply, 'He has them.'

'He?'

'My brother.' He still held the note to the milkman in his hand. She said. 'You are so fond of investigation, aren't you? The first time I saw you you came to the office about a cake. You were so determined to get to the bottom of things. You've got to the bottom now.'

'I remember. He seemed so helpful. He took me to that house . . .'

She took the words out of his mouth. 'He staged a murder for you and helped you to escape. But afterwards he thought it safer to have you murdered. That was my fault. You told me you'd written a letter to the police, and I told him.'

'Why?'

'I didn't want to get him into trouble for just frightening you. I never guessed he could be so thorough.'

'But you were in that room when I came with the suitcase?' he said. He couldn't work it out. 'You were nearly killed too.'

'Yes. He hadn't forgotten, you see, that I telephoned to you at Mrs Bellairs. *You* told him that. I wasn't on his side any longer— not against you. He told me to go and meet you—and persuade you not to send the letter. And then he just sat back in another flat and waited.'

He accused her, 'But you are alive.'

'Yes,' she said, 'I'm alive, thanks to you. I'm even on probation again—he won't kill his sister if he doesn't feel it's necessary. He calls that family feeling. I was only a danger because of you. This isn't *my* country. Why should I have wanted your memory to return? You were happy without it. I don't care a damn about England. I want you to be happy, that's all. The trouble is he understands such a lot.'

He said obstinately, 'It doesn't make sense. Why am I alive?'

'He's economical.' She said, 'They are all economical. You'll never understand them if you don't understand that.' She repeated wryly, like a formula, 'The maximum of terror for the minimum time directed against the fewest objects.'

He was bewildered: he didn't know what to do. He was learning the lesson most people learn very young, that things never work out in the expected way. This wasn't an exciting adventure, and he wasn't a hero, and it was even possible that this was not a tragedy. He became aware of the note to the milkman. 'He's going away?'

'Yes.'

'With the photographs, of course.'

'Yes.'

'We've got to stop him,' he said. The 'we' like the French *tu* spoken for the first time conveyed everything.

'Yes.'

'Where is he now?'

She said, 'He's here.'

It was like exerting a great pressure against a door and finding it ajar all the time. 'Here?'

She jerked her head. 'He's asleep. He had a long day with Lady Dunwoody about woollies.

'But he'll have heard us.'

'Oh no,' she said. 'He's out of hearing, and he sleeps so sound. That's economy too. As deep a sleep and as little of it . . .'

'How you hate him,' he said with surprise.

'He's made such a mess,' she said, 'of everything. He's so fine, so intelligent—and yet there's only this fear. That's all he makes.'

'Where is he?'

She said, 'Through there is the living-room and beyond that is his bedroom.'

'Can I use the telephone?'

'It's not safe. It's in the living-room and the bedroom door's ajar.'

'Where's he going?'

'He has permission to go to Ireland—for the Free Mothers. It wasn't easy to get, but your friends have made such a sweep. Lady Dunwoody worked it. You see, he's been so grateful for her woollies. He gets the train tonight.' She said, 'What are you going to do?'

'I don't know.'

He looked helplessly round. A heavy brass candlestick stood on the oak chest; it glittered with polish; no wax had ever sullied it. He picked it up. 'He tried to kill me,' he explained weakly.

'He's asleep. That's murder.'

'I won't hit first.'

She said, 'He used to be sweet to me when I cut my knees. Children always cut their knees . . . Life is horrible, wicked.'

He put the candlestick down again.

'No,' she said. 'Take it. You mustn't be hurt. He's only my brother, isn't he?' she asked, with obscure bitterness. 'Take it. Please.' When he made no move to take it, she picked it up herself; her face was stiff and schooled and childish and histrionic. It was like watching a small girl play Lady Macbeth. You wanted to shield her from the knowledge that these things were really true.

She led the way holding the candlestick upright as though it were a rehearsal: only on the night itself would the candle be lit. Everything in the flat was hideous except herself; it gave him more than ever the sense that they were both strangers here. The heavy furniture must have been put in by a company, bought by an official buyer at cut rates, or perhaps ordered by telephone—suite 56a of the autumn catalogue. Only a bunch of flowers and a few books and a newspaper and a man's sock in holes showed that people lived here. It was the sock which made him pause; it seemed to speak of long mutual evenings, of two people knowing each other over many years. He thought for the first time, 'It's her brother who's going to die.' Spies, like murderers, were hanged, and in this case there was no distinction. He lay asleep in there and the gallows was being built outside.

They moved stealthily across the anonymous room towards a door ajar. She pushed it gently with her hand and stood back so that he might see. It was the immemorial gesture of a woman who shows to a guest after dinner her child asleep.

Hilfe lay on the bed on his back without his jacket, his shirt open at the neck. He was deeply and completely at peace, and so defenceless that he seemed to be innocent. His very pale gold hair lay in a hot streak across his face as though he had lain down after a game. He looked very young; he didn't, lying there, belong to the same world as Cost bleeding by the mirror, and Stone in the strait-jacket. One was half-impelled to believe, 'It's propaganda, just propaganda: he isn't capable . . .' The face seemed to Rowe very beautiful, more beautiful than his sister's, which could be marred by grief or pity. Watching the sleeping man he could realize a little of the force and the grace and the attraction of nihilism—of not caring for anything, of having no rules and feeling no love. Life became simple . . . He had been reading when he fell asleep; a book lay on the bed and one hand still held the pages open. It was like the tomb of a young student; bending down you could read on the marble page the epitaph chosen for him, a verse:

> *'Denn Orpheus ists. Seine Metamorphose*
> *in dem und dem. Wir sollen uns nicht mühn*
>
> *um andre Namen. Ein für alle*
> *Male ists Orpheus, wenn est singt . . . '*

The knuckles hid the rest.

It was as if he were the only violence in the world and when he slept there was peace everywhere.

They watched him and he woke. People betray themselves when they wake; sometimes they wake with a cry from an ugly dream: sometimes they turn from one side to the other and shake the head and burrow as if they are afraid to leave sleep. Hilfe just woke; his lids puckered for a moment like a child's when the nurse draws the curtain and the light comes in; then they were wide open and he was looking at them with complete self-possession. The pale blue eyes held full knowledge of the situation; there was nothing to explain. He smiled and Rowe caught himself in the act of smiling back. It was the kind of trick a boy plays suddenly, capitulating, admitting everything, so that the whole offence seems small and the fuss absurd. There are moments of surrender when it is so much easier to love one's enemy than to remember . . .

Rowe said weakly, 'The photographs. . . .'

'The photographs.' He smiled frankly up. 'Yes. I've got them.' He must have known that everything was up—including life, but he still retained the air of badinage, the dated colloquialisms which made his speech a kind of light dance of inverted commas. 'Admit,' he said, 'I've led you "up the garden". And now I'm "in the cart".' He looked at the candlestick which his sister stiffly held and said, 'I surrender,' with amusement, lying on his back on the bed, as though they had all three been playing a game.

'Where are they?'

He said, 'Let's strike a bargain. Let's "swop",' as though he were suggesting the exchange of foreign stamps for toffee.

Rowe said, 'There's no need for me to exchange anything. You're through.'

'My sister loves you a lot, doesn't she?' He refused to take the situation seriously. 'Surely you wouldn't want to eliminate your brother-in-law?'

'You didn't mind trying to eliminate your sister.'

He said blandly and unconvincingly, 'Oh, that was a tragic necessity,' and gave a sudden grin which made the whole affair of the suitcase and the bomb about as important as a booby-trap on the stairs. He seemed to accuse them of a lack of humour; it was not the kind of thing they ought to have taken to heart.

'Let's be sensible civilized people,' he said, 'and come to an agreement. Do put down the candlestick, Anna: I can't hurt you here even if I wanted to.' He made no attempt to get up, lying on the bed, displaying his powerlessness like evidence.

'There's no basis for an agreement,' Rowe said. 'I want the photographs, and then the police want you. You didn't talk about terms to Stone—or Jones.'

'I know nothing about all that,' Hilfe said. 'I can't be responsible—can I?—for all my people do. That isn't reasonable, Rowe.' He asked, 'Do you read poetry? There's a poem here which seems to meet the case . . .' He sat up, lifted the book and dropped it again. With a gun in his hand he said, 'Just stay still. You see there's still something to talk about.'

Rowe said, 'I've been wondering where you kept it.'

'Now we can bargain sensibly. We're both in a hole.'

'I still don't see,' Rowe said, 'what you've got to offer. You don't really imagine, do you, that you can shoot us both, and then get to Ireland. These walls are thin as paper. You are known as the tenant. The police would be waiting for you at the port.'

'But if I'm going to die anyway, I might just as well—mightn't I?—have a massacre.'

'It wouldn't be economical.'

He considered the objection half-seriously and then said with a grin, 'No, but don't you think it would be rather grand?'

'It doesn't much matter to me how I stop you. Being killed would be quite useful.'

Hilfe exclaimed, 'Do you mean your memory's come back?'

'I don't know what that's got to do with it.'

'Such a lot. Your past history is really sensational. I went into it all carefully and so did Anna. It explained so much I didn't understand at first when I heard from Poole what you were like. The kind of room you were living in, the kind of man you were. You were the sort of man I thought I could deal with quite easily until you lost your memory. That didn't work out right. You got so many illusions of grandeur, heroism, self-sacrifice, patriotism . . .' Hilfe grinned at him. 'Here's a bargain for you. My safety against your past. I'll tell you who you were. No trickery. I'll give you all the references. But that won't be necessary. Your own brain will tell you I'm not inventing.'

'He's just lying,' Anna said. 'Don't listen to him.'

'She doesn't want you to hear, does she? Doesn't that make you curious? She wants you as you are, you see, and not as you were.'

Rowe said, 'I only want the photographs.'

'You can read about yourself in the newspapers. You were really quite famous. She's afraid you'll feel too grand for her when you know.'

Rowe said, 'If you give me the photographs . . .'

'And tell you your story?'

He seemed to feel some of Rowe's excitement. He shifted a little on his elbow and his gaze moved for a moment. The wristbone cracked as Anna swung the candlestick down, and the gun lay on the bed. She took it up and said, 'There's no need to bargain with him.'

He was moaning and doubled with pain; his face was white with it. Both their faces were white. For a moment Rowe thought she would go on her knees to him, take his head on her shoulder, surrender the gun to his other hand . . . 'Anna,' Hilfe whispered, 'Anna.'

She said, 'Willi,' and rocked a little on her feet.

'Give me the gun,' Rowe said.

She looked at him as if he were a stranger who shouldn't have been in the room at all; her ears seemed filled with the whimper from the bed. Rowe put out his hand and she backed away, so that she stood beside her brother. 'Go outside,' she said, 'and wait. Go outside.' In their pain they were like twins. She pointed the gun at him and moaned, 'Go outside.'

He said, 'Don't let him talk you round. He tried to kill you,' but seeing the family face in front of him his words sounded flat. It was as if they were so akin that either had the right to kill the other; it was only a form of suicide.

'Please don't go on talking,' she said. 'It doesn't do any good.' Sweat stood on both their faces: he felt helpless.

'Only promise,' he said, 'you won't let him go.'

She moved her shoulders and said, 'I promise.' When he went she closed and locked the door behind him.

For a long time afterwards he could hear nothing—except once the closing of a cupboard door and the chink of china. He imagined she was bandaging Hilfe's wrist; he was probably safe enough, incapable of further flight. Rowe realized that now if he wished he could telephone to Mr Prentice and have the police surround the flat—he was no longer anxious for glory; the sense of adventure had leaked away and left only the sense of human pain. But he felt that he was bound by her promise; he had to trust her, if life was to go on.

A quarter of an hour dragged by and the room was full of dusk. There had been low voices in the bedroom: he felt uneasy. Was Hilfe talking her round? He was aware of a painful jealousy; they had been so alike and he had been shut out like a stranger. He went to the window and drawing the blackout curtain a little aside looked out over the darkening park. There was so much he had still to remember; the thought came to him like a threat in Hilfe's dubious tones.

The door opened, and when he let the curtain fall he realized how dark it had become. Anna walked stiffly towards him and said, 'There you are. You've got what you wanted.' Her face looked ugly in the attempt to avoid tears; it was an ugliness which bound him to her more than any beauty could have done; it isn't being happy together, he thought as though it were a fresh discovery, that makes one love—it's being unhappy together. 'Don't you want them,' she asked, 'now I've got them for you?'

He took the little roll in his hand: he had no sense of triumph at all. He asked, 'Where is he?'

She said, 'You don't want him now. He's finished.'

'Why did you let him go?' he asked. 'You promised.'

'Yes,' she said, 'I promised.' She made a small movement with her fingers, crossing two of them—he thought for a moment that she was going to claim that child's excuse for broken treaties.

'Why?' he asked again.

'Oh,' she said vaguely, 'I had to bargain.'

He began to unwrap the roll carefully; he didn't want to expose more than a scrap of it. 'But he had nothing to bargain with,' he said. He held the roll out to her on the palm of his hand. 'I don't know what he promised to give you, but this isn't it.'

'He swore that's what you wanted. How do you know?'

'I don't know how many prints they made. This may be the only one or there may be a dozen. But I do know there's only one negative.'

She asked sadly, 'And that's not it?'

'No.'

3

Rowe said, 'I don't know what he had to bargain with, but he didn't keep his part.'

'I'll give up,' she said. 'Whatever I touch goes wrong, doesn't it? Do what you want to do.'

'You'll have to tell me where he is.'

'I always thought,' she said, 'I could have both of you. I didn't care what happened to the world. It couldn't be worse than it's always been, and yet the globe, the beastly globe, survives. But people, you, him . . .' She sat down on the nearest chair—a stiff polished ugly upright chair: her feet didn't reach the floor. She said, 'Paddington: the 7.20. He said he'd never come back. I thought you'd be safe then.'

'Oh,' he said, 'I can look after myself,' but meeting her eyes he had the impression that he hadn't really understood. He said, 'Where will he have it? They'll search him at the port anyway.'

'I don't know. He took nothing.'

'A stick?'

'No,' she said, 'nothing. He just put on his jacket—he didn't even take a hat. I suppose it's in his pocket.'

He said, 'I'll have to go to the station.'

'Why can't you leave it to the police now?'

'By the time I get the right man and explain to him, the train will have gone. If I miss him at the station, then I'll ring the police.' A doubt occurred. 'If he told you that, of course he won't be there.'

'He didn't tell me. I didn't believe what he told me. That was the original plan. It's his only hope of getting out of here.'

When he hesitated she said, 'Why not just let them meet the train at the other end? Why do it all yourself?'

'He might get out on the way.'

'You mustn't go like this. He's armed. I let him have his gun.'

He suddenly laughed. 'By God,' he said, 'you have made a mess of things, haven't you?'

'I wanted him to have a chance.'

'You can't do much with a gun in the middle of England except kill a few poor devils.' She looked so small and beaten that he couldn't preserve any anger. She said, 'There's only one bullet in it. He wouldn't waste that.'

'Just stay here,' Rowe said.

She nodded. 'Good-bye.'

'I'll be back quite soon.' She didn't answer, and he tried another phrase. 'Life will begin all over again then.' She smiled unconvincingly, as though it were he who needed comfort and reassurance, not she.

'He won't kill me.'

'I'm not afraid of that.'

'What are you afraid of then?'

She looked up at him with a kind of middle-aged tenderness, as though they'd grown through love into its later stage. She said, 'I'm afraid he'll talk.'

He mocked at her from the door. 'Oh, he won't talk *me* round,' but all the way downstairs he was thinking again, *I* didn't understand her.

The searchlights were poking up over the park; patches of light floated like clouds along the surface of the sky. It made the sky seem very small; you could probe its limit with light. There was a smell of cooking all along the pavement from houses where people were having an early supper to be in time for the raid. A warden was lighting a hurricane-lamp outside a shelter. He said to Rowe, 'Yellow's up.' The match kept going out—he wasn't used to lighting lamps; he looked a bit on edge: too many

lonely vigils on deserted pavements; he wanted to talk. But Rowe
was in a hurry: he couldn't wait.

On the other side of the bridge there was a taxi-rank with one
cab left. 'Where do you want to go?' the driver asked and considered, looking up at the sky, the pillows of light between the
few stars, one pale just visible balloon. 'Oh, well,' he said, 'I'll
take a chance. It won't be worse there than here.'

'Perhaps there won't be a raid.'

'Yellow's up,' the driver said, and the old engine creaked into
life.

They went up across Sloane Square and Knightsbridge and into
the Park and on along the Bayswater Road. A few people were
hurrying home; buses slid quickly past the Request stops; Yellow
was up; the saloon bars were crowded. People called to the taxi
from the pavement, and when a red light held it up an elderly
gentleman in a bowler hat opened the door quickly and began to
get in. 'Oh,' he said, 'I beg your pardon. Thought it was empty.
Are you going towards Paddington?'

'Get in,' Rowe said.

'Catching the 7.20,' the stranger said breathlessly. 'Bit of luck
for me this. We'll just do it.'

'I'm catching it too,' Rowe said.

'Yellow's up.'

'So I've heard.'

They creaked forward through the thickening darkness. 'Any
land-mines your way last night?' the old gentleman asked.

'No, no. I don't think so.'

'Three near us. About time for the Red I should think.'

'I suppose so.'

'Yellow's been up for a quarter of an hour,' the elderly gentleman said, looking at his watch as though he were timing an express train between stations. 'Ah, that sounded like a gun. Over
the estuary, I should say.'

'I didn't hear it.'

'I should give them another ten minutes at most,' the old gentleman said, holding his watch in his hand, as the taxi turned into
Praed Street. They swung down the covered way and came to
rest. Through the blacked-out station the season-ticket holders

were making a quick get-away from the nightly death; they dived in earnest silence towards the suburban trains, carrying little attaché-cases, and the porters stood and watched them go with an air of sceptical superiority. They felt the pride of being a legitimate objective: the pride of people who stayed.

The long train stood darkly along number one platform: the bookstalls closed, the blinds drawn in most of the compartments. It was a novel sight to Rowe and yet an old sight. He had only to see it once like the sight of a bombed street, for it to take up its place imperceptibly among his memories. This was already life as he'd known it.

It was impossible to see who was in the train from the platform; every compartment held its secrets close. Even if the blinds had not been lowered, the blued globes cast too little light to show who sat below them. He felt sure that Hilfe would travel first class; as a refugee he lived on borrowed money, and as the friend and confidant of Lady Dunwoody he was certain to travel in style.

He made his way down the first-class compartments along the corridor. They were not very full; only the more daring season-ticket holders remained in London as late as this. He put his head in at every door and met at once the disquieting return stare of the blue ghosts.

It was a long train, and the porters were already shutting doors higher up before he reached the last first-class coach. He was so accustomed to failure that it took him by surprise, sliding back the door to come on Hilfe.

He wasn't alone. An old lady sat opposite him, and she had made Hilfe's hand into a cat's cradle for winding wool. He was handcuffed in the heavy oiled raw material for seamen's boots. His right hand stuck stiffly out, the wrist bandaged and roughly splinted, and round and round ever so gently the old lady industriously wound her wool. It was ludicrous and it was sad; Rowe could see the weighted pocket where the revolver lay, and the look that Hilfe turned on him was not reckless nor amused nor dangerous: it was humiliated. He had always had a way with old ladies.

Rowe said, 'You wouldn't want to talk here.'

'She's deaf,' Hilfe said, 'stone deaf.'

'Good evening,' the old lady said, 'I hear there's a Yellow up.'

'Yes,' Rowe said.

'She's deaf,' Hilfe said, 'stone deaf.'

'Shocking,' the old lady said and wound her wool.

'I want the negative,' Rowe said.

'Anna should have kept you longer. I told her to give me enough start. After all,' he added with gloomy disappointment, 'it would have been better for both . . .'

'You cheated her too often,' Rowe said. He sat down by his side and watched the winding up and over and round.

'What are you going to do?'

'Wait till the train starts and then pull the cord.'

Suddenly from very close the guns cracked—once, twice, three times. The old lady looked vaguely up as though she had heard something very faint intruding on her silence. Rowe put his hand into Hilfe's pocket and slipped the gun into his own. 'If you'd like to smoke,' the old lady said, 'don't mind me.'

Hilfe said, 'I think we ought to talk things over.'

'There's nothing to talk about.'

'It wouldn't do, you know, to get me and not to get the photographs.'

Rowe began, 'The photographs don't matter by themselves. It's you . . .' But then he thought: they do matter. How do I know he hasn't passed them on already? if they are hidden, the place may be agreed on with another agent . . . even if they are found by a stranger, they are not safe. He said, 'We'll talk,' and the siren sent up its tremendous howl over Paddington. Very far away this time there was a pad, pad, pad, like the noise a fivesball makes against the glove, and the old lady wound and wound. He remembered Anna saying, 'I'm afraid he'll talk,' and he saw Hilfe suddenly smile at the wool as if life had still the power to tickle him into savage internal mirth.

Hilfe said, 'I'm still ready to swop.'

'You haven't anything to swop.'

'You haven't much, you know, either,' Hilfe said. 'You don't know where the photos are . . .

'I wonder when the sirens will go,' the old lady said. Hilfe moved his wrists in the wool. He said, 'If you give back the gun, I'll let you have the photographs . . .'

'If you can give me the photographs, they must be with you. There's no reason why I should bargain.'

'Well,' Hilfe said, 'if it's your idea of revenge, I can't stop you. I thought perhaps you wouldn't want Anna dragged in. She let me escape, you remember . . .'

'There,' the old lady said, 'we've nearly done now.'

Hilfe said, 'They probably wouldn't hang her. Of course that would depend on what I say. Perhaps it would be just an internment camp till the war's over—and then deportation if you win. From my point of view,' he explained dryly, 'she's a traitor, you know.'

Rowe said, 'Give me the photographs and then we'll talk.' The word 'talk' was like a capitulation. Already he was beginning painfully to think out the long chain of deceit he would have to practise on Mr Prentice if he were to save Anna.

The train rocked with an explosion; the old lady said, 'At last we are going to start,' and leaning forward she released Hilfe's hands. Hilfe said with a curious wistfulness, 'What fun they are having up there.' He was like a mortally sick man saying farewell to the sports of his contemporaries: no fear, only regret. He had failed to bring off the record himself in destruction. Five people only were dead: it hadn't been much of an innings compared with what they were having up there. Sitting under the darkened globe, he was a long way away; wherever men killed his spirit moved in obscure companionship.

'Give them to me,' Rowe said.

He was surprised by a sudden joviality. It was as if Hilfe after all had not lost all hope—of what? escape? further destruction? He laid his left hand on Rowe's knee with a gesture of intimacy. He said, 'I'll be better than my word. How would you like to have your memory back?'

'I only want the photographs.'

'Not here,' Hilfe said. 'I can't very well strip in front of a lady, can I?' He stood up. 'We'd better leave the train.'

'Are you going?' the old lady asked.

'We've decided, my friend and I,' Hilfe said, 'to spend the night n town and see the fun.'

'Fancy,' the old lady vaguely said, 'the porters always tell you 'ong.'

You've been very kind,' Hilfe said, bowing. 'Your kindness rmed me.'

'Oh, I can manage nicely now, thank you.'

It was as if Hilfe had taken charge of his own defeat. He moved purposefully up the platform and Rowe followed like a valet. The rush was over; he had no chance to escape; through the glassless roof they could see the little trivial scarlet stars of the barrage flashing and going out like matches. A whistle blew and the train began to move very slowly out of the dark station; it seemed to move surreptitiously; there was nobody but themselves and a few porters to see it go. The refreshment-rooms were closed, and a drunk soldier sat alone on a waste of platform vomiting between his knees.

Hilfe led the way down the steps to the lavatories; there was nobody there at all—even the attendant had taken shelter. The guns cracked: they were alone with the smell of disinfectant, the greyish basins, the little notices about venereal disease. The adventure he had pictured once in such heroic terms had reached its conclusion in the Gentlemen's. Hilfe looked in an L.C.C. mirror and smoothed his hair.

'What are you doing?' Rowe asked. 'Oh, saying good-bye,' Hilfe said. He took off his jacket as though he were going to wash, then threw it over to Rowe. Rowe saw the tailor's tag marked in silk, Pauling and Crosthwaite. 'You'll find the photographs,' Hilfe said, 'in the shoulder.'

The shoulder was padded.

'Want a knife?' Hilfe said. 'You can have your own,' and he held out a boy's compendium.

Rowe slit the shoulder up and took out from the padding a roll of film; he broke the paper which bound it and exposed a corner of negative. 'Yes,' he said. 'This is it.'

'And now the gun?'

Rowe said slowly, 'I promised nothing.'

Hilfe said with sharp anxiety, 'But you'll let me have the gun?'

'No.'

Hilfe suddenly was scared and amazed. He exclaimed in his odd dated vocabulary, 'It's a caddish trick.'

'You've cheated too often,' Rowe said.

'Be sensible,' Hilfe said. 'You think I want to escape. But the train's gone. Do you think I could get away by killing you in Paddington station? I wouldn't get a hundred yards.'

'Why do you want it then?' Rowe asked.

'I want to get further away than that.' He said in a low voice, 'I don't want to be beaten up.' He leant earnestly forward and the L.C.C. mirror behind him showed a tuft of fine hair he hadn't smoothed.

'We don't beat up our prisoners here.'

'Oh no?' Hilfe said. 'Do you really believe that? Do you think you are so different from us?'

'Yes.'

'I wouldn't trust the difference,' Hilfe said. 'I know what we do to spies. They'll think they can make me talk—they will make me talk.' He brought up desperately the old childish phrase, 'I'll swop.' It was difficult to believe that he was guilty of so many deaths. He went urgently on, 'Rowe, I'll give you your memory back. There's no one else will.'

'Anna,' Rowe said.

'She'll never tell you. Why, Rowe, she let me go to stop me. . . . Because I said I'd tell you. She wants to keep you as you are.'

'Is it as bad as that?' Rowe asked. He felt fear and an unbearable curiosity. Digby whispered in his ear that now he could be a whole man again: Anna's voice warned him. He knew that this was the great moment of a lifetime; he was being offered so many forgotten years, the fruit of twenty years' experience. His breast had to press the ribs apart to make room for so much more; he stared ahead of him and read—'Private Treatment Between the Hours of . . .' On the far edge of consciousness the barrage thundered.

Hilfe grimaced at him. 'Bad?' he said. 'Why—it's tremendously important.'

Rowe shook his head sadly: 'You can't have the gun.'

Suddenly Hilfe began to laugh: the laughter was edged with hysteria and hate. 'I was giving you a chance,' he said. 'If you'd given me the gun, I might have been sorry for you. I'd have been grateful. I might have just shot myself. But now'—his head bobbed up and down in front of the cheap mirror—'now I'll tell you gratis.'

Rowe said, 'I don't want to hear,' and turned away. A very small man in an ancient brown Homburg came rocking down the steps from above and made for the urinal. His hat came down over his ears: it might have been put on with a spirit-level. 'Bad night,' he said, 'bad night.' He was pale and wore an expression of startled displeasure. As Rowe reached the steps a bomb came heavily down, pushing the air ahead of it like an engine. The little man hastily did up his flies; he crouched as though he wanted to get farther away. Hilfe sat on the edge of the wash-basin and listened with a sour nostalgic smile, as though he were hearing the voice of a friend going away for ever down the road. Rowe stood on the bottom step and waited and the express roared down on them and the little man stooped lower and lower in front of the urinal. The sound began to diminish, and then the ground shifted very slightly under their feet at the explosion. There was silence again except for the tiny shifting of dust down the steps. Almost immediately a second bomb was under way. They waited in fixed photographic attitudes, sitting, squatting, standing: this bomb could not burst closer without destroying them. Then it too passed, diminished, burst a little farther away.

'I wish they'd stop,' the man in the Homburg said, and all the urinals began to flush. The dust hung above the steps like smoke, and a hot metallic smell drowned the smell of ammonia. Rowe climbed the steps.

'Where are you going?' Hilfe said. He cried out sharply, 'The police?' and when Rowe did not reply, he came away from the wash-basin. 'You can't go yet—not without hearing about your wife.'

'My wife?' He came back down the steps; he couldn't escape now: the lost years waited for him among the wash-basins. He asked hopelessly, 'Am I married?'

'You *were* married,' Hilfe said. 'Don't you remember now? You poisoned her.' He began to laugh again. 'Your Alice.'

'An awful night,' the man in the Homburg said; he had ears for nothing but the heavy uneven stroke of the bomber overhead.

'You were tried for murder,' Hilfe said, 'and they sent you to an asylum. You'll find it in all the papers. I can give you the dates . . .'

The little man turned suddenly to them and spreading out his hands in a gesture of entreaty he said in a voice filled with tears, 'Shall I ever get to Wimbledon?' A bright white light shone through the dust outside, and through the glassless roof of the station the glow of the flares came dripping beautifully down.

It wasn't Rowe's first raid: he heard Mrs Purvis coming down the stairs with her bedding: the Bay of Naples was on the wall and *The Old Curiosity Shop* upon the shelf. Guilford Street held out its dingy arms to welcome him, and he was home again. He thought: what will that bomb destroy? Perhaps with a little luck the flower shop will be gone near Marble Arch, the sherry bar in Adelaide Crescent, or the corner of Quebec Street, where I used to wait so many hours, so many years . . . there was such a lot which had to be destroyed before peace came.

'Go along,' a voice said, 'to Anna now,' and he looked across a dimmed blue interior to a man who stood by the wash-basins and laughed at him.

'She hoped you'd never remember.' He thought of a dead rat and a policeman, and then he looked everywhere and saw reflected in the crowded court the awful expression of pity: the judge's face was bent, but he could read pity in the old fingers which fidgeted with an Eversharp. He wanted to warn them—don't pity me. Pity is cruel. Pity destroys. Love isn't safe when pity's prowling round.

'Anna . . .' the voice began again, and another voice said with a kind of distant infinite regret at the edge of consciousness, 'And I might have caught the 6.15.' The horrible process of connection went on; his Church had once taught him the value of penance, but penance was a value only to oneself. There was no sacrifice, it seemed to him, that would help him to atone to the dead. The dead were out of reach of the guilty. He wasn't interested in saving his own soul.

'What are you going to do?' a voice said. His brain rocked with its long journey; it was as if he were advancing down an interminable passage towards a man called Digby—who was so like him and yet had such different memories. He could hear Digby's voice saying, 'Shut your eyes . . .' There were rooms full of flowers, the sound of water falling, and Anna sat beside him, strung up, on guard, in defense of his ignorance. He was saying, 'Of course you have a brother . . . I remember . . .'

Another voice said, 'It's getting quieter. Don't you think it is?'

'What are you going to do?'

It was like one of those trick pictures in a children's magazine: you stare at it hard and you see one thing—a vase of flowers—and then your focus suddenly changes and you see only the outlined faces of people. In and out the two pictures flicker. Suddenly, quite clearly, he saw Hilfe as he had seen him lying asleep—the graceful shell of a man, all violence quieted. He *was* Anna's brother. Rowe crossed the floor to the wash-basins and said in a low voice that the man in the Homburg couldn't hear, 'All right. You can have it. Take it.'

He slipped the gun quickly into Hilfe's hand.

'I think,' the voice behind him said, 'I'll make a dash for it. I really think I will. What do you think, sir?'

'Be off,' Hilfe said sharply, 'be off.'

'You think so too. Yes. Perhaps.' There was a scuttling on the steps and silence again.

'Of course,' Hilfe said, 'I could kill you now. But why should I? It would be doing you a service. And it would leave me to your thugs. How I hate you though.'

'Yes?' He wasn't thinking of Hilfe; his thoughts swung to and fro between two people he loved and pitied. It seemed to him that he had destroyed both of them.

'Everything was going so well,' Hilfe said, 'until you came blundering in. What made you go and have your fortune told? You had no future.'

'No.' He remembered the fête clearly now; he remembered walking round the railings and hearing the music; he had been dreaming of innocence . . . Mrs Bellairs sat in a booth behind a curtain . . .

'And just to have hit on that one phrase,' Hilfe said. ' "Don't tell me the past. Tell me the future." '

And there was Sinclair too. He remembered with a sense of responsibility the old car standing on the wet gravel. He had better go away and telephone to Prentice. Sinclair probably had a copy . . .

'And then on top of everything Anna. Why the hell should any woman love you?' He cried out sharply, 'Where are you going?'

'Can't you give me just five minutes?'

'Oh no,' Rowe said. 'No. It's not possible.' The process was completed; he was what Digby had wanted to be—a whole man. His brain held now everything it had ever held. Willi Hilfe gave an odd little sound like a retch. He began to walk rapidly towards the lavatory cubicles, with his bandaged hand stuck out. The stone floor was wet and he slipped but recovered. He began to pull at a lavatory door, but of course it was locked. He didn't seem to know what to do: it was as if he needed to get behind a door, out of sight, into some burrow . . . He turned and said imploringly, 'Give me a penny,' and everywhere the sirens began to wail the All Clear; the sound came from everywhere: it was as if the floor of the urinal whined under his feet. The smell of ammonia came to him like something remembered from a dream. Hilfe's strained white face begged for his pity. Pity again. He held out a penny to him and then tossed it and walked up the steps; before he reached the top he heard the shot. He didn't go back: he left him for others to find.

4

One can go back to one's own home after a year's absence and immediately the door closes; it is as if one has never been away. Or one can go back after a few hours and everything is so changed that one is a stranger.

This, of course, he knew now, was not his home. Guilford Street was his home. He had hoped that wherever Anna was there would be peace; coming up the stairs a second time he knew that there would never be peace again while they lived.

To walk from Paddington to Battersea gives time for thought. He knew what he had to do long before he began to climb the stairs. A phrase of Johns' came back to mind about a Ministry of Fear. He felt now that he had joined its permanent staff. But it wasn't the small Ministry to which Johns had referred, with limited aims like winning a war or changing a constitution. It was a Ministry as large as life to which all who loved belonged. If one loved one feared. That was something Digby had forgotten, full of hope among the flowers and *Tatlers*.

The door was open as he had left it, and it occurred to him almost as a hope that perhaps she had run out into the raid and been lost for ever. If one loved a woman one couldn't hope that she would be tied to a murderer for the rest of her days.

But she was there—not where he had left her, but in the bedroom where they had watched Hilfe sleeping. She lay on the bed face downwards with her fists clenched. He said 'Anna.'

She turned her head on the pillow; she had been crying, and her face looked as despairing as a child's. He felt an enormous love for her, enormous tenderness, the need to protect her at any cost. She had wanted him innocent and happy . . . she had loved Digby . . . He had got to give her what she wanted . . . He said gently, 'Your brother's dead. He shot himself,' but her face didn't alter. It was as if none of that meant anything at all—all that violence and grace-lessness and youth had gone without her thinking it worth atten-tion. She asked with terrible anxiety, 'What did he say to you?'

Rowe said, 'He was dead before I could reach him. Directly he saw me he knew it was all up.'

The anxiety left her face: all that remained was that tense air he had observed before—the air of someone perpetually on guard to shield him . . . He sat down on the bed and put his hand on her shoulder. 'My dear,' he said, 'my dear. How much I love you.' He was pledging both of them to a lifetime of lies, but only he knew that.

'Me too,' she said. 'Me too.'

They sat for a long while without moving and without speak-ing; they were on the edge of their ordeal, like two explorers who see at last from the summit of the range the enormous dangerous plain. They had to tread carefully for a lifetime, never speak with-out thinking twice; they must watch each other like enemies be-cause they loved each other so much. They would never know what it was not to be afraid of being found out. It occurred to him that perhaps after all one could atone even to the dead if one suffered for the living enough.

He tried tentatively a phrase, 'My dear, my dear, I am so happy,' and heard with infinite tenderness her prompt and guarded reply, 'I am too.' It seemed to him that after all one could exaggerate the value of happiness . . .

AVAILABLE FROM
PENGUIN CLASSICS

Brighton Rock
Introduction by J. M. Coetzee
ISBN 978-0-14-243797-1

Burnt-Out Case
ISBN 978-0-14-018539-3

The Captain and the Enemy
Introduction by John Auchard
ISBN 978-0-14-303929-7

The Comedians
Introduction by Paul Theroux
ISBN 978-0-14-303919-8

Complete Short Stories
Introduction by Pico Iyer
ISBN 978-0-14-303910-5

The End of the Affair
Introduction by Michael Gorra
ISBN 978-0-14-243798-8

England Made Me
ISBN 978-0-14-018551-5

A Gun for Sale
Introduction by Samuel Hynes
ISBN 978-0-14-303930-3

The Heart of the Matter
Introduction by James Wood
ISBN 978-0-14-243799-5

The Honorary Consul
Introduction by Mark Bosco
ISBN 978-0-14-310555-8

The Human Factor
Introduction by Colm Toibin
ISBN 978-0-14-310556-5

Journey without Maps
Introduction by Paul Theroux
ISBN 978-0-14-303972-3

PENGUIN
CLASSICS

AVAILABLE FROM
PENGUIN CLASSICS

Lawless Roads
Introduction by David Rieff
ISBN 978-0-14-303973-0

Loser Takes All
ISBN 978-0-14-018542-3

The Man Within
Introduction by Jonathan Yardley
ISBN 978-0-14-303921-1

The Ministry of Fear
An Entertainment
Introduction by Alan Furst
ISBN 978-0-14-303911-2

Monsignor Quixote
Introduction by John Auchard
ISBN 978-0-14-310552-7

Orient Express
Introduction by Christopher Hitchens
ISBN 978-0-14-243791-9

Our Man in Havana
Introduction by Christopher Hitchens
ISBN 978-0-14-243800-8

The Portable Graham Greene
Introduction by Philip Stratford
ISBN 978-0-14-303918-1

The Power and the Glory
Introduction by John Updike
ISBN 978-0-14-243730-8

The Quiet American
Introduction by Robert Stone
ISBN 978-0-14-303902-0

The Third Man and
The Fallen Idol
ISBN 978-0-14-018533-1

Travels with My Aunt
Introduction by Gloria Emerson
978-0-14-303900-6

Twenty-one Stories
ISBN 978-0-14-018534-8

PENGUIN
CLASSICS